"THIS COUNTRY'S GETTIN' DOWNRIGHT TAME."

"Funny thing, I was just thinkin' the same thing," Smoke responded.

Suddenly, just behind them a new voice, harsh and slurred by whiskey, interrupted their camaraderie.

"Well, well, what have we got here?" said one voice.

Another answered, "Looks to me like a couple of old farts blockin' the street."

A third joined in. "Yeah. You old geezers better get out of the way and make room for some real *men*."

The menace in the voices froze Smoke Jensen and Monte Carson in their tracks. Slowly they turned as one to face their tormentors. Arctic coldness covered Smoke's words. "If you *men* are looking for a lesson, I'll be glad to oblige."

All three of the young drunks burst into laughter.

Smoke Jenson's eyes turned a dangerous gray, while he pulled on a pair of think black leather gloves. Quietly, he said, "Looks like I'm going to have to kick some butt."

And that did it . . .

BOOK YOUR PLACE ON OUR WEBSITE AND MAKE THE READING CONNECTION!

We've created a customized website just for our very special readers, where you can get the inside scoop on everything that's going on with Zebra, Pinnacle and Kensington books.

When you come online, you'll have the exciting opportunity to:

- View covers of upcoming books
- Read sample chapters
- Learn about our future publishing schedule (listed by publication month *and author*)
- Find out when your favorite authors will be visiting a city near you
- Search for and order backlist books from our online catalog
- Check out author bios and background information
- Send e-mail to your favorite authors
- Meet the Kensington staff online
- Join us in weekly chats with authors, readers and other guests
- Get writing guidelines
- AND MUCH MORE!

**Visit our website at
http://www.kensingtonbooks.com**

POWER OF THE MOUNTAIN MAN

William W. Johnstone

PINNACLE BOOKS
Kensington Publishing Corp.

http://www.kensingtonbooks.com

PINNACLE BOOKS are published by

Kensington Publishing Corp.
850 Third Avenue
New York, NY 10022

All Kensington Titles, Imprints, and Distributed Lines are available at special quantity discounts for bulk purchases for sales promotions, premiums, fund-raising, and educational or institutional use. Special book excerpts or customized printings can also be created to fit specific needs. For details, write or phone the office of the Kensington special sales manager: Kensington Publishing Corp., 850 Third Avenue, New York, NY 10022, attn: Special Sales Department, Phone: 1-800-221-2647.

Pinnacle and the P logo Reg. U.S. Pat. & TM Off.

First Printing: February 1996
20 19 18 17 16 15 14 13 12 11

Printed in the United States of America

ONE

Winter had poised to blow its way across the High Lonesome. Most of the aspens had lost their leaves. Those that remained glowed in a riot of yellow and red. The maples and scrub oak resisted stubbornly, greenness proclaiming their independence dotted in among the less hearty trees. Smoke Jensen took a draw on the flavorful cigar and sent his gray gaze out across the vista of his beloved Sugarloaf Ranch while the white ribbons rose from around the stogie.

It wouldn't be long, he mused, before a thick blanket of snow covered everything in sight. Which reminded him of the letter he held in his hand. It had come from San Francisco that morning, brought by a ranch hand who had gone to Big Rock for the weekly mail run. Smoke cut his eyes to the brief message, only a single line.

"Come at once. Meet me at Francie's." It was signed simply with a bold L.

Because of where they were to meet and of whom he suspected as the sender, Smoke refrained from mentioning the cryptic message to his wife Sally. That he would go went without question. Despite the harsh winter looming over them, he would not suggest that his lovely wife accompany him to the more hospitable clime. He sighed gustily and ran long, strong fingers through his hair, pleased to reflect that only thin threads of gray showed at his temples. As to breaking the news of his departure, he had better get to that right away.

Smoke Jensen lifted himself out of the cane-bottom chair he had tilted back against the outer wall of his home on the

Sugarloaf. Once a tight, square cabin of fir logs, it now sprawled with the additions brought on by a large family. He crossed to the door and entered. At once his nostrils twitched and swelled to the delicious scent of a pie baking. Drawn by that tempting aroma, he gained the kitchen with a broad grin on his face, his unpleasant mission forgotten for the moment. He negotiated the floor on cat feet and caught Sally with both big hands around her still-trim waist. She gave only the slightest of starts at the contact, then looked over her shoulder, long curls dancing.

"It's the last of the blackberries. I thought you'd like it."

"I know *I* will," young Bobby Jensen chirped from the big, round oak table in the center of the expanded room.

Smoke turned to the boy, surprise written on his face. "I thought you were out with the hands."

"I woulda been, but . . ." Bobby elevated a bare foot, a strip of white rag tied around his big toe. "I got this big ol' splinter when I went to wash up this morning."

"You'll live," Smoke told him with a grin.

Smoke and Sally had adopted Bobby Harris several years ago, after Smoke had been forced to kill the boy's abusive father. The elder Harris had been a brute, a drunk who'd tormented both people and animals. He had gone after Smoke Jensen with a pitchfork while Smoke's back had been turned. Bobby's shout of alarm had saved Smoke's life.

On an important mission to help old friends in Mexico, Smoke had sent the orphaned lad to the Sugarloaf and put him in Sally's charge. What had forged that decision had been Bobby's revelation that Harris, Sr., had killed the lad's mother some months previous. For all his reputation as a deadly gunfighter—the best ever, many maintained—his past did not harden Smoke from compassion for the boy. Sally would take care of Bobby, since there was no way he could go where Smoke was headed. Bobby's sunny smile recalled Smoke to the kitchen. By God, the lad would soon be thirteen.

"Oh, I know that. It just stings, and my toe swelled up too much to put in a boot."

Sally recognized the distracted expression Smoke wore and

came right to the point. "There's something in that letter I don't know about," she challenged.

"I was coming to tell you. Maybe you ought to check on that pie and then get a cup of coffee and come sit at the table."

Sally frowned. "Bad news." Then she added, "As always." She complied, however, and when seated, Smoke revealed the summons to San Francisco. When he concluded, Sally fought back her disappointment and provided, "You're going, of course."

"I have to, Sally. You know as well as I who probably sent that."

Sally's scowl deepened. "I've no doubt. And that always spells danger."

"Danger for who?" Bobby piped up.

Smoke and Sally shot him a look. "For *whom,*" She corrected automatically, then answered his question. "Smoke, of course," she advised him. "But mostly for anyone who gets in his way."

That made Bobby's day. His face lit up with expectation. "You're goin' gunnin' for someone, huh, Smoke?"

Smoke Jensen sighed wearily and shook his head. "Not if I can help it. I really don't know what to expect. But I'll be leaving early in the morning. Sally, make sure there's plenty of firewood and supplies laid in, who knows when I'll be back?" He shrugged. "Then all I can think of is that you all bundle up tight for the winter."

Shortly after sunrise, Smoke Jensen fastened the last strap on his saddlebags and swung atop his 'Palouse stallion, Thunder. He had kissed Sally goodbye minutes earlier and had left her at the kitchen table, her eyes bright with suppressed tears. Now, as he turned his mount south, toward the main gate of the ranch and the town of Big Rock beyond, Sally came from the back door, a shawl over her shoulders to stave off the morning chill.

She hurried to his side, calling his name. Smoke turned and

bent low as Sally reached him and stood on tiptoe, arms out to embrace the man she loved with all her heart. Deeply moved by her affection, Smoke kissed her ardently. When their embrace ended, he spoke gruffly.

"Always did have to have the last word, woman."

"Goodbye, Smoke, dearest. Be careful."

"You, too. And keep your friend close at hand."

"I will." Sally turned away so as not to have to witness the actual moment of Smoke's departure. When Thunder's hoofbeats faded down the lane to the ranch, she turned to wave at Smoke's back.

Mountain man instincts, imbued in him by his mentor, Preacher—who some were starting to call, rightly or not, the First Mountain Man—alerted Smoke Jensen to the presence of others even before Thunder twitched his big, black ears and swiveled them forward to listen down the trail. The stallion's spotted gray rump hide rippled in anticipation. Always cautious, even in this settled country, Smoke drifted off the trail, thankful that snow had not yet fallen. He dismounted and put a big, hard hand over Thunder's muzzle to prevent an unwanted greeting to others of the stallion's kind. Five minutes later, two young men rode into view.

They had the look about them of ranch hands and an air of that wandering fraternity loosely described as drifters. Smoke Jensen noted that their clothing was a cut above average. They wore their hats at a jaunty angle and rode easy in the saddle. Their conversation, when it reached his ears, convinced Smoke of the accuracy of his surmise.

"It's gettin' close to winter, Buck."

"Sure is, Jason. I sure hope there's a spread out here somewhere that'll take us on for the winter. Be dang cold tryin' to get by on our own."

"No foolin', Buck. But you know, I hear there's old cabins hereabouts, shanties put up by the fur traders. We could settle down in one of them."

"What are we gonna use to buy supplies?" Buck challenged.

Jason considered it in silence as they approached the spot where Smoke Jensen had concealed himself off the trail. "I reckon that's why we should find us a place to earn some cash money."

"Don't no moss grow on you, Jase."

That decided Smoke. He led Thunder by the headstall onto the trail. Startled, the riders reined abruptly, then raised their hands, eyes wide." You ain't gonna rob us, is you, Mister?"

Smoke chuckled. "No—nothing like that. I overheard you talking about looking for work. As it happens, I could use a couple of hands right now." Smoke took stock of their location. Less than three miles from Big Rock. Couldn't take them back. "I can't take you there and introduce you around. I'll write you a note. Take it to Cole Travis, my winter foreman, and to my wife, Sally."

"Why, that's mighty generous of you, Mister . . . ?"

"The name's Jensen."

"Right, Mr. Jensen," Buck said. "We're obliged. I'm Buck Jarvis, an' this is Jason Rucker. We'll work hard for you, that I promise."

"I know you will, boys." Smoke's steely gray eyes told them why he did. "The Sugarloaf is ten miles up this trail, in a large highland valley. You'll make it about in time for dinner. Walk your horses slow. Takes time to accustom them to the altitude."

"Thank you, Mr. Jensen. You'll not regret this."

"Fine, boys. Let me do that note." Smoke delved in a shirt pocket for a scrap of paper and a stub of pencil.

After Smoke had parted from Buck and Jason, the young drifters pondered over the name. "Jensen, huh?" Buck intoned. "I wonder if he's any relation to you know who?"

"Naw, he couldn't be. That Smoke Jensen's a gunfighter and a cold-blooded killer. Ain't no way a man that nice would be related," Jason assured his partner.

* * *

In Big Rock, Smoke Jensen had a three hour wait for the D&RG daily train north to the Union Pacific junction. He left Thunder to be loaded on a stock car and walked down Main Street to the sheriff's office. Although Smoke was a skilled woodsman, the horse was an integral part of the life of a mountain man as in later years it became for the Texas cowboys. Old Preacher always grumbled when put to walking.

When Smoke had met Preacher, his life changed forever.

Mountain men invented rugged individualism. They personified self-reliance. And the man known to all as Preacher outdid them all. Preacher had named him Smoke the first day they'd met.

And "Smoke" he became from that day. Now, walking along the muddy, rutted central avenue in Big Rock, Smoke Jensen savored all that. Yet he missed Thunder's slab flanks between his legs more than he would admit, even to himself. Gratitude flooded him as he reached the open doorway to the sheriff's office.

"Don't you ever do any work?" Smoke bellowed at the man behind the desk inside, whose newspaper concealed his face, and whose ubiquitous black hat topped a thick mane of silver hair.

The boots came down from the desk with a thud and the copy of the Denver *Post* fluttered to the desk top. "Dang it now, Smoke Jensen. What the devil you mean, sneakin' up on a body like that?"

"Monte, you never change. I'm on my way to San Francisco, thought I'd stop by and let you know I'd be gone from the Sugarloaf."

"Glad you did. I've been hopin' for an excuse to go after a cup of coffee with a shot of rye in it. Let's go down to the Gold Field."

"Might as well. I've got a three-hour wait."

Out of doors again, the two old friends ambled down the street, lawman fashion—out in the middle, where no one could come at them suddenly from a doorway. Smoke Jensen had often trod both sides of the law. Yet he had always returned, passionately, to the side of decency. The main thing that had kept him from settling down and accepting a permanent badge, as Monte had done, was all the infernal walking a man had to do in the job. One could not rattle doorknobs from horseback. Of course, the deputy U.S. marshal's badge he carried in the fold of his wallet was another matter entirely.

None of the mundane details of a peace officer's routine stifled his freedom of movement or action. Smoke rarely used it, and he thought of it even less. Yet it was a comfort, given the reputation he had acquired, much of it the fanciful blathering of the authors of the penny dreadfuls and dime novels. More than once, his marshal's badge had gotten him out of tight spots. In the last few years he had not needed to resort to it often.

Perhaps the world had indeed passed him by while he'd languished in the beautiful valley that housed his ranch. He banished such thoughts when he realized Monte had been talking to him for some while.

". . . Like I said, this country is getting downright tame."

"Uh—yep. Funny thing, I was just thinking the same thing," Smoke responded.

"Used to be, it was wild fights. Now, I don't bust the head of more than one rowdy drunk a week."

Smoke gave his friend a puzzled look. "You're complaining, Monte?"

Monte sucked his cheeks hollow as he contemplated that. "Well, now, I 'm not sayin' that I object all that much. Bruises take longer to heal at my age. I caught me a winner of a shiner three weeks ago. The last of the yaller an' green faded out yesterday."

Smoke joined him in a hearty laugh. Abruptly, new voices, harsh and slurred by whiskey, interrupted their camaraderie. "What we got here?"

"Couple of old farts hoggin' the street, I'd say."

"You be right, Rupe. Hey, Grandpa, ain't you got horses? Or cain't you git up in the saddle anymore?"

"That's the ticket, Bri. You geezers get over on that boardwalk. The street is for *men.*"

Brian's fourth companion joined in. "That big 'un's packin' iron, boys. S'pose he knows how to use it?"

The menace in his words froze Smoke Jensen and Monte Carson in their steps. Slowly, they turned as one to face their drunken tormentors. Arctic glaciers covered Smoke's words. "If you are looking for a lesson, I would be glad to oblige."

Monte laid a hand on Smoke's forearm. "No need for that, ol' hoss. Remember, you have a train to catch in less than three hours."

Brian got back into it. "D'ya hear that, Casey? This doddering idiot is calling you out."

Rupe got his two cents in, as well. "Fin, you think we oughta back up ol' Casey? That feller looks mighty mean."

Truth to tell, the years had been kind to Smoke Jensen. He still retained the barrel chest and large, powerful muscles of his youth. His face was creased, but with the squint lines of an outdoorsman. Only the faintest traces of gray could be seen at his temples. Those, and the streak of pure white where a bullet had once gouged his scalp, provided the only indications that he was not a man in his early thirties. The legendary speed of his draw had not diminished a jot. Still, he had no quarrel with these intoxicated louts. Smoke raised a hand in a gesture of peace.

"There'll be no gunfighting," he declared, in as soft a tone as he could manage.

With a skin full of liquor, Fin just had to push it. "Oh, yeah? You insulted my friends, and I'm not going to let you get away with it, old man."

Smoke cut his eyes to Monte and sighed heavily. "I don't see as how there's much you can do about it. My friend and I simply will not draw on you."

Swinging a leg over his mount, Brian issued a new challenge. "Then, what say we step down and pound you into the ground like a fence post?"

Smoke Jensen had run out of all his nice guy attitude. His eyes turned a dangerous ice-gray and narrowed while he drew on a pair of thin black leather gloves he carried folded over his cartridge belt. "If you try it, I'll have to kick your butt up between your shoulder blades."

That did it. Fin, Rupe, Brian, and Casey cleared their saddles and rushed at Smoke Jensen and Monte Carson. Brian swung a hard fist that did not connect. With surprising speed, Smoke had stepped back. Confused, Brian hesitated. Which gave Smoke time to set himself for a hog-stopper of a punch. A blissful smile lighted his face as he rapped Brian solidly in the teeth.

Blood flew from one tooth that broke off. Brian rocked back on his feet and shook his head. A red haze misted his eyes. To his left, Fin threw a punch that landed hard against Smoke's ribs. Without taking his gaze from Brian, Smoke snapped a sharp sideways right that landed in the center of Fin's sternum and put him on his butt. Smoke cut a quick glance Monte's way.

The marshal had all he could handle in Rupe and Casey. Arms windmilling, the young louts rained a series of blows down on Monte that drove him backward. While Smoke watched, the quick-moving youths drove Monte to one knee. This wouldn't be as easy as he had thought, Smoke realized, as he set himself to receive Brian's charge.

TWO

Brian came at him like a furious bull. The punches he had gleefully planned a moment before did not land. Smoke Jensen received the young bully with a series of stinging, punishing blows to the face, left . . . right . . . left . . . right . . . left. A cut opened above Brian's left eye that sent a sheet of blood to blind him. His nose smashed, more crimson fountains joined the flow. Already damaged lips grew fatter and scarlet ribbons of tinted saliva hung in long strands. Brian's knees buckled when the hard leather-encased knuckles of Smoke Jensen crashed solidly against his jaw.

Taking a step back as Brian toppled, Smoke brought up a knee with blurring speed. It cracked under the point of Brian's chin. He went to the ground twitching and unconscious. That didn't slow Fin any. He had recovered enough to fly at Smoke, arms held wide, to grab the older man around the waist. They crashed to the dirt of the street together. Fin's arms tightened, squeezing Smoke's intestines painfully. Air gushed from his lungs. Dark dots danced before Smoke's eyes. Fin drove a shoulder into Smoke's gut.

Sharp agony shot through Smoke's liver. Smoke rolled slowly to the side until Fin was on top. Then he drove a fist into Fin's right kidney. It brought forth a grunt and a howl. A second hammer blow brought another grunt and a loosening of Fin's grip. Smoke smacked him soundly on the top of the head. Fin's arms fell away. Smoke grabbed Fin by the chin and the back of his head. His slackened neck muscles gave little resistance as Smoke twisted violently to his right. Just short of breaking Fin's neck, he let off pressure.

Fin began to twitch and jerk like a demented marionette. Arms and legs flew akimbo as he did a crab scuttle in the dust. In the next second, Smoke Jensen turned to aid his older friend. Monte Carson had one of the punks bent over a tie-rail, pounding the exposed, taut belly of Rupe like a drum. Clutching an abandoned length of tow-by-four, Casey began a swing at Monte's head.

Smoke got to him first. Before Casey could launch his attack, Smoke grabbed the chunk of lumber and yanked backward. Casey went off his feet. He struck the ground on his shoulders. Give him credit, Smoke thought, he bounded right back. Snarling, the bully swung the board at Smoke. The last mountain man anticipated that and dodged. With his opponent off balance, Smoke kicked him in the knee. Wobbly, Casey doubled over, to catch a fist in his face. He backpedaled two painful steps and then sat down. Hands at the ready, Smoke Jensen surveyed their accomplishments.

Fin still jittered on the street, his face in a pile of horse dung. A groggy Brian tried to regain his feet. His face a mass of red gore, he shook his head, which released a shower of droplets. Bleary-eyed, he located his enemy and stumbled toward Smoke Jensen. His arms weighted a ton each. In aching slow motion, he raised his fists and set himself for a punch.

It came not from Brian, but from Smoke. Brian's head snapped back, his knees buckled and he toppled like a fallen tree. Smoke stepped in to finish him. Monte Carson released the drunken lout he had been pounding and turned to Smoke Jensen.

"That's enough, Smoke."

"Whaaa?" Rupe bleated. Clutching his badly pounded belly, Rupe looked up as though from a deep bow. "What'd you call him?"

"Smoke," Monte answered simply. "His name is Smoke Jensen."

"Aaah, Gaaad!" Rupe wailed. "Please, Mr. Jensen, please don't kill us."

Smoke turned to the youth. "I didn't start this."

"I know—I know," Rupe babbled. "Only we was just fun-nin'. Please spare us, Mr. Jensen. I—I know who you are."

"Obviously," Smoke replied icily. "Too bad you didn't before you started this."

Fin had stopped twitching and now came to all fours with a groan. "Didn't mean no harm, Mr. Jensen," he whined, whey-faced.

Smoke glowered at them. "It sure as thunder didn't look like it."

"I should lock the four of you up until you get sober."

"Who are you? The marshal?"

"No. I'm Sheriff Monte Carson."

"Oh, Jesus, now I know we're dead," Rupe sobbed.

"Like I said, I *should* lock you up, but I figure you've had enough punishment for one day. Now, get your partners on their horses and get the hell out of Big Rock. You have a quarter hour."

"Yes, sir—yes, sir, oh, yessir!" Rupe gobbled in terror and relief.

They managed it in less than five. Their humiliation-reddened ears still rang with the sound of hearty laughter from Smoke Jensen and Monte Carson as they cleared the city limit.

Out in California, in the gold fields on the Sacramento River, a miner worked his claim alone under the shade of huge, ancient live oaks. A crafty man and a proficient prospector, Ray Wagner had forged higher up the river than those who had been attracted by the magnet of the Sutter's Mill discovery more than thirty years before. Logic and a basic knowledge of physics told him that the gold found farther down had to have a source higher up. As a result, he had a prosperous claim that produced three-fold what the next most productive outfit took from the river. He had just dumped a shovel-load of mud and gravel into his riffle-box sluice when he sensed the presence of others.

Always a cautious man, Wagner had a bulky, superbly made 10mm Mauser tucked in the waistband of his trousers. He set the shovel aside, and instead of reaching for the gold pan to work the finings, he put his long, strong fingers around the parrot-bill butt of the revolver. Then he turned to confront his uninvited guests.

"Won't be no need for that, Mister," a runty, bow-legged specimen, who had Cornish miner written all over him, declared in a crusty voice.

Level nut-brown eyes fixed on the intruder. "I didn't hear you howdy m' claim," Ray Wagner challenged tightly.

"Well, we did. Likely you didn't hear us for the water rushing through that sluice. If you be Raymond Wagner, we have something important for you."

"Yeah, I am," Wagner replied.

The runty one produced a sheaf of documents in a stiff, blue paper legal binder. "These are for you. All you need do is sign where the x-marks are."

Suspicious, Wagner did not reach for the papers, but kept his grip on his Mauser. "What is it I'm signing?"

"No need to read through 'em. Just sign."

Wagner's eyes narrowed and he shook his head. "I never sign anything I haven't read."

"All right," came the testy response. "Take 'em and read."

Wagner reached left-handed and took the documents. He quickly learned that they were a quit-claim deed and transfer of title for his claim. His thin lips hardened into a stubborn line. Tethering his anger, he pushed the papers back toward the former Cornishman.

"I will not sign these. I do not wish to leave this place, or give up my gold find."

Meanness revealed itself in the runt's face and he and his companions spread out, away from their horses. "You really don't have a choice. Now, sign them like a good boy, pack up, and be on your way."

"And what am I to be paid for my claim?"

"Paid?" the runt repeated. "Why, with the enjoyment of the rest of your life."

That brought the Mauser out with respectable speed. *"Unglüclicher Bastarben!* Get off my claim, you miserable bastards," Wagner repeated his curse in English. "I will give you two minutes to get out of sight."

Shaking with rage, the runty one stalked to his horse and mounted. "We'll be back. And when we come, you will regret this."

"I think not," Wagner countered. "Now, move, or be buried here."

Smoke Jensen got up from the table considerably better off than when he had taken a seat some two hours earlier. "Thank you, gentlemen, for an entertaining evening."

With that, he departed the smoking car of the Union Pacific *Daylight Flyer,* westbound for California. Two men, modest winners in their own right, left behind him. The carriage was provided for the convenience of gentlemen who wished to indulge in tobacco or spirits, or both, while making the long journey from their homes to their distant destinations. Three round baize-covered tables also accommodated those who wished to wager on a game of skill. In this case, poker, to be exact. Over the time Smoke had been in the game, the fortunes of those in the game had declined steadily, three of them quite sharply. One of the heavy losers spoke bitterly, his tone one of whining complaint.

"I still say he cheated."

"No," an older man said. "Only a matter of real skill, I would say."

"But, it ain't fair; he took all of me an' Billy's money," the complainer sniveled.

"Teddy's right," a pouting Billy added to the whining. "He done cleaned us out, near on eight hundred dollars. Money we earned fair and square." Earned in this case by driving cattle to market and selling them. *Other people's* cattle.

Smarting from his own substantial loss, the elder man could bear their childish petulance no further. "If you really feel that way, why don't you go take it away from him?" he asked sarcastically.

Billy and Teddy exchanged surprised glances. They hadn't thought of that. Now, with Smoke out of the room, the sheer size and latent menace forgotten, the idea presented enormous appeal. A wicked light of cupidity shone in Billy's eyes as he cut them to the older man.

"You're a smart man, Mr. Rankin. We'd of never though of that. What say, Teddy? You game for it?"

Teddy was already out of his chair. "You bet I am. Let's git on with it."

A teasing light of cynicism flickered in Rankin's eyes. "Of course, you'll replace my losses in return for finding the solution?"

"Oh, sure, Mr. Rankin. You can count on that," Teddy burbled.

When pigs start to fly, Rankin thought. But, never mind; he had his own idea of how to retrieve his portion, and with considerable interest. He wished the youthful rustlers well and watched them on their way.

Billy and Teddy caught up with Smoke Jensen on the platform between the parlor car behind the smoker and the Pullman beyond that. Through the beveled glass lattice window of the car door they saw him crossing over to the far platform, hand out to grasp the brass latch lever. Teddy was aslobber in eagerness, his hand on the grip of the underpowered Colt .38 Model '77 Lightning in the Furstnow/Zimmerman "Texas" style shoulder holster in his left armpit. When Billy yanked open the door on their side, he also drew his .44 Colt.

Yelling to be heard over the rattle and clatter of the steel-wheeled trucks, he called to Smoke, "Hold it right there, Jensen!"

Smoke risked a quick look over one shoulder and noted that both had weapons in hand. "What seems to be the problem?"

"You cheated, and we want our money back," Teddy enlightened him.

"Sorry. I don't cheat and you don't get anything back."

"You think because we're young, we'll bluff easy," Teddy snarled. "You don't even know who we are."

"Two boys in way over their heads, I'd say," Smoke said.

"We're *danger*. We're the biggest, meanest, smartest rustler gang in Wyoming, Colorado, and Kansas, that's who we are."

Smoke had all he could take of this pair. "Frankly, I think you are full of crap. Grow up, Sonny-Boy and take your loss like a man."

"Then we'll take it from you if we have to kill you to do it," Billy railed.

"You'll never make it, Sonny."

"Goddamn you, Jensen!" Billy shrieked.

Smoke could not hear the sear notches on Billy's six-gun ratchet to full-cock over the noise of the train, but he knew it happened. He flexed his knees and pivoted on his left boot heel. His .45 Colt Peacemaker appeared in his right fist as though by magic. Even with their six-guns at the ready, Smoke's prediction came true. He put his first bullet into Teddy's shoulder. His second took Billy in the gut.

Teddy dropped his Lightning and began to scream and cry like a girl. For all the speed of the double-action revolver, he had not been able to get it in play. Billy tried to raise his Colt again and Smoke shot him a second time. An expression of surprised disbelief fixed his features in a pinched, puckered mouth and blankly staring eyes. Slowly he sagged to his knees, then toppled sideways. His six-gun forgotten, he began to writhe in agony. Smoke stepped quickly across and kicked the revolver away from the young thug. Suddenly the door behind Billy flew open and Rankin appeared in the entrance, backlighted by the yellow glow of kerosene lamps. The blue steel barrel of the Merwin and Hulbert .44 in his left hand glittered wickedly.

Before Smoke Jensen could react, Rankin's weapon barked. The slug cracked loudly past Smoke's head an instant before Smoke obliged Rankin with a slug in the brain. Rankin went down in a rubber-limbed heap. Half a heartbeat later, the wide-eyed, badly shaken conductor arrived.

"Oh m'god, what happened here?"

"These three tried to kill me," Smoke answered.

Crouched by the corpse of Rankin, the conductor gaped up at Smoke. "But, why?"

"They figured to rob me."

Indignation rang in the supervisor's voice. "Not on *my* train."

Smoke lifted the corners of his mouth in a fleeting smile. "That's how I saw it, too."

"This is terrible, simply terrible. All this mess. And the passengers. What will we do about them?"

"Well, we could spare them the awful sight."

"How's that?"

"We could simply dump this garbage off the train."

The round eyes went wider. "Oh, no, we could never do that. There will have to be an inquiry into the shooting," the conductor insisted.

Right then, Billy ceased his groans and gasps. With a little shudder, he stopped writhing. The trainman eyed the newly made corpse and the other, and the wailing youth with the bloody shoulder. Then he looked back at Smoke and correctly read the steely gray eyes. He swallowed hard to get his words past the hard lump in his throat.

"Well," he said meekly, "if Mr. Smoke Jensen will say nothing about the incident, I certainly won't." To his surprise, Smoke frowned and pointed at the wounded Teddy.

"One's still alive."

"D-do you want that taken care of?"

"Noo," Smoke drawled. "We'll stop off at the county seat and have that little inquiry."

Relieved, the conductor sighed deeply. "I'll go make arrangements to have the bodies wrapped up and moved to the baggage car."

Early morning reached San Francisco in a pink haze. Starlings twittered in the cornices of the public buildings off Market Street. Pigeons cooed indignantly at this invasion by their smaller, sleek cousins. On the wide front porch of his splendid home on Knob Hill, Cyrus Murchison gave his wife a buss on her peaches-and-cream cheek.

"I'll be late tonight, Agatha, my dear."

"Oh, Cyrus, you've been working so hard lately. Can't anyone else run that railroad of yours?"

"Yes. And there are a lot of them doing that day and night," the portly Murchison assured her. "This is . . . other business."

Agatha frowned. "You're seeing Titus and Gaylord again." It came out a statement.

Abashed, Murchison sputtered his reply. "But they're my friends. They are also my only peers in commerce and industry."

"Empire building, you mean," Agatha charged pettishly.

Murchison brushed vacantly at the thick gold watch chain that hung in twin loops from the pockets of his dark navy pinstriped vest. Grown portly from good living, he had the florid face to go with the rich diet and ample spirits he consumed. In his early fifties, he had a layer of fat right under his skin that gave him the youthful appearance of a man ten years his junior. Often hailed in the pages of the San Francisco *Chronicle* as a "captain of industry," Murchison had reached the pinnacle of his enterprise through hard, if often dishonest, effort. His sole weakness was his relationship with his wife.

Put frankly, Agatha terrified him. One of her looks, a gesture, or a soft, deprecating word could swiftly unman him. While he was a tyrant to every subordinate and lived life like an autocrat, Cyrus Murchison quailed at the mildest rebuke from the woman he adored above all things save power. Now he shot a quick look over his shoulder. His carriage, complete with liveried driver, waited to take him to his office.

"Be that as it may, my dear. But this meeting is important. Tell cook not to hold supper."

He bent to give her another quick peck, then put his hat firmly on his head and turned to negotiate the steps. He strolled briskly down the flagstone walk to a gate in the white-painted, wrought-iron picket fence. The driver opened the carriage door and touched fingers to the brim of his hat, a tugging the forelock gesture.

Seated in the brougham, Cyrus Murchison mentally reviewed the events of the past few days. Gaylord Huntley was a fool to believe they could use those people and get out of it unaffected; they'd invented the squeeze. He sighed heavily.

But they need them. Not all of the employees in their various enterprises could be corrupted. Another thing rankled even more. So they let that sourdough run them off, eh? One man against three, and not a one had had forethought or fortitude enough to force him to sign? Next time, it might be well to have Tyrone Beal take charge of gaining that mining property.

Stubborn man, that Raymond Wagner. A German, and block-headed. Titus Hobson simply had no idea of how to properly delegate authority. He made his way to the top in the gold fields by himself, and never learned how to rely on the judgment and performance of other men. On the other hand, Murchison mused, he had learned that lesson early in the building of his California Central railroad empire. He would have some hot words for his companions that evening. Something he felt certain they would not like to hear.

An early riser by habit from his time in the gold fields of Central California, Titus Hobson already sat at his desk. Although he was a good five years older than Cyrus Murchison, he retained powerful shoulders and arms from his years of working at mining and prospecting. Every bit as rich as Murchison, he remained a bit rough around the edges. His clothes might be of the best cloth and perfectly fitted, but they lost their luster on his burly frame. He eased himself forward in the leatherbound swivel chair to gaze down on San Francisco from his office on the fourth floor of the Flatiron Building. His eyes settled on the oddly peaked roofs of Chinatown. A smile played across his craggy face and set his bushy brows to waggling.

This thing with the Chinese—he liked it. Yes, let those little yellow devils take the lumps, if indeed any were to be handed out. But would they take orders from a white man? They should; thousands of them had labored on Cyrus's railroad. They would settle the Chinese question tonight. Cyrus still had to be brought around. Gaylord had convinced him yesterday. It was up to the two of them to sway Cyrus. He smacked a hard hand on the glowing mahogany desktop.

"Hell, we should be able to handle this ourselves," he said aloud, startling himself. To cover speaking to an empty room, he called out to his male secretary, "Alex, bring me a cup of coffee."

"Right away, Mr. Hobson."

Hobson picked up the report once more. Neat rows of numbers ran down the page in columns. Looking at them irritated him. He could read and write; he'd taught himself after he'd made that big strike on Rush's Mountain. He could do his figures right enough, too. Only, this many numbers tended to blend together into a single indecipherable mass. If this accountant of Cyrus's was right, they were all going to become a whole lot richer than their wildest dreams. That comforting thought made his belly rumble. He always had a little snack at mid-morning. Why not a little early?

"Oh, and Alex, bring me a piece of that cream cake."

Gaylord Huntley stepped catfooted up to the bull-necked bruiser who stood defiantly in the gateway of pier 7. The gigantic longshoreman held a cargo hook in one huge fist and a wicked filleting knife in the other. He seemed not the least intimidated by the presence of the overlord of all San Francisco dockworkers.

"When I say you don't work these docks," Huntley growled, "I mean you are out, even in times of emergency. Now, get your butt out of my sight."

"You're not throwing me out, Huntley. I come to work, and I aim to finish it."

Lightning fast, Huntley's ham fist flashed from his side and cracked into the center of the longshoreman's chest. The dockworker's eyes crossed and air gushed out of him. Huntley followed up with a left to the jaw, then reversed to backhand the hook out of his way. Half a dozen onlookers remained frozen in place.

To them it appeared Huntley had forgotten the knife. He hadn't. As it flashed forward, his right hand filled with the parrot-bill grip of a .44 Colt Lightning, which he snapped free of a high hip holster and squeezed through the double-action trigger to send a round square into the belligerent longshoreman's heart. He fell dead at Huntley's feet.

"Dump this trash in the bay," he commanded his other workers.

"Yes, sir, Mr. Huntley," one blurted.

All of them had long ago been intimidated by this ferret-faced man with the bulging shoulders and arms of their trade. Gaylord Huntley's oily black hair, slicked straight back on his elongated head, added to the ratlike visage created by black, close-set eyes and protruding yellowed teeth. Seen from behind, Huntley's stature was laughable.

Some few had made the mistake of laughing. His oversized upper torso dwindled rapidly to a narrow waist and short legs planted on small feet. It gave him the appearance of a soaked wharf rat. Those who had sniggered at that sight had paid for it . . . painfully. Not a few had paid with their lives. Huntley did not waste time on watching the disposal. He reholstered his Colt and turned from the dock. His mind went at once to the meeting with Cyrus and Titus.

Over dinner, they would settle the idea of using the Chinese instead of his longshoremen or Cyrus's railroad detectives to enforce their will. It had been his idea. He considered himself to be a remarkable judge of the abilities and the reliability of other men. He found Xiang Lee to be capable and trustworthy, if a little full of himself. He believed he had sold Titus on it the previous day. Only Murchison objected strongly. Perhaps that could be changed. He smiled in anticipation as he entered his office.

"Ah, my dear Millie," he greeted the young woman seated in a comfortable chair beside a large potted palm. "Won't you come in, please? I have need of your special talents." Killing always made him hunger for a woman's charms.

THREE

At Rock Springs, the county seat of Sweetwater County, Wyoming, the train pulled to its scheduled stop and Smoke Jensen readied himself for the inevitable questions he had encountered so many times before. The conductor, a man named Ames, had arranged for the sheriff and the doctor who served as coroner to come aboard the train to conduct their inquiry.

That gave Smoke a little more confidence. The railroad would back him. Unfortunately, some bogus Wanted posters might still circulate in Wyoming. That harkened back to the time when dark forces had combined to have him marked as a man wanted for murder. It had brought him literally years of grief. He looked up now as the trainman and the law returned to the baggage car.

"I know you," the sheriff growled, his eyes narrowing as he entered.

"I don't know you," Smoke quipped back.

"Sheriff Harvey Lane. You're a wanted man, Smoke Jensen."

Smoke answered simply, "No, I'm not."

"I have a wanted flyer . . ." Lane began, to be cut off by a raised hand and a sharp bark from Smoke.

"It's all crap, Sheriff. You should know that by now. Those were fraudulent when they were printed and they were recalled a month after being issued. Let's get on to this shooting."

"Why did you kill them?" Lane quickly changed gears.

"Like I told Mr. Ames here, they were trying to kill me."

Lane spoke drily. "Of course there could be no possible reason for that?"

"I had just finished nearly cleaning them out at poker. The punk kids turned out to be part of a rustling gang. The whole gang, I suspect."

"You have any proof of that?"

"Ask our boy Teddy. He's locked up in the strong room," Smoke snapped.

Sheriff Lane cut a sharp eye to the conductor, who nodded. "Yep. Once I got him away from Smoke—er—Mr. Jensen, he wouldn't stop babbling. Confessed to all sorts of things. Claimed the dead boy, Billy, forced him to participate. Said they'd rustled cattle in five states."

"Well, well," Lane mused aloud. "There anyone else I can ask?"

"The other players in the poker game," Smoke suggested.

Wrath darkened the lawman's hawklike visage. "Now I got a gunfighter and killer tellin' me my business."

Tired from the fight the previous day and strained to the limit by the attempt on his life, Smoke Jensen had absorbed all of this he could. "No," Smoke countered as he produced his wallet and badge. "You have a deputy U.S. marshal telling you your business."

Lane's jaw sagged. "Well, I'll . . . be . . . damned. You working on somethin' now, Marshal Jensen?"

Amazing, how his tone changed, Smoke mused. "If I am, it does not involve your jurisdiction. I'm sure Mr. Ames has told you I am ticketed through to San Francisco."

"I think I am beginning to see. Well, then, I'm off to talk to those players and this yonker rustler. Enjoy your journey, Marshal Jensen."

After the sheriff left the car, Ames looked blankly at Smoke. "What was that all about?"

"I ask you," Smoke shot back.

Three men met the eleven o'clock local of the California Central when it rolled into Parkerville, California. Their leader, the bandy-legged one who had confronted Ray Wagner, wore a surly expression and spoke with false bravado.

"Whoever the boss is sending had better be in the mood to take orders."

"But didn't the telegram from San Francisco say he was to be in charge?" one of his henchmen asked ingenuously.

"Button that lip, Quint. *I'm* the boss around here. And this sissy city dude had better know it."

With a final hiss, screech, and groan, the train came to a stop. The first to bound down the folding iron steps was a huge, burly man with flame-red hair and a big walrus mustache that drooped around thick, tobacco-stained lips. He had a saddle slung over one massive shoulder that made the rig look tiny. It became obvious he could not be someone for whom any of the delicate women and small children waited. He made a quick study of those on the platform and walked directly to the trio.

"You must be Spencer. I'm Beal. Get me a horse," he commanded the erstwhile leader.

Swallowing with difficulty, the bow-legged hard case surrendered his captaincy and responded humbly. "Yes, sir. Right away."

Tyrone Beal had arrived.

Cyrus Murchison had chosen well. Beal led a company of twenty-five railroad detectives, under the direct order of his boss, Hector Grange, Chief of Railroad Police for the California Central. Always big for his age, Beal had killed his first man at the age of thirteen, beaten him to death with his fists. The man was his stepfather, a brute and drunk who alternately beat his stepchildren and his wife. The authorities sent Tyrone Beal to a school for errant boys for six months while the family moved to another county, and then Beal was released.

Since that time, he had never let anyone back him down. Never. No two-bit gold chaser was about to be the first. He had heard of the failure of Spencer and his underlings. They should have taken ax handles to the stupid German and beaten some sense into him. He privately gave himself ten minutes to convince Wagner. He dismissed this as he studied the two henchmen who accompanied Spencer.

"Can either of you count to twenty without taking off your boots?" he growled.

They exchanged puzzled glances. "Uh—what's that mean?" one asked.

Beal gave them a contemptuous sneer. "I gather that means no. Now, get this straight, I don't like to repeat myself. You are going to take me out to this Wagner claim and we are going to get his signature. There will be no failure. Clear?"

They nodded their heads dumbly. Spencer returned then and took in the display. Anger rose again. He stomped over and put his face up in that of Tyrone Beal. "Those are my men. They take their orders from me."

Beal's answer came back heavy with menace. "Not . . . any . . . more. Now, saddle my horse and let's head for that claim."

The humiliation of that was more than Spencer could bear. "You can go to hell. C'mon, boys, we're out of this. Let the *big man* handle it himself"

Beal's right ham fist came up with a blur of speed. He mushed Spencer's mouth and knocked the smaller man on his butt. "When I give an order, it is obeyed."

He turned on one heel and started for the tie-rail at one end of the station. Spencer's underlings followed him, gaping.

Sally Jensen stood in the shade of the porch roof. Small fists on hips, she looked across the yard at the hands gathered near the breaking corral. Young Bobby had crowded in among them. Ordinarily, that would not trouble her. But of late, the boy had taken to the newcomers as his idols. It wasn't often that Sally questioned the judgment of her husband.

In his life of enforced caution, Smoke sometimes made bad judgments about people. Sally had recently begun to hold a mild distrust toward the drifters Smoke had sent with that note. At least, he would be in San Francisco the next day and she would know where to contact him. Only thing, would she pass on her distress to worry him? He would think her taken with old maidish vapors, she scoffed at herself. A loud shout drew her attention closer to the ranch hands.

At the urging of Buck Jarvis and Jason Rucker, the new hands, Bobby Jensen had climbed over the top rail and made for a particularly fractious young stallion who stood splay-legged at the tie-rail. Foam flecked its black lips and hung in strings nearly to the ground. Its buckskin hide glistened with sweat and its bellows chest heaved from exertion. So far he had dumped three hands. A sharp pang of concern shot through Sally and she hoisted her skirts to make room for her boots to fly faster.

Running brokenly, Sally streaked toward the corral. "Bobby!" she yelled. "Bobby, don't you dare get on that horse."

Most of the hands, the old-timers, turned to look and said nothing. Buck and Jase sneered and Buck turned his head to shout encouragement to the boy. "Go on, Bobby. You know you can do it.

"That's enough!" Sally commanded. "If that boy gets on that horse, you can pick up your time as of now."

"Awh, come on, Miz Jensen. You're gonna make a sissy out of him," Jason Rucker brushed off the threat.

"Cole, you hear me?" Sally called to their winter foreman, Cole Travis.

"Sure do, Miss Sally," Travis responded, a tight smile on his face.

"I mean what I say. If Bobby gets on that horse, you throw them off the Sugarloaf."

An uncomfortable silence followed in which Sally reached the cluster of hands at the corral. Buck would not meet her eye. Jase turned his back insolently. Sally marched to the gate, slid the bar, and entered. She raised an imperious hand toward the lad who stood before her, the pain of humiliation written on his face.

"Come on out of here, Bobby," she ordered quietly.

"But I *can* ride him. I know I can."

"I'm not going to argue with you. Come with me."

"Please? He's worn down some now. At least let me try?"

"Not another word. Come along."

Outside the corral again, with Bobby in tow, Sally had the first pang of regret as she looked at his miserable expression. Huge, fat tears welled up and threatened to spill down his face. She knew she had done right! Then another part of her mind mocked her; *How would Smoke have handled it?*

"Saaan Fraaaan-cisssco. Last stop. Saaan Fraaan-ciiisssco!" the conductor brayed as he passed through the cars of the *Daylight Express*.

Smoke Jensen, who had been snoozing, tipped up the brim of his hat and gazed out the window of the Pullman car. A row of weathered gray shanties—shacks, actually—lined the twin tracks. A gaggle of barefoot, shirtless boys of roughly eight to ten years old made impudent gestures to the passengers as the train rolled past their squalid homes. How different from youngsters in the High Lonesome, Smoke mused. There they would be clean as Sunday-to-meeting, bundled up to their ears in coats and scarves and in rabbit-fur-lined moccasins or boots to protect them from the cold. Already the car felt warm, after their descent from the low costal range. Gradually the speed drained off the creaking, swaying coaches.

Now grim factories and warehouses took the place of the shacks. No doubt those youngsters' fathers toiled in these places, Smoke reasoned. How could any man labor day after day with the only light from windows too high up to see out of and only dingy inner walls to look at. How could they stand it? He wondered again if Thunder had received proper care.

His twice-daily visits to the stock car had not provided time enough to make a thorough check. Smoke had acquired the 'Palouse stallion from an old Arapaho horse trader to add new vitality to the bloodline of his prize horses. The Arapaho had obtained Thunder from the Nez Perce who had raised him from a colt and gently broken him. The beast proved to be better as a saddle horse than as a breeder. Accordingly, Smoke had ridden him for more than three years now. A sturdy mountain horse, Thunder could cover ground with the best of them. For years Smoke had worn smooth-knob cavalry spurs out of respect for his horses. As a result, not a scar showed on Thunder's flanks. A huge rush of steam and a jolt of compressing couplers announced the arrival at the depot as the locomotive braked to a stop.

Smoke roused himself and retrieved his saddlebags from a rack overhead. At night, the same rack served as frame for the fold-down bed that he had occupied for two nights. Not the most comfortable arrangement, Smoke acknowledged, but it beat the daylights out of a chair car. A trip back East with Sally several years ago had spoiled him. They had ridden in luxury in the private car of the president of the Denver and Rio Grande.

They had their own room, and a big, soft bed that did not even creak when they made love. Now, *that* was the way to travel. Until man learned to fly—a foolish notion!—Smoke would prefer the pleasures of a private car for long-distance journeys. When the Pullman finally came to a jerking halt, Smoke walked down the aisle to the open vestibule door and outside, to descend from the train.

He had a short wait while the crew positioned a ramp and opened the stock car. A vague hunger gnawed him, so Smoke availed himself of a large, fat tamale from a vendor with a large white box fitted on the front of a bicycle. The thick cornmeal roll was stuffed with a generous portion of shredded beef and lots of spices, including chili peppers, Smoke soon found out. Mouth afire, Smoke rigidly controlled his reaction, determined not to give the Mexican peddler the satisfaction of seeing a *gringo* suffer.

Ten minutes later, as Smoke finished the last bite of the savory treat, a trainman walked Thunder down the ramp. Smoke hastened forward, but not fast enough. Typically, Thunder, like most 'Palouse horses, liked to nip. With a jubilant forward thrust of his long, powerful neck, Thunder sank his teeth into the shoulder of the crewman in a shallow bite.

A bellow resulted. "Tarnation, you damn nag!" the handler

roared, as he broke free and turned to drive a clinched fist into the soft nose of the stallion.

Smoke Jensen's big hand closed on the offended shoulder in an iron clamp. "Don't hit my horse," he rumbled.

"I'll hit any damn' animal that bites me," the man snarled. Then he whirled and got a look at Smoke's expression. *Jeez!* It looked as though *he'd* bite him, too. "Uh—er—sorry, Mister. Here, you hold him an' I'll go fetch your saddle."

Somewhat mollified, Smoke accepted the reins from the trainman and walked Thunder down off the ramp onto the firm ground. Fine-grained, the soil held thousands of broken bits of seashell. Smoke studied the curiosity. The station was some distance from the bay and even further from the ocean. Could it be that this area had once been under water? He ceased his speculation, rubbed Thunder's nose, and slipped the big animal a pair of sugar cubes.

Crunching them noisily and with great relish, Thunder rolled his big, blue eyes. The pink of his muzzle felt silken to Smoke's touch. The 'Palouse flared black nostrils and whuffled his gratitude for the treat. Shortly the trainman returned with the saddle and blanket, which he fitted to Thunder's back with inexpert skill. Amused, Smoke wondered how someone could get through life without acquiring the ability to properly saddle a horse. He took over when the man bent to fasten the cinch.

"Here, I'll do that. You hold him."

With a dubious look at Thunder, the man hesitated. "You sure he won't bite me again?"

"Positive. I gave him some sugar cubes."

"That's all it takes?"

Smoke chuckled. "That's all it will take this time."

He tightened the cinch strap and adjusted his saddlebags, tying them in place with latigo strips. Then he swung into the saddle and rode off toward the far side of town.

Narrow, steep streets thronged with people made up the hilly city of San Francisco. Horse-drawn streetcars clanged noisily to scatter pedestrians from the center of the thoroughfares. Smoke Jensen steered his mount though the crowds with a calming hand ready to pat the trembling neck that denoted the creature's dislike of close places and milling, noisy humanity.

"Easy, boy, use your best manners," he murmured. "We'll be out of here soon."

The center of town consisted of tall buildings, four and five stories each, like red-brick and wooden canyon walls. Even Smoke Jensen felt hemmed in. Too many people in far too little space. He passed the opera house, its marquee emblazoned with bold, black letters.

TONIGHT!
MADAME SCHUMAN-HINKE

Whoever she was, she must be important, Smoke thought. Those letters were *big*. Beyond the commercial district, which appeared to be growing with all the frenzy of a drowned-out anthill, tenements stood in rows, rising to small duplexes and single-family dwellings. Smoke found the street he sought and began to climb another hill. This one was wider, and led to a promontory that overlooked the bay. The higher he went, the better the quality of the houses.

At last he came to an opulent residence that had a spectacular view of the Golden Gate, as the harbor was being called lately. Tall masts billowed with white bellies, a stately, swift clipper ship sailed toward port, a snowy bone in her teeth so large it could be seen from Smoke's vantage point. He watched her for a while, captivated by her grace. Then he nudged Thunder and rode on to his destination.

When he got there, his instincts kicked in and his hackles rose. Smoke cast a guarded gaze from side to side and along the street. What roused his sixth sense was the sight of a black mourning wreath that hung below the oval etched-glass portion of the large front door of the stately mansion. He slowed Thunder and eased off the safety thong on the hammer of his right-hand Colt.

When he reached the wide, curving drive, he halted and

looked all around. Not even a bird twittered. Smoke could feel
eyes on him—some from inside the mansion, others from hidden places along the avenue. A cast-iron statue of a uniformed
jockey stood at the edge of a portico. Smoke reined in there,
dismounted, and looped his reins through the ring in the metallic boy's upraised hand. Four long strides brought him to
the door. A brass knocker shone from the right-hand panel.
Smoke had barely reached for it when the door opened.

A large, portly black woman, dressed in the black-and-white
uniform and apron of a housekeeper, gave him a hard, dis-
trustful look. "We's closed. Cain't you see the wreath?"

"I'm not a—ah—client. I'm Smoke Jensen. Here to see
Miss Francie."

Suddenly the stern visage crumpled and large tears welled
in the eyes. "Miss Francie, she dead, suh."

"What?" Smoke blurted. "When? What happened?"

"We's ain't supposed to talk about it, the po-lice said. Miss
Lucy, she in charge now. Do you wish to talk to her?"

"Yes, of course."

He followed her into the unfamiliar hallway. Although
Smoke had known of the place, and known Francie Delong
for years, he had never visited the extravagant bordello. The
housekeeper directed the way to a large, airy room, darkened
now by the drawn drapes. A large bar occupied one long wall,
a cut-crystal mirror behind it. Comfortable chairs in burgundy
velvet upholstery surrounded small white tables.

"Wait here, if you will, Mr. Jensen. Miss Lucy will join
you shortly."

"Thank you." Hat in hand, Smoke waited.

Lucy Delong arrived a few minutes later. She wore a high-
necked black dress set off with a modest display of fine white
lace. Her eyes, red and puffy from crying, went wide when
she took in the visitor. "You have to be Smoke Jensen. Francie
speaks—spoke—so highly of you." The tears came again.

"Miss Lucy, I'm sorry. I didn't know something had happened to Francie. Was she sick for long?"

"It—wasn't sickness. She was—she was run down by a stolen carriage." An expression of horror crossed her face and she covered it with both hands, sobbing softly.

So that's why the police said not to discuss it. Lips tight, Smoke laid his hat on the bar and stepped to Lucy, putting a big hand on her shaking shoulder. "It must have been terrible for you. For all the girls," Smoke said helplessly, unaccustomed to words of condolence. "When did it happen?"

"Three days ago. It was a foggy day. Francie went out to see her banker. She never came back." Lucy drew a deep breath and shuddered out a sigh in an effort to regain control.

"I received a note saying someone would meet me here."

"I don't know anything about that. I'm sorry."

"We'll wait here a while, then."

"Oh, we cannot. There's to be a reading of Francie's will at half past noon. I am to be there, and you are expected, too." She looked confused. "I sent you a telegram when I learned. We barely have time to get there as it is."

"I still want to confirm who wrote me to meet him here."

"I'll leave word with Ophilia as to where we'll be."

"Your housekeeper?"

"Yes. All the girls are to be at the reading of the will."

"All right. Let me write a little note."

Lucy took paper, a pen, and an inkwell from behind the bar. Smoke wrote briefly. He gave it to Ophilia and turned to Lucy. "How are you getting to this?"

"We have a carriage. You're welcome to come along."

"I have my horse outside. I'll accompany you."

"I'll be relieved if you do." She frowned slightly, her eyes gone distant. "Something doesn't seem . . . right about the way Francie died. It will feel nice to have a strong man around. We will meet you on the drive."

Raymond Wagner looked up from his study of the flake gold and several rice-sized nuggets he had retrieved from his sluice. The splash and rumble of water racing down the riffles and screens of his sluice box had masked the sound of hoofbeats. He stared into the ugly, impassive faces of the three men whom he had run off his claim not four days ago. They had another one with them.

This time it was he who came forward and thrust the deed for him to sign. "Sign this," Tyrone Beal demanded.

"I told them fellers I would not and I say the same to you. Get off my claim."

"Sign it and save us all a lot of trouble."

"Gehen Sie zu Hölle!" a red-faced Wagner snarled in German.

Beal sighed. "Go to hell, huh? Well, I tried to be nice."

With that, he whipped the pick handle off his left shoulder and swung it at Wagner's head. The prospector ducked and lashed out a hard fist that caught an off-balance Beal in the chest. He staggered backward, recovered, and waded in on his victim. Another swing broke the bone in Wagner's upper left arm. Beal rammed him in the gut, then the chest, and cracked the dancing tip off the stout German's chin. Teeth flew.

Wagner had not a chance. Methodically, Beal beat him with the hickory cudgel. Driven to his knees, Wagner feebly raised his arms to shield his head. Beal broke three of Wagner's ribs with the next blow. Then came a merciful pause while Beal looked over his shoulder at the others.

"Don't just stand there. Give him a good lesson."

Kicks and punches pounded Raymond Wagner into a bleeding hulk curled on the ground in an attempt to protect his vital spots. The pick handle in Beal's hands made a wet smack against Wagner's back and the prospector rolled over to face upward. His eyes had swollen shut and a flap of loose skin hung down over his left eye. His mouth was ruined and large lumps had distorted his forehead. Beal prodded him with the bloody end of the handle.

"We'll be back when you've healed enough to sign this deed."

Without another word, they left. Raymond Wagner lay on his side again and shivered in agony. Slowly the world dimmed around him.

FOUR

Buck Jarvis and Jason Rocker looked up from the generous slabs of pie on their noon dinner plates. They fixed long, hungry, speculative looks on Sally Jensen as she distributed more of one of her famous pastries to the other hands. Only four days and Sally had grown to dislike them intensely. Forcing herself to ignore their lascivious stares, she turned away.

Jason leaned toward Buck and whispered softly into his ear, "Wonder what her body looks like under that dress?"

"I wonder what it would look like *without* a dress," Buck responded.

"I bet them legs go on forever," Jason stated wistfully.

"Shoot, man, she's too old for you."

Jason thrust out his chin. "I'm willin' to find out. Some of them older wimmin is the best ride you can get. They appreciate it more."

"You be blowin' smoke, Jason."

"Am not. My pappy tole me that when I was a youngin."

Buck sighed regretfully. "Well, neither one of us will get a chance to find out, you can be sure of that."

"Don't count on it, Buck. I reckon her man is gonna be gone a long time. Wimmin get to needin' things, know what I mean?"

Smoke Jensen had half the hall yet to cover when a loud pounding came on the door. Ophilia materialized out of a small drawing room and beat Smoke to the entrance. She opened the portal to reveal six tough-looking men.

"I wanna see whoever's runnin' this fancy bawdy house," a wart-faced man at the center of the first rank demanded.

"I'm sorry, we are not receiving clients at this time. There's been a death."

"Yeah. We know. An' we're here to throw you soiled doves out. This place don't belong to you."

Icily Ophilia defied them, drawing up her ample girth like a fusty old hen. "That is to be determined at the reading of Miss Francie's will this afternoon. Until then, no one is going anywhere."

"I have the say on that, Mammy," the unpleasant man barked, as he pushed past the housekeeper.

"I think not," Smoke Jensen's voice cracked in the quiet of the hall.

"Who the hell are you?"

"A man who does not like rude louts." Smoke advanced and the intruder retreated.

Back on the porch, the knobby-faced man regained his belligerence. "We come to evict them whores and we're gonna do it," he snarled.

"Who do you work for?" Smoke demanded.

"That's none of your business."

Smoke bunched the man's shirt in his big left fist and hauled him an inch off the ground. "I think it is. Is it the city? If so, by what right do they say these ladies must leave?"

A carriage had pulled around from the stable behind the house and nine lovely young women peered out with surprise at the scene before them. Lucy dismounted and stormed across the lawn and drive to the front steps. Hands on hips, she confronted the six unwelcome visitors.

"What exactly is going on here?"

"You're out in the street. My boss is taking over this place."

"Who is your boss?"

"Gargantua here asked me the same thing. I didn't tell him and I won't tell you."

Smoke Jensen shook him like a terrier with a rat. "You do

a lot of talking to say so little. Maybe I should loosen your jaw a little and rattle something out of you."

The thug turned nasty. "Put me down or I'll blow a hole clear through you."

If only to better get to his six-gun, Smoke set the man on his feet again. At once, the ruffian, a head shorter than Smoke Jensen, shot out a hand and pushed Smoke in the chest. Smoke popped him back, then two more of the evictors jumped him.

Smoke planted an elbow in the gut of one and rolled a shoulder in the way of the other so that he punched his boss instead of Smoke. He took in the remaining three standing in place on the bottom step, staring. That wouldn't last long, Smoke rightly assumed. Time to give them something to worry about.

Smoke Jensen spun to his left and drove a hard, straight right to the chest of the bruiser who kept punching him. He followed with a left, then swung his right arm in a wide arc to sweep the smaller man on that side off his feet. By then, their leader had recovered himself enough to return to the scuffle. He lowered his head and came at Smoke with a roar.

Roaring back, Smoke met him with a kick to one knee. Something made a loud pop and the thug howled in pain and abruptly sat down. Smoke returned his attention to the last upright opponent. He moved in obliquely, confusing the brawler as to his intent. The man learned quickly enough what Smoke had in mind when big, powerful hands closed into fists thudded into his chest and gut. Wind whistled out of his lungs and black spots danced before his eyes. Wobble-legged, he tried to defend himself only to be driven to his knees. Smoke finished him with a smash to the top of his bowed head. The other three, Smoke noted, had been suitably impressed.

They remained where they had been, eyes wide and mouths agape. Not so their leader. Unwilling to face that barrage of fists again, he decided to up the ante. A big, wicked knife appeared in his hand from under his coat. Sunlight struck gold off the keen edge as he forced himself upright, wincing at the pain in his leg. He took a wild swipe at Smoke Jensen, expecting to see his intended victim back up in fright.

Smoke obliged him instead with a swift draw of his .45 Peacemaker and quick discharge of a cartridge. The bullet shattered the thug's right shoulder joint.

"D'ja see that?" one of the less belligerent ones croaked. "Let's get out of here."

"Help me, you idiots!" their wounded leader bellowed. "Get me away from here."

They moved with alacrity, eyes fixed on the menace of the six-gun in Smoke's hand. Ignoring the continued yelps of discomfort, they dragged their leader away. With order restored, Smoke Jensen reholstered his revolver and tipped his hat to the soiled doves in the carriage.

"I apologize for the unpleasantness, ladies," he told them politely.

"Quite all right," Lucy replied. "I enjoy seeing scum like that get their come-uppance. We'll lead the way to Lawyer Pullen's office."

Brian Pullen had his office over the Bank of Commerce on Republic Street. Smoke Jensen was able to tie up at a public water trough, which Thunder appreciated. The ladies had to place their oversized vehicle in a lot next door to the bank. Smoke walked there and escorted them to the outside staircase that led to the lawyer's office. The sight of all those painted ladies turned more than a few heads.

Rising from behind a cluttered desk, Brian Pullen extended a hand in greeting. "You must be Mr. Jensen. Lucy—uh—ladies, I'll send my law clerk for more chairs. Please, make yourselves at home."

The lawyer turned out to be younger than Smoke had expected. His well-made and stylishly cut suit showed his prosperity without being ostentatious. Pullen wore his sandy-blond hair in a part down the middle. Not one to make snap judgments, Smoke Jensen found himself liking the youthful attorney. Chairs began to arrive and with a twitter of feminine voices the soiled doves seated themselves.

Smoke noted that Pullen had mild gray-green eyes, which he imagined could become glacial when arguing before a jury, against a prosecutor in defense of a client. He spoke precisely, addressing them in an off-hand manner.

"There is another gentleman expected, though he appears to be late. We'll give him until one o'clock."

They passed the time in small talk. Pullen made an effort to draw Smoke out about his circumstances. "I understand you are in ranching?"

"Horse breeding. I have a good, strong line of quarter horses and another of 'Palouse horses."

"Weren't they first bred by Indians?"

"Yes, Mr. Pullen. The Nez Perce," Smoke answered precisely.

"Please, call me Brian. I'm not old enough to be *Mister* Pullen. You are in Montana, or Colorado, is it?"

"Colorado, Brian," Smoke replied.

Pullen frowned and checked his big turnip watch. These short answers weren't getting him anywhere. If only the other man would arrive so they could get on with the reading of the will. He'd give it one more try.

"You've been a lawman, is that right?"

"Yes. Off and on."

"On the frontier?"

"Of course."

Brian sighed. "I suppose you have some exciting tales to tell."

"Nothin' much to tell. At least, not in mixed company. Blood and violence tends to upset the ladies." Smoke gave Lucy a mischievous wink.

Another look at the watch. "Well, it's the witching hour, you might say. I don't believe we can delay any longer. Very well, then, let's proceed. We are here for the reading of the last will and testament of Frances Delong. As her attorney, I am well aware of the contents, and feel she exercised excellent judgment in the disposal of her estate."

He paused and opened a folded document. From a vest pocket, he produced a pair of half-glasses and perched them on his generous patrician nose. Then he began to read in a formal tone. " 'I, Frances Delong, being of sound mind and body, do hereby bequeath all my worldly possessions as follows: to my dear friends at the San Francisco Home for Abandoned Cats, the sum of one thousand dollars. To my faithful employees,' " here, Brian Pullen read off the names. " 'I leave the sum of five hundred dollars each. To my ever faithful assistant, Lucy Glover, I leave in perpetuity the revenue from the saloon bar at my establishment. All my other property, liquid assets, and worldly goods I leave to the man who once saved my life, Kirby Jensen.' This was dated and signed six months ago," Brian added.

Smoke had always hated his first name and had not used it except under the utmost necessity for many years, so the shocking import of what the lawyer read did not strike him at once—not until the door opened and a jocular voice advised him, "What do you think of being the proprietor of the most elaborate sporting house in San Francisco, *mon ami?*"

Just as he had expected. Louis Longmont, his old friend and fellow gunfighter, stood in the doorframe with a broad grin on his face. Smoke came to his boots quickly and crossed the short space. Both men gave one another a back-slapping embrace.

"I thought it was you who sent me that mysterious message. Now, tell me about it."

"I will, *mon ami*, but not here or now. We need some place to be alone for what I have to say."

Sally Jensen stood over the boy seated at the kitchen table. Bobby had his face turned up to hers, though he would not meet her eyes. Not ten minutes ago Sally had caught the twelve-year-old behind the big hay barn, a handmade quirley in his lips, head wreathed in white tobacco smoke. Now, rather than the hangdog expression of shame, his face registered defiance. His explanation of the smoking incident had shocked and angered her.

"Buck made it for me. Jason said I was big enough to take up smokin'."

She hadn't liked the looks of them when they'd first arrived, and she hadn't grown any fonder of them since. This was just about the last straw.

This morning, they had both remained in the bunkhouse, claiming sickness, when the hands had ridden out to check the prize horses on graze in the west pasture. Not long ago they had come out and moseyed around the barnyard. Bobby, who had been laid up with his bunged-up toe since three days ago, had joined them. The three of them had gone around behind the barn.

Sally, at work at the kitchen sink, had kept an eye on the barn, wondering what they might be doing. When enough time had passed to arouse her suspicions, she wiped her hands on her apron and walked out to check on them. She had found Bobby alone, smoking a cigarette. She descended on him in a rush and snatched the weed from his mouth. Crushing it with a slender boot toe, she had demanded to know what he thought he was doing. His explanation only increased her pique.

"Well, Buck Jarvis and Jason Rucker are neither your mother nor your father. Smoke would have a fit if he knew what you've done. Come with me to the kitchen."

Seated now, with Sally over him, Bobby said, "Does it mean you are not going to tell Smoke? You know? What you said? That he would have a fit if he *knew* what I had done?"

"I'm disappointed in you, Bobby. I don't know now if I will tell Smoke or not. But you are staying inside for the rest of the day, young man."

"Awh, Miss Sal—Mom, I feel okay now. No more sore toe. Please let me eat with the hands. It's goin' on noon anyhow."

Sally considered it. "All right. But you stay away from Buck and Jason, hear?"

"Yes, ma'am."

"You may go to your room now."

"Yes, ma'am." Feet dragging, Bobby headed for the staircase that led to the second-floor bedrooms.

Although he ordinarily slept in the bunkhouse with the hands, since the arrival of Buck and Jason, Sally had insisted that Bobby return to his room in the main house. Something about them made her mighty uncomfortable.

She had good reason to recall that when the hands arrived at noon, Buck and Jason joined them. The two drifters stuffed themselves, then begged off work on the pretext that they still ailed a mite. After the hands rode off and Bobby came back inside, they lounged around on a bench outside the bunkhouse. When she went outside to hang up a small wash, they gave her decidedly lascivious looks.

Aware of that, Sally thought to herself it was a good thing she was not entirely alone.

Dinner for Smoke Jensen and Louis Longmont was at the Chez Paris on the waterfront, near the huge pier that people were already calling Fishermen's Wharf. The fancy eating place catered to San Francisco's wealthy and near-wealthy. White linen cloths covered the tables, their snowy expanse covered with matching napkins in silver rings, heavy silverware, and tall, sparkling candleholders, complete with chalky candles. Thick maroon velvet drapes framed the tall windows, each foot-square pane sparkling from frequent cleaning. Paintings adorned the walls, along with sconces with more tapers flickering in the current sent up by scurrying waiters.

The staff wore black trousers and short white jackets over brilliant lace-fronted shirts and obsidian bow ties. The maitre d' was formally attired in tails. He led Smoke and the New Orleans gunfighter to a table in an alcove. Seated, they ordered good rye. While it was being fetched, Louis perused the menu.

"I'll order for us both, if you don't mind, Smoke," he offered with a fleeting smile. The menu was in French.

Smoke took a glance and smiled back. "Yes, that would be fine."

When the waiter returned with their drinks on a silver tray, Louis was ready to order. "We'll start with the escargots.

Then . . ." He went on to order a regular feast. He added appropriate wines for each course and sat back to enjoy his whiskey.

After an appreciative sip, he inclined his long, slim torso toward Smoke, seated across from him. "You are no doubt wondering why I so summarily summoned you here, *non?*"

Smoke pulled a droll expression. "I will admit to some curiosity."

Louis pursed his lips and launched into his explanation. "Francie was still alive when I sent that letter. It is not about her rather—unusual—demise. Something is afoot among the big power brokers of Northern and Central California. There are rumors of a secret cabal recently formed that includes Cyrus Murchison, the railroad mogul, Titus Hobson, the mining magnate, and Gaylord Huntley, the shipping king."

"Hummm. That's some big guns, right enough. Murchison is the biggest fish, of course. Even in Colorado we have read of his doings in the newspapers."

"Well, yes. Word is that they are out to establish a monopoly on all transportation and gold mining. But, that's not all, *mon ami.* Phase two of their scheme, I have learned since coming to San Francisco, is to then go after title to all of the land in private hands.

"They will strangle out all the small farmers and shop owners with outrageous shipping rates by rail, water, or freighting company." Louis paused and nodded sagely. "Part of it, too, is to take control of all forms of entertainment: theaters, saloons, and bordellos."

"Not too unusual for captains of commerce," Smoke observed drily. "A bit ambitious, but I'd wager any group of powerful men might seek to eliminate competition."

"Quite true," Louis agreed. "Yet this is no ordinary power play. The cabal is supposed to have made an unholy alliance, which has prompted me to seek your help. Murchison and company are believed to have made an accommodation with the dreaded Triad Society." At Smoke's quizzical expression, he explained, "The Tongs of Chinatown."

Smoke raised an eyebrow and his eyes widened. A certain

darkness colored his gray gaze. "Of course I'll help, Louis. I think I've already had an encounter with some of the cabal's henchmen." He went on to describe the incident at Francie's.

Louis listened with interest and nodded frequently. "That sounds like their methods, all right. Must be the railroad police."

"Are you staying at Francie's?" Smoke asked, as the waiter arrived with their succulent, garlicky-smelling snails. Smoke took one look and made a face.

"Try them. You'll like them."

"I don't eat anything that crawls on its belly and leaves a trail of slime behind."

"Smoke, my friend, you must become more worldly. Escargots are a delicacy."

"Sally squashes them when they show up in her garden."

"These are raised on clean sand and fed only the best lettuce and other vegetable tops."

"They are still snails."

"Suit yourself," Louis said, as he picked up the tongs and fastened them onto one of the green-brown shells.

With a tiny silver fork he plucked the mollusk from its shelter and smacked his lips in appreciation. His hazel eyes twinkled in anticipation as he popped the snail onto his tongue. His eyes closed as he chewed on it thoughtfully. Smoke made a face and sipped from the glass of sherry the waiter had poured. Not bad. The aroma of the escargots reached his nostrils and they flared. His stomach rumbled. He had not eaten since the depot cafe that morning, he recalled. Tentatively, he reached for the tongs and clamped them on a snail shell.

"Aha! You have joined the sophisticates. Enjoy. Now, in answer to your question, no. I am staying at Ralston's Palace."

"I haven't taken a room. But I think one of us should stay at Francie's. The trash that showed up might come back."

"Since you own it now, it sounds reasonable to me that it is you who stays there, *mon ami*. I'll meet you there in the morning."

"Make it early. The way I see it, we have a lot to accomplish."

* * *

When they had finished the lemon *gelato,* Louis Longmont offered to accompany Smoke Jensen back to the bordello. Smoke gladly accepted; he enjoyed the company of his friend. Their route took them past the pagoda gateway that marked the entrance to Chinatown. Beyond it, a dark alley mouth loomed. They had barely passed it when the men in black pajama-like clothes attacked.

Tong hatchets whirred in the moonlight, striking a myriad of colors from the cheerful lanterns bobbing in the light onshore breeze behind Smoke and Louis. Both gunfighters had been walking their horses and now mounted swiftly. A man on horseback had it all over one afoot. With eight Oriental thugs rushing at them, it became even more critical.

In the lead, one snarling, flat-faced Tong soldier swelled rapidly. Smoke reared Thunder and prodded with a single spur in a trained command. The black cap flew one way and the cue flung backward as Thunder flicked out a hoof and flattened the Tong face. Then the others swarmed down on Smoke and Louis.

FIVE

The Chinese gangsters soon discovered that their Tong hatchets might well strike terror into the merchants of Chinatown, but they proved no match for blazing six-guns in the hands of the two best gunfighters in the West. Smoke Jensen and Louis Longmont opened up simultaneously with their .45 Colts. Hot lead zipped through the air. Louis's first round rang noisily off the blade of a hatchet descending on the head of his horse.

Its owner howled in pain and dropped the weapon. Smoke put a bullet through the hollow of another Tong soldier's throat and blew out a chunk of his spine. Suddenly limp, the Asian thug went down to jerk and twitch his life away. Louis fired again. Another Tong fight master screamed and clutched his belly in a desperate attempt to keep his intestines from squirting through the nasty hole in his side where the slug had exited. Alarmed, others shrank back momentarily.

"Where did they come from, Smoke?" Louis asked cheerily, as he lined his sights on another enemy.

"I'd say that alley behind us." Smoke paused as Louis fired again. "I believe we can safely say you heard the right of it about the Tongs."

"Why is that?"

Smoke Jensen loosed a round at a squat Chinese who had recovered his nerve enough to foolishly charge the two gunfighters. "They don't even know I'm in town. You're the one who has been asking questions around San Francisco."

"I see what you mean, *mon ami*. Smoke, we had better make this fast, *non?*"

"Absolutely," Smoke agreed, as he dropped another hatchet shaker.

Wisely, the surviving pair, one of them wounded, turned and ran. The wide street held a litter of bodies and a sea of blood. Longmont's horse flexed nostrils and whuffled softly, uneasy over the blood smell. Both men reloaded in silence.

"Shall we go on to Francie's?" Smoke asked lightly.

"Hadn't we better report this to the police?" Louis asked.

"If the police haven't showed by now, I imagine they already know and don't want to get involved. We'll leave these here for whoever wants them."

Freshly ground Arabica beans usually made the day for Cyrus Murchison. This morning, his coffee tasted bitter in his mouth. The reason was the presence of Titus Hobson and Gaylord Huntley in his breakfast room—that, and the news they brought. The news came in the form of Xiang Wai Lee. The slight-statured Chinese could barely suppress his fury.

"The first time we are to perform a service for you, we are sent out against men of inhuman capability." His queue of long black hair bobbed in agitation as he hissed at Murchison. "You told us that Louis Longmont was a fop, a dandy, a gambler, an easy target. Not so," Lee informed the wealthy conspirators. "Then there was the other man with him. Such speed and accuracy with a firearm."

"Who was that?" Murchison demanded.

"What does it matter?" Xiang snapped. "Only two of the men sent after Longmont and his companion survived the encounter."

"That doesn't answer my question. Who is this other man?" Ordinarily, this Oriental would not be in this part of his house. Would not even gain access, except by the servants' entrance to the back hallway and pantry. Murchison took his presence as an insult.

"My two soldiers who lived informed me that Longmont used the word 'smoke' as though it was a name."

Hobson paled and gasped. "He can't still be alive."

"Who?" Murchison barked.

"Smoke Jensen," Hobson named him. "He is reputed to be the best gunfighter who ever lived. If he still *is* alive, we have a major problem on our hands."

"Preposterous," Murchison dismissed.

Hobson would not let it go. "He has killed more men and maimed many more than any other three shootists you can name. His name is legend in Colorado. When I was there last, Smoke Jensen had devastated a force of forty men who hunted him through the mountains for a month. It was they who died, not Jensen. He has been an outlaw and a lawman.

"There are some who say he has back-shot many men he has killed." Hobson paused to catch his breath. "Personally, I don't believe that. I have also heard that to say so to his face is to get yourself dead rather quickly. He is mean and wild and totally savage. He's lived with the Indians. He was raised by another total barbarian, a mountain man named Preacher. The pair struck terror into the hearts of the men in the mountains for years."

Murchison snorted derisively, totally unimpressed. "What impact can a couple of aging gunfighters have on our project?" His small, deep-set blue eyes glittered malevolently in his florid face as he cut his gaze to Xiang. "If your men cannot handle this, Tyrone Beal and his railroad detectives can take care of a mere two men, no matter that they are good with their guns. Now, get out of here, all of you, and let me finish my breakfast."

Smoke Jensen punched back his chair from the round oak table in the breakfast nook of the Delong mansion. Frilly lace curtains hung over the panes of the bay window, with plump cushions on the bench seats under them. This excess of the feminine touch made Smoke a bit uneasy. If he kept the place, there would have to be some changes. No. That was out of the question. Sally would be bound to find out. When she did, she would skin him alive.

Amusement touched his lips as he recalled the time Sally had herself inherited a bordello from a favored aunt who had passed away. That and a big ranch that stood in the way of the ambitions of powerful, greedy men who needed some lessons in manners. Smoke Jensen had given those lessons, with fatal results. No, Sally would never favor him owning a bawdy house. Lucy Clover's entrance banished the images of the past.

"Mr. Longmont is here, Smoke."

"Thank you, Lucy. Have Ophilia show him in. Join us—we have a little strategy to discuss."

"Oh?"

"Yes. About protection for this establishment, among other things," Smoke informed her.

Lucy left him alone to return with Louis Longmont. *"Bonjour, mon ami,"* Louis greeted.

"Oui, c'est tres bon," Smoke answered back with almost his entire French vocabulary.

Louis chuckled. "They must have fed you well. What is in order for today?"

"First, we must make provisions for someone to protect this place." He paused to sip the marvelous coffee.

"You think there will be trouble?" Lucy asked anxiously.

"Those louts who came yesterday will be back, count on it. And we can't stay here all the time. Now that I own the place, I want to make sure all of you are safe."

"You make it sound ominous," a pale-faced Lucy observed.

Smoke was disinclined to play it down. "Believe me, it is."

Ophilia appeared in the doorway. "Those nasty gentlemen from yesterday are here again, Miss Lucy. And they brung friends."

Smoke's lips tightened. "How many?"

"They's about a dozen, Mister Smoke."

Smoke came to his boots. Louis started to rise. "I'll take care of it, Louis."

"If you say so, *mon ami,*" he answered with a shrug.

"This way, Mister Smoke," Ophilia directed. Although richer by $500, thanks to Francie, she still performed her duties as housekeeper flawlessly.

At the door, Smoke quickly counted the twelve men standing in a semicircle at the foot of the porch steps in three ranks. Several of them held stout hickory pick handles. Tyrone Beal, who had returned only that morning on the early train, acted as spokesman this time.

"Tell those girls that they are to be out of here within half an hour. This place has been sold for back taxes and the new owner, the California Central Railroad, wants immediate occupancy."

After seeing all the books and ledgers on Francie's establishment the previous day in Pullen's office, Smoke knew that there were no back taxes. "I have some bad news for you, whoever you are."

Beal drew himself up. "Captain Tyrone Beal of the Railroad Police. I'm not interested in any news you might have. I said out they go, and that's what I mean."

"The bad news, *Captain* Bean," and Smoke put a sneer on the title, "is that you are a liar. All taxes have been paid up through next year. I'm the owner now, so you had best back off so no one gets hurt."

Goaded by the insult, Beal launched himself at Smoke. Jensen waited for him to the precise second, then powered a hard right into the face of the railroad detective. Beal, his feet off the ground, flew down the steps faster than he had ascended them. His pick handle clattered after him. The others similarly armed, pressed forward, dire intent written on their faces.

Smoke turned slightly and called over his shoulder, "Louis, would you like to join the dance?"

"I would be delighted," Louis said from the doorway, where Smoke had anticipated he would be.

Back-to-back, they met the railroad thugs. The first to attack came at Smoke. When he swung his pick handle, Smoke ducked and kicked him in the gut. The billet of wood went flying. Smoke finished him with a left-right combination to the right side of his head and jaw. He fell like a rumpled pile of clothes. Another stick-wielder went for Louis.

The New Orleans gunhand gave his hapless assailant a quick lesson in the French art of *la Savate*. He kicked the brawler three times before the man could get set to swing his hickory club. His swing disturbed, he staggered drunkenly when he missed. Louis kicked him twice in the back, once in each kidney. Grunting in misery, he went to his knees, one hand on the tender flesh at the small of his back. Louis swung sideways and put the toe of his boot to the bully's temple. He went down like a stone.

Smoke popped a hard right to the mouth of an ox of a man who only shook his head and pressed his attack. Smoke went to work on the protruding beer gut. His hard fists buried to the wrists in blubber. Still he failed to faze his opponent. Instead, he launched a looping left that caught Smoke alongside his ear. Birdies twittered and chimes tinkled in the head of Smoke Jensen. He shook his head to clear it and received a stinging blow to his left cheek that would produce a nasty yellow, purple, and green bruise.

Another pick handle whizzed past his head and pain exploded down his back when it struck the meaty portion at the base of his neck.. Left arm numbed, he cleared tear-blurred eyes and snapped a solid right boot toe to the inner side of his attacker's thigh. A squeal of pain erupted from thick, pouting lips. Smoke sucked in air and stepped close.

With a sizzling right, he pulped those flabby lips. The blow had enough heft behind it to produce the tips of three broken teeth. *Finish him fast,* thought Smoke, as feeling returned to his left arm. Two powerful punches to the gut brought the man's guard, and the gandy stick, down. Smoke felt the cheekbone give under the terrible left he delivered below the man's eye. His right found the vulnerable cluster of nerves under the hinge of the jaw and the man went to sleep in an instant.

Louis had four men down in front of him and worked furiously on a fifth. Not bad, Smoke thought. He sought his fourth. The sucker came willingly to the slaughter. Wide-eyed and yelling, he rushed directly at Smoke. The last mountain man sidestepped him at the proper moment and clipped him with a rabbit punch at the base of his skull. His jaw cracked when he struck the lowest marble step. Suddenly Smoke had no more enemies. The remaining three thugs hung back, uncertain, and decidedly impressed by what these two men could do. Smoke gestured to the fallen men.

"Drag this trash off my property and don't bother to come back," he commanded hotly.

Satisfied with the results, he and Louis turned to walk back in the mansion. Enraged at this ignominious defeat, Tyrone Beal wouldn't leave it alone. Mouth frothing with foam, he shrieked at his henchmen. "What's the matter with you three? Finish them off. Kill the bastards!"

Six-guns exploded to life and a bullet took the hat off Louis Longmont's head. Instantly the two gunfighters turned to meet the threat. Crouched, they spun and drew at the same time. Smoke's .45 Colt spoke first. He pinwheeled the middle hard case, who did a little jig with the devil and expired on his face in the grass. Louis took his man in the stomach, doubling him over with a pitiful groan. Smoke's Peacemaker barked again.

The slug burned a mortal trail through the lower left portion of the railroad policeman's chest and burst his heart. He tried to keep upright, but failed. Slowly he sank into a blood-soaked heap. Powder smoke still curling from the muzzle of his Colt, Smoke Jensen addressed Tyrone Beal.

"Take this garbage out of here. You would be smart not to report this to the police. We have a building full of witnesses who saw what happened. If your boss wants to verify what I said about the taxes and owning this place, he can check with Lawyer Pullen." He turned away, then paused and spoke over his shoulder. "Oh, and don't bother coming back."

Up on the porch, Louis Longmont opened the loading gate on his revolver and began to extract expended cartridges. "Now that we have finished our post-breakfast exercise, what's next?"

"Easy," Smoke said with a slow grin. "We look into this

Tong business from last night and find some reliable men to guard this place while we are gone."

"They did it again," Sally Jensen testily said.

Both of those saddle tramps, as she now saw Buck and Jason, remained behind, professing illness again. She looked up sharply from the elbows-deep soap suds when their coarse laughter reached her in the wash house attached to the outer kitchen wall. Through the small, square window she saw them lolling around, obviously in perfect health. She had sent Bobby out with the hands today. Now she was thankful she had. While she watched, Buck and Jason drew their lanky frames upright and ambled in the direction of the bunkhouse well pump. She gave her washing an angry drubbing on the washboard and abandoned it.

Wiping her arms, she headed to the kitchen. She had pies in the oven, and biscuits yet to do. When she stepped out of the wash house, Buck and Jason were nowhere in sight.

"What are they up to now?" she asked herself, mildly disturbed by this disappearance.

In the kitchen she pulled the four large deep-dish pies from the oven and slid in two big pans of biscuits. That accomplished, she dusted her hands together in satisfaction. Now, she had better cut vegetables for the stew. She strode to the sink and pumped water into a granite pan. Bending down, she pulled carrots, potatoes, turnips, and onions from their storage bins. As she came upright, her eye caught movement through the window.

Buck and Jason were back. The two young saddle tramps were headed directly toward the kitchen.

Tyrone Beal and his battered henchmen sat nursing their wounds in a saloon on Beacon Street. After they'd downed several shots of liquid anesthetic, their bravado found new life.

"We're not gonna let two country hicks get the best of us, are we, Boss?" Ned Parker growled.

"Not on your ass," Tyrone Beal growled.

Parker poured another shot from the bottle. "I want a piece of that Frenchie bastard."

"Me, too," Earl Rankin piped up.

"Sam's got a busted jaw," Beal reminded them.

"They say only sissies fight with their feet," Monk Diller observed.

"Maybe so, but that Longmont broke five of Ham's ribs with a kick," Beal continued to list their injuries.

" 'Twern't nothin' compared to what the big guy with him did to the boys," Ned Parker summed up.

Tyrone Beal had enough of this. "No, boys, we're not going to let them get away with it. We'll get 'em both, even if we have to shoot them in the back."

Monk Diller's tone came out surly. "You tried that. There's three of us dead for it."

Tyrone Beal wanted to keep them on the subject. "What's done is done. The thing is, we drop everything else until we can fix their wagon."

Beal had no idea of how soon the opportunity would come. Even while he detailed a plan for ambushing Smoke Jensen and Louis Longmont separately, a young Chinese entered the saloon. The bartender noticed at once.

"Get out. We don't allow your kind in here."

"I got message for thisee gentleman, Bossee," he sing-songed in pidgen, pointing to Tyrone Beal.

"Okay. Deliver your message and get out."

Walking softly in his quilted shoes, the Chinese youth approached the table. "Arrogant *qua'lo* disgust me," he muttered in perfect English, as he came before the railroad detective.

"What was that?"

"I said bigots like that bartender make me angry. I have a message for you from Xiang Lee. Here it is." He offered a scrap of rice paper.

Beal opened the folded page and read carefully. *"Smoke Jensen and Louis Longmont are strolling around Chinatown bold as brass dragons. It is an insult to the Triad. The Tong leaders have met and consider it wise, and more convenient, if other* qua'lo *take care of them. You and your railroad police are to come at once. The messenger who brought this will lead you to your quarry. Xiang."*

Boyle looked up at the young Chinese. "This says you can take us to some men we want rather badly. Is that so?"

"Oh, yes."

"Then do so," he rumbled as he rose, and adjusted the hang of his six-gun.

The door to the Jensen kitchen flew open and the two young drifters swaggered in. Sally looked askance at them from where she stood washing vegetables. She dropped the paring knife in the bowl and rubbed her arms furiously on her apron. Nursing her rising anger, she turned to them with a stony face.

"What is the meaning of this?" she demanded harshly.

Buck Jarvis cut his eyes to Jason Rucker. Then they both ogled her boldly, slowly, up and down in an insolent, lewd manner. "We're here to get some of what you must have under that dress," the smirking lout nearest to Sally brayed.

Sally took two purposeful steps to the table and picked up her clutch purse. Men had seen the expression in her eyes and known fear. This pair hadn't a clue. Her scorn aimed directly at Jason, she calmed herself as she shoved a hand into the open purse. Her voice remained level when she answered his insolence.

"No, you're not."

Buck, the bolder of the two, reached for her. His eyes, slitted with lust, widened to white fear and disbelief when the bottom of the purse erupted outward toward him, a long lance of flame behind the shattered material. An unseen fist slammed into Buck's gut an inch above his navel and an instant of hot, soul-shriveling pain raked his nerves raw. He doubled over so rapidly that Sally's second round, double-actioned from her Model '77 Colt Lightning .44, smacked into the top of his head.

A giant starburst went off in the brain of Buck Jarvis and he fell dead at her feet.

White men alone on the streets of Chinatown stood out markedly in the daytime. Particularly ones as big, strong, and purposeful as Smoke Jensen and Louis Longmont. The denizens of the Chinese quarter gave them blank, impassive faces. The few who would talk to them, or even acknowledge they understood English, made uniformly unsatisfactory replies.

"So solly, no Tongs in San Francisco," one old man told Smoke, his face set in lined sincerity. He was lying through his wispy mustache and Smoke knew it.

"I know nothing of such things, gentlemen," a portly merchant in a flowing silk robe stated blandly. "The Triads did not come with us from China."

More horse crap, Smoke and Louis agreed. They moved on, creating a wake behind them. More questions and more denials. One young woman in a store that sold delicate, ornately decorated china did register definite fear in her eyes when Smoke mentioned the Tongs. Like the rest, though, she denied their existence in San Francisco.

"This is getting nowhere," Louis complained. "We waste our time and make a spectacle of ourselves, *mon ami.*"

"We'll give it another quarter hour, then try the local police," Smoke insisted.

When the quarter hour ended, they had come to the conclusion it would be a good idea to give it up. They had turned on the sidewalk to retrace their steps when Tyrone Beal and his black-and-blue henchmen located them.

"There they are! Let's get 'em!" Beal shouted. This time they had the forethought to bring along guns. A shot blasted the stately murmur of commerce in Chinatown. A piercing scream quickly followed.

Six

Hot lead whipped past the head of Smoke Jensen. More screams joined the first as women, clad in the traditional Chinese costume of black or gray pegged-skirt dresses that extended to their ankles, awkwardly ran in terror from the center of violence. Louis Longmont overturned a vendor's cart heaped high with dried herbs and spices. A sputtering curse in Cantonese assailed him. Bullets slammed into the floor of the hand cart and silenced its owner.

"Smoke, on your left!" Louis shouted as he triggered a round in the direction of the shooter who riddled his temporary, and terribly insubstantial, cover.

Smoke Jensen reacted instantly, swiveled at the hips, and pumped a slug into the protruding belly of Ned Parker. Parker's mouth formed an "O," though he did not go down. He raised the Smith American in his left hand and triggered another shot at Smoke Jensen. Another miss. Smoke didn't.

His second bullet shattered Parker's sternum and blasted the life from the corrupt railroad policeman. "We've got to move, pard," he advised Louis. "There's too many of them."

"Exactement," Louis shouted back over the pandemonium that had boiled along the street in the wake of the first shots.

With targets so plentiful, they had no problem with downing more of Beal's men as they emptied the cylinders of their six-guns. More Chinese women and children ran shrieking as havoc overtook their usually peaceful streets. Bent low, Smoke and Louis sprinted from cart to cart. They reloaded on the run. Chinese merchants yelled imprecations after them. Blundering along behind, the furious railroad police overturned carts of produce and dried fish. Smoke spotted a dark opening and darted into a pavilioned stall to replace the last cartridge in his .45 Colt.

A squint-eyed hard case saw Smoke duck out of sight and came in after him—his mistake. His first wild shot cut through the cloth of the left shoulder of Smoke's suit coat, not even breaking skin. Facing him, his face a cloud of fury, Smoke pumped lead into the chest of the slightly built gunman. Flung backward by impact and reflex, the dying man catapulted himself through the canvas side of the vendor's stall. The material tore noisily as the already cooling corpse sagged to the ground, partway into the street. It forced Smoke Jensen to abandon his refuge, though.

"He's over there," voices shouted from outside.

Smoke slid his keen-edged Green River knife from its sheath and cut his way to freedom through the back of the stall. The Chinese owner gobbled curses after him, his upraised fist and his long black pigtail shaking in rhythm. Smoke moved on. Then, from behind him, he heard yelps of pain and surprised curses. A quick glance over his shoulder showed him the cause.

Wielding a long, thick staff, the irate merchant took out his frustration on the rush of thugs who poured into his establishment. He struck them swiftly on shoulder points, legs, and heads. Two went down, knocked unconscious. Smoke produced a grim smile and moved on.

Tyrone Beal looked on in disbelief as his magnificent plan began to disintegrate. How could two lone men create such havoc among his men? Granted they were a wild, wooly lot, but he had managed to instill enough discipline in them that they fought together, as a unit. Yet here and now they seemed to forget all they had learned.

"Get them, you stumbling idiots!" he railed at his men, who darted around the central market square of Chinatown in confusion. "They went down the main street."

Five or six obeyed at once. Others continued to mill around. They poked six-guns into the faces of the frightened Chinese and overturned their displays of goods. "You'll not find them that way, you worthless curs," he bellowed at them.

He had sent to the railroad yards for reinforcements. It looked to Beal as though the stupidest of the lot had responded to the summons. He had no time to stay here and reorganize this mob-gone-wild. He headed along the central artery that led to this marketplace. Ahead he saw three of his better men closing in on the one called Longmont. Well and good. Put an end to him, and then go after Jensen.

Louis Longmont had a revolver in each hand, the left one a double-action Smith and Wesson Russian .44. He crouched, eyes cutting from one hard case to the other. Only one of them had a firearm. The other two wielded knives and pick handles. One of those lunged at Louis and he leaped catlike to the side and discharged his right-hand Colt. The roar of the .45 battered at him from the wall to his left. His target fared far worse.

Shot through the hand, the bullet lodged in his shoulder, the railroad thug howled in agony and pawed at the splinters from the hickory handle that stuck in his face. On weakened legs he tottered to the side and sat down heavily on a doorstep. Believing Louis to be distracted by this, the remaining pair moved as one.

First to act, the gunman raised his weapon for a clear shot. He never got the sights aligned. Louis shot him in the forehead with the .44 Russian in his left hand. Automatically he had eared back the hammer on the .45 Peacemaker in his right and tripped the trigger a split second later. The fat slug punched into the belly of the other thug. Before he plopped on the street, Louis went into rapid motion.

A rickety cart piled high with racks of delicate bone china loomed in his vision. Louis jinxed to avoid it, only to feel the hot path of a slug burn along the outside of his left arm. That threw him off balance enough that he crashed into the moun-

tain of tablewear. Cascading down, the fragile pieces gave off
a tinkling chorus as they collided and rained onto the cobblestones to shatter into a million fragments.

"Go, qua'lo!" the owner shouted after Louis, uselessly
shaking a fist. Then he repeated his insult as two of the railroad
thugs blundered through the ruin. "Barbarian dog!"

Warned by this renewed outburst, Louis turned at the hips
and fired behind him. The sprint of one of the hard cases
turned into a stumbling shamble that sent him into the window
of a shop that dispensed Chinese medicinal herbs. Shards of
glass flew in sparkling array. The largest piece fell last and
decapitated the already dying man. His companions hung back,
mouths agape, while Louis disappeared from their view.

Slowly Smoke Jensen began to notice a change in the people
of Chinatown. When they had recovered enough composure
to look at the men being pursued and their pursuers, they recognized old enemies. Shouts of encouragement came from a
trio of elderly men on one street corner when Smoke plunked
a slug smack in the middle of one thug's chest. He had shot
his one Colt dry and now used the one from the left-hand
holster, worn at a slant at belt level, butt forward. Singly and
in pairs, Smoke noticed, he and Louis were gunning down the
trash sent to kill them.

A volley of praise in Cantonese rose when Smoke shot a
stupidly grinning hard case off the top of a Moon gate. The
volume of gunfire had diminished considerably. Smoke found
he had to look for targets. Unfazed by this, he continued on
his way toward the main entrance to Chinatown.

"Impossible!" Tyrone Beal shouted to himself. It was all
over. He could see that clearly. Only five of his men remained
upright, and three of them had been wounded.

Self-preservation dictated that he get the hell out of there—
and fast. He didn't delay. He would report to Heck Grange;

Heck would know what to do. These two were inhuman. Nobody was *that* good. But his eyes told him differently. Quickly, Tyrone Beal turned away from the scene of carnage and broke into a trot, departing Chinatown by the shortest route.

His course took him to the railyard of the California Central. There he banged in the office of his superior, Chief of Railroad Police Hector Grange. "Heck, God damn it, we got wiped out."

Heck Grange looked up sharply, startled by this outburst. "Did the Chinks turn on you?"

"Some of them did, near the end. But it was Longmont and Jensen. I saw it with my own eyes. We've got to do something to stop them."

Heck considered that a moment. "We can start by filing a complaint with the city police."

"What good will that do?" Beal protested.

"You've got cotton between your ears?" Heck brayed. "Mr. Murchison is a pillar of the community, right? He owns the mayor, the police, the city fathers, even the judges. So you put together a story as to how these two troublemakers, wanted for crimes against the railroad, were located by some of your men. They opened fire without warning and killed our policemen. You follow so far?"

A light of understanding glowed in Beal's eyes. "Yeah, yeah. I think I do. We put the blame on them, send the regular police after them."

"And when we get them in court, they get convicted and hanged. End of problem. Now, get on it."

Inspired by Heck's confidence, Beal departed faster than he'd arrived.

"Stay on your knees, if you want to live," Sally Jensen coldly told Jase, the would-be rapist.

The instant Buck Jarvis had fallen dead to the kitchen floor, Jason Rucker had gone alabaster white and dropped to his knees, his hands out in appeal, and begun to beg for his life. Sally had been sufficiently aroused by their brazen attempt that she had yet to simmer down enough to ensure that this worthless piece of human debris *did* survive.

"Oh, please, please, don't hurt me. We didn't mean nothin'."

The former schoolteacher in Sally Jensen made her wonder if Jase understood the meaning of a double negative. The wife of Smoke Jensen in her made her wonder why she had not already shot him. Driven by a full head of steam, she formed her answer from her outrage.

"If I turn you over to the sheriff, you will most likely hang. Why not take the easier way out with a bullet?" she coldly told him.

Jase cut his eyes to his partner, lying dead on the floor. *"Please!"* he begged in desperation, "please. I'll do anything, take any chances with the law. Just—don't—shoot—me."

Sally considered that a moment, eyes narrowed, then told him, "Drag that filth out of my kitchen and clean up the mess while I think about it."

Gulping back his terror, he hastily crawled on hands and knees to comply.

Slowly at first, the solemn-faced residents of Chinatown came forward. Stooped with age, one frail man with a wispy, two-strand beard and long, drooping mustache approached Smoke Jensen.

"You were acting in defense of your life, honored sir," he said softly. "The damage done is inconsequential. I am Fong Jai. It shames me that our own people have not stood up to these *qua'lo* bandits like you have done."

"I am called Smoke Jensen, and this is Louis Longmont," Smoke introduced the two of them. "You know them, then?"

"Ah, yes. To my regret, we of Chinatown know them all too well. I recognized the one who led them. He is called Tyrone Beal. He is an enforcer for the greedy *qua'lo* who owns the California Central Railroad . . . and, regrettably, most of the land in Chinatown. He and his villainous rabble have broken legs and made people disappear for a long time."

Smoke gave him his level gray gaze. "Then I am doubly glad we could be of service."

Fong Jai folded his hands into the voluminous sleeves of his mandarin gown and bowed low. "It is we who have a debt to you. Earlier you asked about the Triad Society. We behaved badly toward one who is a friend. If you wish to confront the Tongs, the name to use is Xiang Wai Lee."

Smoke and Louis repeated the name several times, committing it to memory. It turned out Fong had more to say. "I would urge that you use that name cautiously. These Tong hatchet men are very dangerous."

"Thank you, Fong Jai," Smoke offered sincerely. He gestured around him. "You can see how we handle danger."

Fong smiled fleetingly and bowed low again. "It is the Tongs, I think, who should take caution if they rain trouble down on your heads. But my warning comes from another case. It is rumored that the Triad has made an arrangement with the villains of Murchison and his two devil allies, Hobson and Huntley. If that is the case, you will encounter them again."

Smoke placed a friendly hand on Fong's shoulder. "My friend, I—we—have every intention of doing so."

"Our great philosopher Confucis said, 'A wise bird never leaves its droppings in its own nest.' By arousing your wrath, I believe that the Triad should consider that carefully. Go in peace, Smoke Jensen, Louis Longmont. Ask what questions you wish. You will get answers."

It took them less than half an hour to learn all they could about the Tongs. Most people remained frightened of the Chinese gangsters and gave scant aid, and none claimed to know where Xiang could be found. When they had what could be gotten out of the residents of Chinatown, Smoke halted Louis on the street with a word.

"We have our name now, and some idea of how the Tongs work," he declared. "Now to get those bouncers for Fran—er—my new place."

"Where to, *mon ami?*"

"Why, to the dockyards, of course. There are always out-of-work longshoremen aplenty."

Tyrone Beal stood in the opulently furnished office he had never before visited. He held his hat in his hands, his head bowed, shame flaming on his cheeks as he repeated the account of his ignominious defeat at the hands of Smoke Jensen and Louis Longmont. Behind the huge desk centered between two tall, wide windows, Cyrus Murchison grew livid as each sentence tumbled out.

"You mean to tell me that twenty men could not stop those two?" Murchison roared. His thick-fingered fist pounded out each word on the desk top.

"Yes, sir. I'm sorry, sir."

"You will be sorrier if you fail again. You behaved stupidly in the matter involving Wagner. You should not have beaten him so badly he could not sign. And now this. Disgusting." He paused, poured a crystal glass full of water, and drank deeply. It successfully masked his ruminations over how to deal with Tyrone Beal. "I'm going to give you a chance to redeem yourself. You will return to the gold fields. Get me Wagner's signature on that deed. You do that, and all will be forgiven."

Relief flooded through Tyrone Beal. He had visions of ending up at the bottom of the bay, wrapped in anchor chain. "Yes, sir. Thank you, sir. I won't mess this one up. I promise you that."

Ice glittered in the deep-set eyes of Cyrus Murchison and his stunning shock of white hair shook violently. "See that you do."

With that dismissal, Tyrone Beal exited the office. When the huge door closed softly behind him, Murchison sighed heavily. "Now, we have to deal with these two gunfighters," he addressed Heck Grange. I want you to drop everything else you're working on. Find a sketchmaker who can draw likenesses of Longmont and Jensen. Go to our company printing plant and have engravings made and flyers printed. I want them by tomorrow morning. Then," Murchison went on, ticking off his points on his stubby fingers, "circulate them to every employee, every informant you've developed among the low-lives of this town, every barkeep—flood the entire city with them." He paused, anger once more flushing his face. He poured and drank off more water and licked his lips fastidiously. "Anyone who finds them is to report directly to you. Then I want you to file a complaint with the police. I'll contact the chief personally, and get them looking for Jensen and Longmont."

"A tall order, sir. But, I am pleased you approve of my idea of bringing in the regular police."

"Harrumph! The idea occurred to me before that idiot Beal got the first two sentences out of his mouth," he dismissed the contribution of his Chief of Railroad Police. "Now, as far as your men are concerned, they are to have orders to shoot to kill Jensen and Longmont on sight. Finally, there are some dirt-scratching farmers in the Central Valley who need convincing that selling to the railroad or to Hobson's Empire Mining and Metal would be good for their health. Send some of Huntley's dockwallopers out there to impress it on them. See to all of it," Murchison commanded. "Jensen and Longmont first."

"This is going to be harder than I thought," Smoke Jensen admitted after their fourth profane refusal.

"It is strange that men out of work, waiting in a hiring hall, would refuse an offer so generous in nature," Louis Longmont agreed.

They had spent the past half hour along the harbor. With scant results, for all that. So far, only a single man had taken up the offer. A burly man with bulging forearms, bulldog face, and thick, bowed legs ambled along a careful two paces behind Smoke and Louis. He had a knit sailor's cap on his huge head, canvas trousers, and a blue-and-white-striped V-neck pullover.

Smoke privately suspected he was not a longshoreman, but that he had recently jumped ship. He would do, though.

"Over there," Louis pointed out. Two men sat astraddle a bench, a checkerboard between them. As Smoke approached, one picked up a black playing piece and made a triple jump.

"You're cheatin', Luke," his opponent growled. "I don't know how, but I know you are."

"No, I ain't," Luke responded. "You just make too many mistakes."

"I don't make mistakes."

"Yes, you do."

"No, I don't."

"Do."

"Don't."

"Now, boys," Smoke addressed them, in a tone he often heard Sally use on their children when they squabbled.

It brought up the both of them, red-faced, their disagreement forgotten. Luke gestured to the playing board. "Doin' nothin' for days on end gets to a feller," he apologized for them both.

"Out of work?" Smoke suggested.

"Sure am. We refused to turn back half our pay to the hall boss."

"Would you like to take a job?"

Luke studied the blue sky above. His eyes wandered to a wheeling dove. "Sure, if we get to keep what we earn and it ain't again' the law."

"It's not, I assure you," Louis Longmont added.

"So, what is this work you have? Cargo to unload? Sure. Warehouse to clean out? Sure. We can do anything."

"Speak for yourself, Luke," his companion snipped.

"This job does entail some danger. You may have to fight to preserve the peace."

"You ain't offering us a place with the police, are you?" Luke objected.

"Far from it," Smoke Jensen assured him. "I have recently inherited a famous sporting house in San Francisco. I need some strong, honest men to keep order. I know nothing about running such a place, but there is a nice young lady who is in charge. She can explain your routine duties to you. As for the other, there are some interests in town who don't want me to keep the place."

Louis joined the outline of what might be expected. "We will not be able to be there all the time. It would then be up to you to eject any of their convincers who happened around."

Luke squared his shoulders and gave them a roll suggestive of readiness. "A bouncer, eh? I've been one before. What's it pay?"

"Right now, fifty dollars a week."

Luke's jaw sagged. "I don't believe you. That's more than a month's wages."

"It is quite correct," Louis said sincerely.

"Why, sure, Mister," Luke addressed Smoke. "Far's I'm concerned, you got yourself another bouncer." He looked beyond Smoke to the big man who intently took in their conversation to illustrate his meaning.

"Count me out," Luke's surly friend stated flatly.

"That's two," Smoke agreed, lightly. "What we need is about six more."

Louis rolled his eyes.

Outside the next hiring hall, Smoke Jensen and his companions came face-to-face with a large group of longshoremen. Smoke noted their mood to be surly at best, if not downright hostile. A barrel-chested inverted wedge of a man stepped forward, a hand raised in a sign to stop.

"That's far enough. You fellers have been pokin' around here long enough. It's time for you to get yourselves out of here. And you, too," he gestured to Luke and the other dockworker. "You ain't workin' for them nohow. Come over here with us."

"Sorry," Smoke answered lightly. "Can't do that. I need about six more good men to work for me."

"Well, you can't have 'em," the spokesman snapped.

Smoke was quickly getting riled. First the running gunfight

with the railway thugs in Chinatown, and now this. "By whose authority?" he asked with deadly calm.

Pointing to the sign over the doorway to the hiring hall, the aggressive longshoreman bit off his words. "D'you see that sign? This here's the North Star Shipping Company. Mr. Huntley heard what you two were up to and told me special to see you got run off from the docks. So take a hike."

Sharp-edged menace covered every word Smoke Jensen spoke. "I don't think so."

"Then we'll have to remove you."

Luke stepped forward and spoke uneasily in Smoke's ear. "What are we gonna do? They got us outnumbered five-to-one."

A taunting grin lighted Smoke's face. "Simple. We surround them."

No stranger to street fighting, Luke understood immediately. "Sure. We spread out and hit them from four places at once. But that don't make the numbers any less."

"I think we have the advantage," Smoke spoke from the corner of his mouth. "I failed to introduce myself and my friend. I'm Smoke Jensen. He's Louis Longmont."

"The Smoke Jensen?" Luke asked in an awe-filled tone.

"There's only one I know of."

"I've heard of you. Read about your doin's in the far mountains. Read about Mr. Longmont, too. The fast gun from New Orleans. I'm honored to be in such famous company." Luke dusted his hands together in eagerness. "We'd better get at it, right?"

"Yes. Before they take it on themselves to start the dance," Smoke agreed.

"Take 'em, boys," Huntley's lead henchman commanded.

At once, the phalanx of longshoremen surged forward. Smoke and company separated. Before the dockworkers realized it, they had been flanked by the two most deadly gunfighters in the nation. Two of them turned to face Smoke Jensen. He stepped in and swiftly punched the nearest one in the mouth.

Shaking his head, the hard case threw a right at Smoke, which the last mountain man took on the point of his shoulder. He rolled with it and went to work on the mouth again. Lips split under a left-right combination. Blood began to flow in a torrent when Smoke hooked a right into the damaged area. His opponent tried for an uppercut and failed to land it. Smoke took him by the upthrust arm and threw him into his companion.

A quick glance told Smoke the other three had their hands full, though they managed to deal with it. Then two more came at him. As they closed in, Smoke extended his arms widely and jumped into the air.

Eager for a quick end to it, the thugs closed in, shoulder to shoulder. Smoke Jensen clapped his hands together, one to the opposite side of each of his attackers' heads. He slammed their noggins together and they went down groggy and aching. Louis had two longshoremen at his feet, out of the battle. Luke had accounted for one and had another in an arm lock around his head. Methodically Luke pounded the man in the face.

Enough of that, the gang of thugs seemed to conclude at once. Fists rapidly filled with cargo hooks and knives.

SEVEN

One pug-faced grappler lunged at Smoke Jensen with a wicked long-bladed pig-sticker. Swiftly Smoke filled his hand with a .45 Colt Peacemaker. The hammer fell and brought a roar of exploding gunpowder. The longshoreman went off to meet his maker. Smoke reckoned the meeting would not be a friendly one. He took note that Louis had his own six-gun in action. While those menacing him backpedaled, confused by this sudden turn of events, Smoke reached left-handed for his second revolver and freed it from leather.

A line of fire blew across Smoke's left forearm. He pivoted in that direction and jammed the muzzle of his right-hand Colt up under the knife-wielder's rib cage and squeezed the trigger. Hot gases shredded the thug's intestines, while the bullet punched through his diaphragm and exploded his heart before exiting his body behind his right collarbone.

"Luke!" he barked in warning as he tossed the Colt to the young dockworker.

Facing three men armed with deadly six-guns changed the outlook of the dock brawlers. Few of them owned a firearm, and fewer had ever been in a gunfight. With a curse, the leader called his men off. They fled down the bayside street. The fight ended as quickly as it had begun. Smoke Jensen had a shallow slash on his left forearm. Louis Longmont was bent slightly, one hand clutching at a ragged tear at the point of one shoulder, which he had received from a cargo hook. His remark showed he felt little of it.

"It is nothing, *mon ami*. A big steak and a shot of brandy will make everything right again."

"Wonder why they didn't stay around?" Smoke asked jokingly. "Let me wrap up that arm for you, Louis. And then it's time for us to find six more good men."

Smoke Jensen and Louis Longmont returned to Francie's with six big, capable men, two less than Smoke had wanted, yet enough, he felt sure, to do the job. He gathered them in the spacious former ballroom, which had been converted into a saloon. Lucy joined Smoke and Louis there. Smoke introduced her and began to outline their duties to the collection of seamen and dockworkers.

"Two of you will be on watch in alternating four-hour shifts, day and night. You are to hold this place against anyone who comes here fixing to throw the ladies out. The weakest places are the back door to the kitchen and the French doors to the drawing room. A twelve-year-old could knock them down. I suggest you put some heavy furniture in front of them. The kitchen door can be blocked with that butcher's block in the middle of the room when needed. No drinking on duty, and only two drinks while off. When the emergency is over, we'll have a rip-roaring party that will be the talk of the town. Until then, I want you all sober.

"In the event someone tries to break in, everyone will respond. You will all be given a rifle or shotgun. Make good use of them, if need be." He paused. "Any questions?"

"Why's someone want to take over this place?"

Smoke smiled at him. "It makes a lot of money. That's not all of it. There are some powerful men who aim to take over every saloon and bawdy house in town. I learned yesterday that they intended to start with this one. I also discovered that Miss Francie refused to sell at a piddling price. Later she was run down by a freight wagon no one saw. I own it now and I don't intend to let these ladies be turned into virtual slaves by anyone."

"Who are these men?" Luke asked.

"Cyrus Murchison, Titus Hobson, and Gaylord Huntley."

Luke's eyes narrowed at the list of names and he gave a slight start. "That's why Huntley's dockyard trash set on us, right?"

"We don't know that for sure," Smoke advised him. "Another thing—don't wear yourselves out on off-duty time. In other words, no sampling of the wares."

That brought six loud groans. Smoke suppressed a smile. He had chosen well, he concluded. "Any other questions?"

"Where will you be while we watch over these pretty doves?" a man called Ox asked.

"Louis and I will be out finding a way to put an end to this cabal's schemes."

"Sure you won't need some help?" Ox asked.

Luke answered for Smoke. "Ox, I know you saw how four of us took care of twenty of Huntley's bully-boys. What do you think?"

Ox produced a gap-toothed grin, the absent teeth the result of more than one brawl. "I think we'll be missing out on a lot of fun."

None of the newly hired protectors had more questions. Smoke Jensen released them to their tasks and strolled to the front door with Louis Longmont. "Old friend, we're going back to Chinatown. I want to get those Tong thugs off our back before we go after Murchison and company."

Monte Carson, hat in hand, stood on the porch of Smoke Jensen's home on the Sugarloaf. Earlier in the afternoon, Sally Jensen had sent a hand to town to summon the lawman. Now he listened to Sally's account of what had happened. His frown deepened and a flush rose to color his face darkly.

"Why, them rotten damn polecats!" he growled, then flushed deeper. "Pardon my language, Miss Sally. I can't help it. You say one's dead and the other is waiting for me inside? How'd that happen?"

"I shot Buck when he made lewd suggestions and took a grab for me."

"Good for you, I don't doubt he deserved it."

"It was not . . . pleasant, Monte."

"I understand. Well," he went on, gesturing to his deputy still astride his lathered mount at the tie-rail, "best put the other one in shackles and get him out of here."

Monte's deputy came forward with an armful of leg irons, chains, and handcuffs. He and Monte entered the house. Sally remained on the porch, preferring not to observe the conclusion of this affair. When the sheriff and his deputy returned, a crestfallen Jason Rucker accompanied them. His appearance shocked Sally.

Leg irons enclosed his ankles, a chain running from the midpoint to another set of links around his waist. His wrists were restrained by thick steel cuffs, and again extended from the coupling bar to his waist. Tear tracks streaked his sallow cheeks, the usual tan faded to a sickly yellow. The corpse of Buck Jarvis had been wrapped in a tarp and draped over his horse by Jason Rucker. The morgan stood knock-kneed at the tie-rail, its loose hide rippling nervously in the presence of death. Monte paused beside Sally while his deputy frog-marched Jase to his waiting mount. She wondered how she could explain all this to Bobby.

"What will happen to him now, Monte?"

Monte Carson paused, weighing how to tell her. "He'll be tried, of course. Most likely he'll hang."

Sally lowered her eyes. "I'm . . . sorry. Oh, not that he will be punished. But I am sorry that this happened in the first place. It seems that there is something terribly wrong with a lot of the younger people these days."

Monte scratched his graying head. "Don't I know it. Well, we'd best be movin' on. It's a long way to Big Rock. And, stop frettin' yourself, Miss Sally. You'll be safe enough."

"Oh, I have no doubt of that, Monte. Though I will need a new purse."

* * *

Tyrone Beal arrived in Parkerville on the late train. He located the incompetent henchmen in the nearest saloon. He accepted that philosophically. They could sober up on the ride to the Wagner claim. He'd be damned if he failed again.

"Why'er we goin' now?" Spencer demanded with a drunken slur.

"Because I say we are," Beal barked.

"It'll be dark before we get there," Quint objected with beery breath.

"That's why we're going now. We didn't do too well in daylight, did we?" Beal taunted.

"Bet your ass," Spencer muttered sullenly.

They rode out ten minutes later. Beal took the lead, the route burned into his mind. They began the climb into the foothills along the Sacramento River as the sun sank below the coastal range. That still left ample light, the afterglow would last for a good two hours. Grumbles came to Beal's ears from the whiskey-soaked hard cases behind him. He kept a strict silence, letting his irritation with these incompetents feed his anger.

That was the good part. Spencer had informed him that Wagner had taken on a partner, a man reputed to be good with a gun. That didn't set too well with Beal. It had caused him to make changes in his plan. He knew what he would do now. It varied little from his original. Of course, that could be a little rough on Wagner.

Ray Wagner had returned to his claim the previous day. Some of the bruises had faded slightly, and he wore his left arm, broken in two places, in a sling. His ribs had been tightly bound and he moved like an arthritic old man. He had taken the precaution to bring along a burly miner friend of his as a minority partner. Let them come again, he thought. Eli Colter had a small reputation as a shootist. He wore a six-gun slung low on his right hip, another tucked into the waistband of his trousers on the left. And he could use them.

Ray had seen Eli face down three rowdy highwaymen who'd tried to rob him. He had killed two of them and wounded the third. Not a one of the robbers had gotten off a shot. He mused on this fact as he added another stick of firewood to the cookfire in a ring of stones. Above him, blue slowly faded into gray, and the first stars twinkled in the black velvet of the East.

A cloud of sparks ascended as he released the piece of firewood. He froze a second when his ears picked out the distinctive sound of a hoof striking a small rock. Slowly he uncoiled his body and came upright. A quick glance located Eli Colter.

"Eli," he cautioned tense and low. "I think we are about to have visitors. Be ready."

A gravelly voice answered him. "No problem, Ray."

"This ought to hold the fire until morning," Ray speculated, as he added another stick. When he came upright again, he directed his hand to the butt of the finely made Mauser revolver in a flap holster at his hip. Constantly alert, he went about preparing to roll up in his blankets.

He glanced away from the treeline for only a moment to do so, yet when he looked back, four men, led by Tyrone Beal, appeared as if by magic at the edge of the firelight. Wagner braced himself, certain a showdown was in the offing. Beal dismounted and came forward. Without a word, he thrust the quit-claim deed at Wagner.

"I told you I would never sign. You are trespassing. Get off my claim or I will bury you here."

Beal sighed gustily. "You failed to profit from my previous lesson, I see. You are feeling very cocky, eh, Fritzie?"

"I will not sign," Wagner ground out in a hard, flat voice, and went for his gun.

Eli Colter slapped leather a split second later. He never got off a shot. Two of the hard cases with Beal gunned him down before the muzzle could clear leather.

"You don't have a chance," Beal warned. "Sign it and be damned."

Raising his Mauser 10mm revolver to chest level, Wagner shook his head in the negative. "I will not."

At once, all four hard cases tore into him with hot lead. When they finished, eleven bullets had struck Ray Wagner. He lay at Beal's feet, quivering on the threshold of death. Tyrone Beal coldly stepped close to the dead man and rolled him over with the toe of one boot. He looked down at the deed in his other hand, shrugged, and signed it himself.

"Got that signed at last," he commented flatly as he walked away. "Mount up. We've got along ride in the dark."

Smoke Jensen and Louis Longmont spent a fruitless afternoon and evening in Chinatown. They picked up Louis's belongings at the Palace Hotel and he moved into the bordello. Morning found them at the breakfast table. Louis took another long draw on his cup of coffee and smacked his lips.

"This is excellent coffee," he remarked.

"They're the same Colombian Arabica beans Cyrus Murchison prefers," Lucy Glover informed him.

That raised some eyebrows. "Murchison? How did Francie get her hands on anything he fancied?" Smoke asked.

"The captain of the ship that brings them to San Francisco was a great admirer of Francie's. He always saw to it that at least one full bag got delivered here. Murchison has never known."

Smoke joined Louis in laughter. When they subsided, Louis asked Smoke the key question. "What do we do today?"

"Go back and try to find a lead to Xiang Lee."

Louis made a face. Before he could make a response, Ophilia came to the doorway to the breakfast room. "Mistah Smoke, they's two po-lice here askin' for you."

Smoke and Louis exchanged glances. "We are not at home, Ophilia."

Eyes twinkling with approval for Smoke, Ophilia left to deliver this message to the lawmen. She liked a man with spunk. This would sure put those officious policemen in their place. Her enjoyment was dampened somewhat by their reaction.

"I'm not sure we believe that. You could be charged with harboring fugitives."

Ophilia controlled herself enough to not show any reaction to that. "What you callin' them gentlemen fugitives for?"

"They are wanted for the murder of fifteen railroad police officers and other crimes."

Ophilia let her outrage flow over. "That ain't true. No, suh, not one bit of it. I don' believe a word you said. Now, you get your flat feet off my porch before I throw you off." She turned her ample back on him and slammed the door.

When they learned the purpose of the visit by the police, Smoke Jensen produced a frown. This could complicate matters considerably. "Murchison is a powerful man. I reckon he's got some higher-ups in the police in his pocket. We'll have to be mighty careful going around outside here."

Louis nodded his understanding. "Perhaps a change of costume is in order," he suggested in a glance at Smoke's buckskin hunting shirt and trousers.

"Umm. I see what you mean. Sorta stands out around here, doesn't it? I don't cotton to the idea of fighting in fancy clothes, but the situation suggests I not look like myself."

"I, too, shall change my appearance," Louis offered. "Perhaps the clothing of a longshoreman would be advisable."

"What?" Smoke jibed. "And give up those fancy shirts you like so much?"

"It was Shakespeare who said, 'All the world's stage.' In this case the actors must blend with the audience."

Smoke quipped back, " 'Faith, that's as well said, as if I had said it myself.' "

Delighted amusement lighted the face of Louis Longmont. "Jonathan Swift. *Polite Conversations,* I believe. From Dialogue Two?"

"Yes," Smoke said with sudden discomfort. "Sally made me read a lot of Swift."

"And for good reason, I would say. His characters and you have a lot in common. Especially in *Gulliver's Travels.*"

"Are you comparing me to a giant among the Lilliputs? Don't wax too literary, old friend. It's too early in the morning." They shared a laugh, and Smoke went on. "Seriously, we're going to find ourselves with our tails in a wringer if the police get too involved in this."

"Why not talk to Lawyer Brian?" Lucy suggested, then flushed furiously.

Louis picked up on it at once. "Aha! So it's *Brian* now, eh?"

"He's been advising me on managing the—ah—business."

"And you have grown close? No doubt," Louis went on gallantly. "You're a lovely woman, *ma cherie.*"

Lucy hastened to protest. "It isn't—I'm just a client. He doesn't even look on me as a woman, let alone have a romantic interest."

Louis cocked an eyebrow and shaped a teasing expression. "Time for our friend Shakespeare again. 'Methinks the lady doth protest too much.' Yet it's entirely understandable, given the circumstances. What do you say, Smoke, my friend?"

"I think they deserve a tad bit less prying. Louis, can't you be serious for two minutes at a time? Lucy, I agree that maybe Pullen can help. I'd be obliged if you'd go see him about all this. As a lawyer, he can look into it, find out what the police have."

Lucy pushed back from the breakfast table, her meal forgotten. "I'll go right away."

"Finish your breakfast first," Smoke urged.

"But those policemen might come back. And they might bring more with them."

"It's a thought, Lucy. Though by then, Louis and I really will not be here."

Liam Quinn had been working for the California Central Railroad since he was a boy—first as a cook's helper and scullion, then as a switchman and telegrapher, and finally as a locomotive engineer. He was enjoying a day off with his buxom wife, Bridget, and their five dark-haired children. A small park, soon to be converted into office buildings and shops, stood across from the entrance to Chinatown. Bridget had packed a huge picnic basket, with cold fried chicken, a small joint of ham, cheese, pickled herring, cold boiled potatoes, and hard-cooked eggs. Liam had sent his eldest, eleven-year-old Sean, for a bucket of beer.

Savoring the arrival of the cool, frothy brew, Liam tore off a hunk of sourdough bread and munched contentedly, a chicken wing in the other hand. Two men, quite tall, caught his attention across the street. Lord, they moved like panthers. A full head above other white men, head and shoulders topping the Chinese who milled about near the large Moon gate, they had an air about them that riveted Liam's attention. Something about them set off an alarm in his head.

Yes, that was it. Those men had the moves of gunfighters Liam had read of in the penny dreadfuls. And, yes, on those flyers that he had seen circulated early this morning when he had checked in at the yard office to be sure he could take the day off. These two sure resembled them. He studied them further, noting the rough dress of the bearded one and the somber cut of the other's suit. Certainty bloomed in Liam's brain.

"That's them, by St. Fiona!" Liam shouted. There was a reward offered, Liam recalled. A fat bounty on those particular gentlemen, sure and wasn't it? He must get the word to Captain Beal or Chief Grange. "Sure an' then that gold will jingle in me pocket," he muttered gleefully.

His beer would have to wait. Nothing for it, though. He had to be the first to report them and where they might be found. Liam tossed a hasty word of explanation to his wife and promised to rejoin them within the hour, then hurried off down the street.

Smoke Jensen and Louis Longmont resumed their search for the elusive Xiang Wai Lee on one of the many bustling new side streets of Chinatown. One shopkeeper, fear clearly written in his seamed old face and tired, ancient eyes, spoke with them while he cast worried glances at the front of the shop.

"Nothing good can come of your search. You arc not *Han.* You have no idea with what, and whom, you are dealing."

"Then the Tongs are here?" Smoke pressed.

"Heyi! Take care in what you say," the frightened elder warned. "They have ears and eyes everywhere. I do not want a hatchet painted on my door. You should not want one on yours, gentlemen."

"I agree," Louis hastened to put in. "What can you tell us of Xiang Wai Lee?"

Eyes wide with fear, the old man blanched so thoroughly that his complexion took on a waxen color. *"Buddah nee joochung!"* he wailed. "To speak the name is to ask for death. Buddha, fortify me," he moaned again.

Smoke Jensen found his patience wearing thin: "Look, this is getting us nowhere. You saw what happened yesterday?" Slowly the aged Chinese nodded. "Then I reckon you should rely upon us to protect you, instead of this Buddha feller. If you know anything at all, tell us how we can find Xiang Lee."

Drawing a shuddering breath, the old merchant stared at a spot above and beyond the shoulder of Smoke Jensen, while he spoke in quiet, broken words. "It is said that there is a secret place, near the opera house."

"The San Francisco Opera?" Smoke asked impatiently.

"No—no, the Chinese opera. It is that large building near the south end of Chinatown. You see it easy, big pagoda, with many peaks and dragon carvings. Near it, it is said, the Triads hold secret meetings. Some say underground. I not know more."

Smoke gave him a warm smile. "You've done enough, old-timer. More than you think. Thank you."

Outside the shop, Louis asked the question that had been troubling Smoke. "Shall we go there straightaway?"

"Don't reckon to. We need to know a lot more about the Tongs. How many are they, for one thing. We don't want to stumble into some nest of wasps. I've been thinking, maybe we're goin' at this the wrong way. There must be some whites who know something about the Tongs. What say we head for those offices built into the wall that runs along Chinatown?"

Louis shrugged. "It's worth a try."

Again, they drew blanks. Not until the filth small, narrow office did Smoke and Louis come upon anyone with specific knowledge. The sign on the outside identified it as an import broker's office. Inside, dusty chairs were littered about and a large, desk-like table had been heaped with invoices and bills of lading. Seated at a cluttered rolltop desk, a slender, bookish young man in shirt sleeves and garters glanced up, his features shadowed by a green eyeshade.

"You here to pick up the shipment of spices? The paperwork's not done yet," he added without waiting for verification.

"No. Actually, we stopped in to ask you a little something about dealing with the folks of Chinatown," Smoke Jensen advised him.

Smoke kept his questions to generalities until the man had relaxed. At that point he directed their conversation towered the area of interest. "Tell me, when you bring in things from the Orient, China in particular, do you have to deal through—ah—shall we say—out-of-the-ordinary agents among the Chinese?"

"Exactly what do you mean?"

"Do you have to make payoffs to one or more of the Tongs?" Smoke asked bluntly.

The broker did not even blink. "Yes. Anyone dealing with Chinatown has to make their—ah—contributions. It's the way they do business. Even though I am not Chinese, I am not exempt from that rule. Tell me, why are you so interested in the Tongs?"

"Idle curiosity? No, you'd never believe that," Smoke went on, as though thinking out loud. "Actually, we need to talk to Xiang Lee."

Blinking, the import broker pushed up his eyeshade and removed his hexagonal spectacles. He wiped the lenses industriously as he spoke. "Whatever for?"

"We have good reason to believe that the Tong hatchetmen are bent upon killing us," Louis informed him.

"Then the last thing you want to do is get anywhere near Xiang Lee. He's the most bloodthirsty of them all. Xiang Wai Lee is a deadly, silent reptile who gives no warning before he strikes. You wouldn't stand a chance."

"Perhaps. Though I would reserve judgment, were I you," Louis Longmont advised.

They got a little more out of the broker. Not enough, and no confirmation of the location of Xiang's lair. Back on the street, they headed again for Chinatown, armed with new facts to prod those they questioned. To appear to be armed with more knowledge than one had often resulted in gaining what one sought, Louis reminded Smoke. They had come abreast of the small park across the street when a shout thrust them into quick action.

"Jehosephat! There they are! There's the men I told you about," a voice, thick with Irish accent, shouted.

Smoke and Louis looked that way to see a burly black-haired man. He stood at the curb, pointing directly at them. Half a dozen railroad police gathered behind him. Two of them carried carbine-length Winchesters, which they swiftly brought to their shoulders. The discharge of the rifles made a *crack-crack* sound. Before they heard the muzzle roar, the deadly bullets passed close enough beside the heads of Smoke Jensen and Louis Longmont that they felt the heat of the lead. It answered one question. These men had been ordered to shoot to kill.

EIGHT

Ten more of the railroad thugs swarmed out of the park. That put Smoke Jensen and Louis Longmont in considerable jeopardy. A quick evaluation of the situation decided Smoke on their wisest course of action.

"Let's get out of here," he said tightly.

With Murchison's hirelings streaming after them, Smoke and Louis bolted into Chinatown. The pursuers rapidly lost ground. Once they entered the throng of Chinese, the two with Winchesters did not fire again. Smoke led the way toward the central marketplace. He noted with satisfaction that many of the residents of the Chinese quarter bustled themselves into the street in a manner that would block the passage of the railroad detectives.

Cursing and shoving their way through the throng, the hired guns fell further behind. Finally the first one broke free of the obstacles and threw a shot in the direction of Smoke and Louis. His bullet passed the gunfighter pair far enough away not to be heard. Two more guns joined the fusillade. Smoke and Louis led them by a block. It forced their attackers to halt to take aim.

Now the slugs cracked past uncomfortably close. One round kicked up rock chips from the cobbles beside Smoke's boots. He drew his Colt Peacemaker and returned fire. His target emitted a weak cry and pitched forward onto his face. It gave those behind him pause. Smoke pounded boot soles on the street as he led the way at a diagonal across the market square. Louis followed. In less than five strides, Smoke and Louis found themselves in even more trouble.

Another ten railroad thugs appeared on their left. They had even less distance to cover than those coming from behind. In an eyeblink, they had their six-guns in action. Before flame lanced from their muzzles, Smoke and Louis responded.

Smoke's .45 roared and sent a slug into the pudgy belly of a buck-toothed hard case who wore the round blue billcap and silver badge of a railroad policeman. He went down in a groaning heap of aching flesh. Smoke cycled the cylinder again and sought another target.

Louis already had his. He put out the lights for a red-faced gunman who bellowed defiance at the formidable pair facing him. He stopped in mid-bellow when Louis's bullet punched a neat hole half an inch below his nose. There was more hell to pay for the "detectives" as they closed on Smoke and Louis from two directions.

Smoke blasted a round into the chest of another of them who had ventured too close. He screamed horribly and flung his Smith and Wesson American high in the air. Beside him, a startled thug triggered a hasty, unaimed round. He did well enough, though, as his slug gouged a shallow trough along the left side of Smoke's rib cage. It burned like the fires of hell. All it did was serve to heighten Smoke's anger.

By then, so many of the hunters had weapons in action it sounded like the Battle of Gettysburg. A Chinese woman screamed shrilly as a slug from one of the hard cases struck her in the chest. An angry mutter rose among the fright-para-lyzed onlookers. A quick glance indicated to Smoke that they had only one way out. A small pagoda fronted on the west side of a small park south of the market square. It rested in stately composure atop a gentle, grassy slope. Smoke touched Louis lightly on one sleeve and nodded toward the religious shrine. Louis understood at once.

Ducking low, the dauntless pair sprinted among the vendors' carts toward their only hope. Two bullets cut holes in the sailor's jacket worn by Louis Longmont and smacked into a cart wall. The pungent odor of spicy Szechuan food filled the air as the contents of a barrel inside poured onto the ground. Once free of the closing ring of hard cases, Smoke settled in to pick individual targets while Louis dashed forward a quarter block. Smoke zeroed in on a florid face and squeezed off a round. The thug went down with a hole in his forehead and the back of his head blown off. Those around him ducked for cover. At once, Smoke set off to close the distance between himself and Louis.

Louis sighted on one of the more daring among the throng of hoodlums and sent his target off to pay for his sins. Smoke joined him a moment later. "Take off, Louis," Smoke panted.

Longmont left without a remark. Smoke turned at once to face their enemies. He had little time to wait for a new target. Two men loomed close at hand. The first shouted an alarm too late. Smoke pinwheeled the other railroad detective and spilled him over backward. Sweat stung the raw wound along Smoke's ribs.

No time to think about that. He banished the discomfort from his consciousness. Halfway to their goal, Louis Longmont took cover behind a cart piled with what looked like small gray-brown stones. A stack had been made on a counter outside one of the barrels from which they had come. Louis opened up on the charging gunmen and immediately Smoke Jensen made a dash to join his companion. Return fire shattered several of the stones and released an abominable odor.

Smoke's nostrils flared at the scent of sulfur and sea salt. He swiveled at the hips and fired almost point blank into the chest of his closest pursuer. The man's arms flung wide and his legs could no longer support him. He hit the ground in a skid. Two more long strides and Smoke rounded the odorous cart. More of the objects had been broken open by gunfire and three of the barrels oozed a malevolent ichor.

Through the distaste in his expression, Smoke asked Louis about them. "What are those?"

"Hundred-year-old eggs," Louis enlightened him. "They are not really a hundred years old, merely duck eggs preserved in sea salt and brine."

Before Louis started off on the next leg of their retreat, Smoke asked, "What are they for?"

"The Chinese eat them," Louis answered and began his sprint.

Left behind to hold off the hoodlums, Smoke could only repeat the last part of Louis's sentence: *"Eat them?"*

Without pausing to consider that, Smoke had his hands full of burly railroad detectives and uniformed yard police. He had emptied his Peacemaker and now used the left-hand Colt to hold them at bay. A well-placed round took down a skinny thug with a huge overbite that made him look like a rabbit. That scattered the two who had been beside him. One of the nearer hard cases caught a whiff of the broken eggs.

"Gawd, that's awful. What is that stink?"

"Them things there," a comrade answered. "Let's get away from here."

"Can't. That's where they're hold up."

"Only one of them, an' you're welcome to him," the disgruntled gunhawk offered. "That stuff would gag a maggot."

Louis had reached his latest shelter and taken the time to reload his six-gun. Now he opened up. Instantly, Smoke was on the run. He concentrated on their goal and found a final dash would make it. He advised Louis of that fact when he skidded to a halt behind a stone lion carved in the Chinese style.

"I figured it that way, too, my friend. Shall I give you time to reload?"

"It would be a good idea. I don't hanker to have them follow us into that place with my iron dry."

Swiftly, without a tremble to his hands, Smoke Jensen reloaded both revolvers. Louis kept up a steady fusillade until he had emptied his own, then ran for the beckoning archway that formed the entrance to the temple. Smoke laid down covering fire, and as soon as he glanced at the pagoda and saw Louis no longer in sight, he made his own hurried rush to the promised safety. Louis blasted two more thugs into perdition while he backed up Smoke. When the last mountain man disappeared into the shrine, a jubilant shout rose from their hunters.

* * *

"We got 'em trapped, boys!" Mick Taggart yelled gleefully.

"How's that, Mick?" one of his underlings asked.

"That Chinee church ain't got no back door, that's how," Taggart told him angrily. He had lost too many men, too many good men at that.

Not all had died, though enough had to make him fume inside. He had heard of Louis Longmont; he was supposed to be a hotshot gunfighter from New Orleans. Well, he sure as hell proved that to be true. The other one really bothered him. Smoke Jensen. How many times had he read of that one's exploits? It was unnerving to see the fabled Smoke Jensen in action.

There had been a time when Mick Taggart had fancied himself good enough to go up against any gunhand west of the Mississippi—and where else were they?—then he had come across an account of Smoke Jensen. Overwhelming pride and self-confidence are necessities for a gunfighter, and Taggart had his full share. Yet he recognized that if even half of what had been written about Smoke Jensen and his fight against the Montana ranching trust was true, he didn't stand a chance. Too late to worry about that secret knowledge.

Now he faced the only man he considered his better. Think fast, he admonished himself. "Pass the word to the rest," he told Opie Engles. "We'll rush that place in a bunch. No way they can get away from us."

"When do we do it, Mick?"

"When you get back, you and me will open up. That'll be the signal."

It worked exactly as Mick Taggart had planned it. Opie returned to tell him the boys were ready. Then Taggart and Engles opened fire on the entrance to the pagoda. The entire force of railroad detectives and police charged as one toward the besieged building. To Taggart and his crew of hard cases and thugs, the shrine held no religious significance. What did it matter if they brought violence and death to its interior? They stormed through the gateway with a shout.

In no time they swarmed into the sanctuary and spread out. They ran and fired as they went. Then Mick Taggart skidded to a stop in the middle of the lacquered floor. A quick glance around verified his suspicion.

Only a smiling faced Buddha witnessed their assault. Smoke Jensen and Louis Longmont had completely disappeared.

Jason Rucker looked up disbelievingly at his visitor to the cell in the Big Rock jail. Dressed in the height of fashion, Sally Jensen cut quite a figure in the dingy corridor of the cellblock. She wore a high-necked, full-skirted dress of deep maroon, edged with black ostrich feathers. A matching hat, small and with only a hint of veil, sat perkily on her head, cocked forward in the latest style.

"Monte told me you were convicted. I—had no reason to stay for the rest of the trial."

"Yep. They're goin' to hang me," Jason said, without even a hint of self-pity.

"That's too bad. You know, this whole thing has broken a small boy's heart?"

Jase brightened, then his lips curled down in genuine sadness. "Bobby? He's a kid with a lot of spunk. He's got sand, that he does. How's it broke his heart?"

Sally hesitated, then forged ahead. "He hasn't spoken to me since he learned about the shooting. He won't even look at me, except with a sulky pout and eyes narrowed with hate."

"That's too bad," Jason said through a sigh. "We weren't neither of us worth that."

Sally's misery wedded the pent-up anger in her heart. "Why did you have to take him into your lives?"

Jason made a helpless gesture. "I ain't sure. It was Buck that shined up to the boy. Said it reminded him of himself at that age."

"Good Lord!" Sally expelled in a rush. "And he wanted to remake Bobby in his likeness?"

"I couldn't say . . . though I suspect you've got the right of it." Suddenly he wanted to change the subject. "You know, your husband is a good man, Miz Jensen. But, he ought to be more careful who he takes on as help. It could get him bad-hurt some time."

"I think not. Do you know who he is, Jason?" Sally responded.

"Just Mr. Jensen, I suppose."

Sadly, Sally shook her head. Maybe if Smoke did not cherish his privacy so much and had told the two of them his first name, none of what had followed would have happened. "His first name is Kirby, but everyone calls him Smoke."

"Oh, my God!" Jase paled and swallowed hard. "That's how come you shoot so good. Honest truth, Miz Jensen, I reckon it's a mercy I'll face the hangman, instead of your—Smoke Jensen."

Sally thought on it a long, silent minute. Slowly, she fixed her features into a mask of genuine concern. "You really regret what was done, don't you, Jason?"

Head hanging, he nodded in agreement. "Yes. Yes, I do."

"Well, then, there's something I must do. Your concern over Bobby and your show of remorse have convinced me that you deserve a second chance. Mind, I'm not promising anything. Nor am I given to feeling sorry for criminals. But you're young, with apparently a will of your own, although it has been long in the shadow of Buck Jarvis, I wager. I'll have a talk with Monte Carson and the judge. Perhaps we can get your sentence commuted to prison time only. Don't get your hopes up, but I will try. Goodbye, Jason."

Jason choked out a farewell through the flood of relieved tears that streamed down his suddenly gaunt cheeks.

"Come this way," a small, old monk in a saffron robe summoned Smoke Jensen and Louis Longmont when they dashed into the center of a large square area with wood floor, red lacquered walls picked out with gold leaf, and a blue domed ceiling.

They cut their eyes to the frail figure, his hands hidden within the voluminous sleeves of a plain yellow silk robe.

Twin, wispy hanks of white hair sprouted from his chin to
mid-chest, matched by a ghost of mustache the same color
and thinness. When they hesitated, he withdrew one skeletal
hand, parchmented with age, from the folds of his sleeve and
beckoned.

"Come this way," he repeated.

Smoke and Louis shifted their gaze to the seemingly solid
wall behind the old man. What good would it do to be against
that wall, as opposed to any other? Impatiently the old monk
gestured again.

"Hurry, there is little time."

"I'm willing," Smoke Jensen told him. "But I sure hanker
to know what good it will do."

"I will take you out of the shrine to safety."

That was good enough for Smoke. He and Louis crossed
the expanse of floor, their boot heels clicking on the high-gloss
floorboards. When they neared the monk, he stepped away in
the direction of a fat statue of a smiling Buddha. There, he
pressed a spot on the wall that looked like any other.

A hidden panel swung open in the side wall of the pagoda.
The priest-monk waited until they reached the opening and
nodded to indicate they should enter. Smoke remembered the
.45 Colt in his hand and thought well of keeping it there. With
a small gasp of impatience at their hesitation, their host preceded them into a dark passageway.

There he used a lucifer to light a torch and return it to its
wall sconce. Smoke and Louis stepped through into what they
soon saw to be a tunnel. Behind them, the secret panel clicked
back into place. Smoke tightened his grip on the plowhandle
butt grip of his Peacemaker. The monk advanced down the
tunnel, igniting more torches. When he had three burning
brightly, he waited for his unexpected guests.

"I am Tai Chiu. I am the abbot of this temple. We have
taken notice of your activities in the past few days. It became
obvious that you are fighting the evil ones. When they out-
numbered you, you took sanctuary in our humble shrine. It is
our duty to protect you." He motioned with the same thin,
frail hand he had used to summon them to the hidden passage.

"Follow in my steps. I will take you to a hidden place and heal your wounds."

Smoke Jensen again became aware of the gouge along his ribs. The bleeding had slowed, but it still oozed his life's fluid. A quick glance apprised him that his wound did not show.

"How did you know we had been shot?"

"I . . . felt your agony. Please to come this way. Those who seek you will be befuddled."

Cyrus Murchison pushed back the picked-clean carcass of the half duck he had enjoyed for his noon meal. Silver bowls held the remains of orange sauce, fluffy mashed potatoes, thick, dark gravy, and wilted salad greens. Beyond this gastronomic phalanx sat a silver platter filled with melting ice and a pile of oyster shells, all that remained of a dozen tasty mollusks on the half-shell. Murchison hid a polite belch behind the back of his hand and dabbed at his thick lips with a white napkin.

"Well, then Judge Batey, did you enjoy your *canard à l'orange?*"

A similar array of plates and utensils covered the tablecloth in front of the judge. He patted a protruding belly and nodded approvingly. "Most excellent, my dear Cyrus. I always look forward to dining with you. Do you eat this well at night?"

Murchison produced a fleeting frown. "Alas, I have been constrained by my stomach, as well as my doctor, to curtail my epicurean adventures in the evening. A chop, a boiled potato, and some fruit and cheese is my limit of late. But I sorely miss the pig's knuckles, sauerkraut, and beer, or roasted venison with *pommes frites,* and strawberries in cream that I used to indulge in."

Judge Batey chuckled softly. "I know whereof you speak. Though I fear we digress."

"Oh? How's that?"

"You are not known to wine and dine persons of influence

without some ulterior motive. What is it I can help you with this time?"

"Right to the point, eh? Your courtroom reputation has preceded you. That is why I dismissed the servants. We'll not be imposed upon." He paused, steepled his thick fingers, and belched again before launching into his proposition. "There are going to be some transfer deeds coming before your court in the near future. Some of them will no doubt be contested. I trust that you can recognize the genuineness of these instruments merely by examining them?"

Judge Batey nodded solemnly. "Is that all? Surely those excellent ducks will have gone begging for so small a favor."

Murchison wheezed stout laughter. "You're the fox, right enough, Judge. You'll be hearing a criminal matter soon—two men charged with murder of railroad police and some of Hector Grange's detectives. The culprits are named Louis Longmont and Smoke Jensen. To be quite up front with you, Judge, I want to see them hanged."

Batey hesitated only a fraction of a second. "That will depend a lot upon the evidence."

A frown flickered on the broad forehead of Cyrus Murchison. "It need not. In order to provide binding evidence, some things might come out that would prove deleterious to the California Central. We like to keep a—uh—low profile. You understand?"

"Quite so." Judge Batey pursed his lips. "That is asking quite a lot, Cyrus." He raised a hand to stave off a protest. "Not that it is impossible. I shall have to examine the circumstances and evidence and perhaps find a way to accommodate you. Whatever the case, I will do my best."

"Fine, fine. Now, help yourself to some of that chocolate cream cake."

NINE

Tai Chiu led Smoke Jensen and Louis Longmont down a long incline that Smoke soon judged put them well below street level. The Chinese priest remained silent, husbanding his thoughts. As he progressed, he paused at regular intervals to light another torch. The flambeaus flickered and wavered, as though in a breeze. Yet the air still smelled dank and musty. Their steps set off echoes as they advanced over the cobblestone flooring of the shaft. When they reached a level space, they had only hard-packed earth beneath them. Their course took them through a twisting, turning labyrinth of intersecting tunnels. Even with his superb sense of direction, Smoke Jensen had to admit that he had not a hint of where the old monk was taking them.

"Where do you think he is taking us, *mon ami?*" Louis voiced Smoke's thoughts in a low whisper.

"I haven't the least idea."

"He could be taking us directly to Murchison," came the source of Louis's worry.

"I doubt that. He could have left us for those railroad thugs."

"Umm. You have a point."

They walked on in silence for a while, ignorant of their destination, or even of where they had been. Then Louis put voice to his concern again.

"He could be taking us to Xiang Lee," he proposed.

Smoke produced a wide, white grin. "Then all the better for us. We can gun down Xiang Lee and end of problem."

Louis got a startled expression. "You do not really mean that, my friend."

Smoke sobered and left only a hint of smile on his full lips. "Only halfway, old pard. I would never kill an unarmed man. But I could gladly tom-turkey-tromp the crap out of him."

Louis looked relieved and pleased. "Now, that's the Smoke Jensen I have always known. Only, I would feel better if I knew where we were going."

"As I said, we will have to wait and see."

They walked along in silence for several lengthy minutes. Suddenly Smoke received a hint of their destination. The sharp tang of salt air reached his nostrils. He cut his eyes to Louis, who nodded his understanding. They made another turn and it came to Smoke's attention that someone had come along behind them to snuff out the torches. Even if they tried, they could not find their way back through the mystifying maze of tunnels.

Ahead of them, Tai Chiu stopped abruptly before what appeared to be the inner side of the wall of a building. When Smoke and Louis came up to him, he lifted a thick iron ring and gave it a twist. A rusty bolt screeched in its latch. Then a section of the "wall" swung inward. Bright sunlight and the stinging tang of sea air, mingled with the fishy smell of the bay, poured in.

"This way, please," Tai urged.

They followed him out of the building onto a street that paralleled a section of San Francisco Bay. Tai Chiu directed them to a tall, wide wire gate in a high fence at the street end of a long pier. Tai used a key to open the fat padlock and ushered them inside. At the far end of the wharf Smoke saw an odd-shaped ship. Its sails had been furled and the masts were stepped at a steep backward angle. The stern rose in the likeness of a turret from a castle in the Middle Ages, even more so than the caravels of fifteenth-century Spain. On a large plank, mounted below the aft weather rail, picked out in Chinese ideograms and English letters, was the name of the ship, the *Whang Fai*.

The bow also jutted high and square, with murlons to accommodate archers. A likeness of a human eye had been painted a couple of feet above the plimsol line. Louis Longmont soon apprised Smoke of its origin and type.

"It is a Chinese junk. The largest one I have ever seen."

"How astute, Mr. Longmont," Tai Chiu complimented him. "It is an oceangoing junk. You will find it curious to see that it appears even bigger from inside. Our Chinese builders have a talent that way."

Tai led them to a rickety gangway that gave access to the deck of the junk. There, he directed them below decks to an aft cabin decorated in an opulent Oriental style. Statuary in the form of dragons and lions, several of them covered in gold leaf, ranged around the bulkheads, which had been hung with heavy silk brocade tapestries. These depicted various subjects, among them, lovely young ladies of the court, solemn mandarins, fierce warriors astride snorting stallions, bows drawn until the wicked barbs of the arrow heads touched the arms of the bow, and a lordly emperor. Incense burned in tall brass braziers. Cushions abounded, though there was nary a chair. Low tables held porcelain bottles and small, footed cups. It truly did look as if it were too large to fit into the junk's aft quarter.

Smoke took it in and found it a bit too fancy for his liking. Fringe-lined lanterns hung from the overhead in bright colors of red, yellow, and green. They swayed slightly with the movement of the water beyond the bulkheads. The junk creaked and groaned like any wooden sailing ship. From beyond the bulkhead that divided the cabin from the rest of the belowdecks area came the twitter of distinctly feminine voices. Tai Chiu clapped his hands in a signal and the owners of those voices appeared.

One bore a tray with a large, steaming pot, and small, handleless cups. The other had a plate of savory smelling tidbits of foods. *"Dim sum,* little bites," Tai explained. "There are Chinese dumplings, steamed wonton, oysters in peanut sauce—oh, and many more things. Refresh yourselves while I summon our doctor."

Lacking any chairs, Smoke and Louis made themselves

comfortable on cushions around the low table on which the young women placed their tea and snacks. Louis made an attempt with chopsticks; Smoke settled for his fingers. He lifted a plump prawn from a scarlet sauce and bit off half of it. At once his tastebuds gave off the alarm. Sweat broke out on his forehead and his eyes began to water as he chose to chew rapidly as the best means of eliminating the fiery morsel. He did not want to spit it out; that, he knew, would be bad manners.

"Szechuan," one of the lovelies provided helpfully.

"I don't know what that is, but it sure is hot," Smoke responded.

They turned their heads away and covered their mouths and broke into a fit of giggles. Smoke noticed in detail how comely they appeared. More than twenty years of fidelity to Sally protected him from their blandishments, a fact for which he gave great gratitude. Louis, however, showed signs of becoming enthralled. He answered Smoke's unasked question in a distant voice.

"She said 'Szechuan.' It's the name of a province in China, and also a style of cooking that uses a lot of garlic and chili peppers."

"More than the Mexicans, I'll grant you," Smoke gasped out.

"Don't use tea to douse the fire," Louis cautioned, "that would only make it hotter. Try some of that rice wine in the ceramic bottle."

Smoke shook his head in wonder. "Is there no place you have not visited, Louis, no one's food you have not sampled?"

Louis produced a depreciating smile. *"Oui.* There are many places I have never gone. Such as Greece, the principalities of Lesser Asia, the islands of the South Pacific, with their dusky maidens . . ." He would have gone on, except that Smoke raised a hand in a warding-off gesture.

"Enough. I get your point. I hope our gracious host hurries. That bullet I took along my ribs left a world of smarting behind it."

"Let me take a look at it."

When Louis removed Smoke's coat, the China dolls turned away in twittering honor at the sight of the bloody shirt worn by Smoke Jensen. Louis cut away the sodden garment and Smoke swore hotly.

"Damn, that's the only Sunday-go-to-meetin' shirt I brought from home."

Louis studied the wound. "Better it is for you that you had it along. Good, clean linen. Less chance of a suppuration. This should heal nicely. But it will leave another nasty scar."

Another scar, Smoke Jensen thought resignedly. His torso and limbs had accumulated a veritable criss-cross of the patterns of violence. He had received wounds from knife and tomahawk, bullet and buckshot, gouges from the sharp stabs of broken branches, flesh ground off by gravel, and painful burns. His body could serve as a roadmap of his many close encounters with death. He shook his head to dislodge the grim images from his mind.

Having recovered from their initial shock, the enchanting Chinese women—hardly more than girls—hovered over their guests once more. In halting English they urged each man to eat more of the delicacies, to drink their tea. There would be a sea of rice wine afterward, they promised. Half an hour went by, according to Smoke's big Hambleton turnip watch, before Tai Chiu returned with a black-clad, bowed older man, his lined face reminiscent of a prune in all but color. With only a perfunctory greeting he set right to work.

From a little, black bag—just like the kind a *real* doctor carried—he produced an assortment of herbs and lotions and a large roll of bandage gauze. He treated both Smoke and Louis, then leaned back on his small, skinny buttocks to chatter in rapid-fire Chinese at the priest.

Tai Chiu translated for the benefit of the Occidentals. "The doctor says you must take this powder in a little rice wine three times a day."

Smoke eyed the packet suspiciously. "What's in it?"

Tai Chiu smiled deceptively. "It is better that you are not knowing," he said through his spread lips.

"No. I want to know."

The priest sighed and named off the ingredients. "Ground rhinoceros horn, dried fungus from the yew tree, and processed gum of the poppy." He gave a little shrug. "There are, perhaps, other things, secrets of the doctor, you understand. The potion will ease any pain, strengthen you until your body overcomes the blood loss, while the unguents he put on the wound will prevent infection."

Dubious, Smoke responded uneasily. "I'm not so sure about all this."

Enigma coated the lips of Tai Chiu. "Do not your *qua'lo* doctors do the same? They mix roots, bark, and herbs and give them to their patients. The gum of the poppy, in your language, is called laudanum. And does it not ease pain?"

Smoke decided to make the best of it. "You've got me there. And, to top it off, our croakers give everything queer foreign names, so a common feller don't know what it is he's getting."

"Just so. There are no mysteries in Chinese healing. Now, to explain why I brought you here. Your courage and your skill with weapons have been observed and have convinced the high council of our humble order, and the elders of the community, that you have been sent by the ancestors to lead a great battle against the evil dragons of the Triad Society."

What a flowery way to say we're here to break up the alliance between the Tongs and Murchison's thugs, Smoke thought. A quick, silent counsel passed between Smoke and Louis. They acknowledged that they weren't too sure about that. The exchange also conveyed that both agreed to go along for the time being.

"How are we to go about this?" Smoke asked.

"You are to wait here. Men will come, young men who wish to rid Chinatown from the curse of the Tongs for all time. They are strong and good fighters. Students at the temple, for the most part. Now that your wounds have been mended, you will eat and rest and wait for the others to join you."

"When will that be?" Louis inquired.

"Later. In the dark of night. It is our hope to catch Xiang Wai Lee by stealth and deal a death blow to his army of hatchetmen. Now, enjoy. These delightful young ladies have

prepared a feast for you. And afterward, you may avail yourselves of the baths in another part of the ship. I will return
with the last of our young warriors to make certain none were
followed."

After Tai Chiu swept out of the cabin, Smoke Jensen went
to one porthole to watch his departure from the wharf.
Strangely, the frail old monk seemed to have completely disappeared. He turned to Louis, who pressed on him a plaguing
question.

"What was that in service of, *mon ami?*"

Smoke flashed an appreciative smile. "I think we have
found the key to dealing with the Tongs, and Xiang Lee in
particular. For now, my stomach thinks my throat's been slit.
Let's eat."

Steaming bowls and platters of exotic Chinese dishes came
one course at a time, in a steady procession. Few, if any, did
Smoke Jensen recognize. He enjoyed the pork and noodles,
the egg foo yong, and the sweet-and-sour shrimp. He balked,
though, at the baby squid in their own ink—another Szechuan
delicacy, which he wisely avoided after his eyes watered from
the chili oil and plethora of peppers, when he sniffed the ped-
estal bowl in which they were served. As was his custom, he
tried to eat sparingly, yet when the parade of food at last
ceased, he felt stuffed to the point of discomfort.

"That was some feed," he remarked, stifling a belch. "The
soup was good, only why did they serve it last?"

"It is their custom," Louis informed him.

Smoke sucked at his teeth a moment. "Tasty, even if it came
as dessert. What was in it?"

"It was bird's nest soup," Louis answered simply.

Smoke swallowed hard, as his stomach gave a lurch. "You're
funnin' me, Louis. Aren't you?"

"Not at all. Of course, they clean them first. I won't go
into how the nests are made."

"No. Please don't." Smoke said no more with the appearance of the sweet young ladies.

"You come bath now?" one of them chirped.

"Sounds good," Smoke agreed, as he came to his boots. All

the way to the small, humid chamber that held the bubbling wooden bath, Smoke Jensen tried to puzzle out the slightly amused, esoteric smile on the lips of Louis Longmont.

When they reached the tiny cabin, Smoke quickly learned the reason why. "You undress now," the charming daughter of Han told them. Both girls and Louis began to remove their clothing.

"What! Whoa, now, hold it," Smoke pleaded. Images of the reaction Sally would have boiled in his mind.

Soft light glowed on the nubile bodies of the delightful creatures while Smoke Jensen continued to gobble his protests. With lithe movements, the girls became water nymphs as they climbed the two short steps and waded into the steaming water. Buck naked, Louis Longmont quickly joined them.

"Louis? What are you doing?"

"I have always appreciated a good bath, *mon ami*. You should join us. There are delights that surpass the imagination that follow the laving."

Smoke gulped down his trepidation and pulled a somber face. "Thanks, partner, I think I'll pass."

Puzzled by this exchange, beyond their capacity for English, one of the girls cut her eyes to the other. "What is this? The barbarian will not clean himself?"

Although the language mystified him, Louis Longmont caught the drift of what had been said. It summoned a deep, rich guffaw. "I think the young ladies are disturbed over your aversion to taking a bath."

"I do have that gouge along my ribs. Wouldn't do to get that wet."

Louis sobered. "You have a point. Ah, well, *mon ami,* I suppose I can force myself to uphold the honor of Western man."

Confounded at last, Smoke Jensen stomped from the room, though not without a backward, longing glance at the precious physical endowments of the giggling girls.

Cyrus Murchison and Gaylord Huntley took their post-prandial stroll through the minute park named after St. Francis of Assisi, patron of the city, in the center of the cluster of municipal buildings. Tall marble columns surrounded them, while pigeons and seagulls made merry sport of the imposing bronze figure on horseback that occupied the center of the swatch of green. It was there that Heck Granger found him and spoiled the repose Murchison had generated from this good meal they had consumed.

In fact, it soured Murchison's stomach. "They whupped the hell out of 'em."

"What?"

"Those two, Jensen and Longmont, blasted their way through twenty-seven of my men and flat disappeared."

Murchison's visage grew thunderous. "That is impossible. I will not accept that. No two men can outgun twenty-five plus."

Fearing the outburst that would be sure to follow, Granger answered meekly, "These two did. They ran into a Chinee temple and when my men got in there, they were nowhere to be seen."

"They went out a back door," Cyrus Murchison suggested.

"There weren't none. No side doors, either. There was . . . no place for them to escape."

"Nonsense. I want you to take more men, go there, and tear that place apart until you find how they got out of there."

"That—wouldn't be wise, Mr. Murchison. That temple is in Chinatown. Even the Tongs would turn on us if we did. We only got them behind us a little while ago. It's touchy, I say."

A ruby color suffused the angry expression on the face of Cyrus Murchison. "Damn the Tongs. I never approved of allying ourselves with them in the first place."

"I hate to mention it, sir. But there are more of them than there are of us. I won't risk my men for that. We'll find those two. And we'll do it our way."

It was blatant defiance, and Granger all but quailed at the boldness he had displayed. To his surprise, it worked. Murchison's expression softened. "All right, Heck. I understand your anxiety. Do it the way you see best. Only . . . don't fail this time."

* * *

Brian Pullen appeared before Judge Timothy Flannery in the judge's chambers. Aware of Flannery's aversion to wasting time on small talk, he came right to the point.

"Your Honor, I have reliable information that several powerful men in this community have conspired to wrest control of a building owned by a client of mine from him. In furtherance of this conspiracy, they have made false representations to the police of this city that the property had been sold for back taxes, which it had not. Also regarding acts committed by my client and an associate. These acts were, in fact, self-defense. The result is that the police are looking for my client and his associate as fugitives from justice."

Judge Flannery steepled his fingers. "What is it you wish me to do, Counselor?"

"Inasmuch as these persons are actively engaged in an attempt to seize my client's property and using police pressure to accomplish their goal, I have here a petition for a restraining order, which will relieve my clients from the loss of said property until such time as the matter can be resolved. It also asks that the police be restrained from hunting down my client and his associate, and to prevent agents of the conspirators from doing the same."

"I . . . see." Judge Flannery considered that a moment. "I'll see your brief and make my decision within two hours. By the way, who are these men you allege are co-conspirators?"

Brian Pullen swallowed hard. "Cyrus Murchison and Titus Hobson. Also Gaylord Huntley."

Flannery's eyebrows rose. "Your client picked some big enemies, I must say." Brian asked, "Will that have an effect on your decision, Your Honor?"

A frown creased Flannery's brow. "Certainly not. Come back in two hours."

* * *

Shortly after sundown, slim, hard-faced young Chinese men began to drift aboard the *Whang Fai.* Smoke Jensen and Louis Longmont inspected them critically. They exchanged worried glances over the odd assortment of weapons these volunteers possessed. Some carried pikes with odd-shaped blades. Several had swords with blades so broad that they resembled overgrown meat cleavers. A few had knives of varying blade length. More than half bore only stout oak staffs.

Smoke cut his eyes to Louis. "They expect to use those to fight the Tong soldiers and any of Murchison's railroad detectives we come across?"

Louis sighed. "It is a most discouraging prospect, *mon ami.*"

Tai Chiu merely smiled and bowed. "Honorable warriors, it is my humble duty to introduce you to Quo Chung Wu." He indicated a fresh-faced youth who could not be past his twentieth year. "He is the leader of these students that it is my humble privilege to instruct."

"Students? Are they studying to be priests?"

"Yes, that, too. What I teach them is *Kung Fu,* which are our words for what you would call martial arts. The Way of the Warrior. Since they are destined to follow the religious life, most of what they learn is unarmed combat. Yet I believe that when you see Wu and his young men in action, you will both marvel at what can be done. Now, the time draws near. We must lay a course of action."

TEN

Tyrone Beal and six thick-muscled railroad detectives sat their horses outside the small, wooden frame building that had been sided with galvanized tin. A pale square of yellow light slanted to the ground from the window in an otherwise blank wall to their left. An angled layer of shingles formed a roof over the narrow stoop that gave to a door, the top third of which was a lattice of glass panes. A hand-lettered sign rested at the junction of porch roof and building front. It read in dripping letters: CENTRAL VALLEY FREIGHT. At a nod from Beal, the thugs dismounted.

"Don't look like much," one hard case grumbled.

"Heck Granger said Mr. Huntley don't want the competition, so we take care of it," Beal told him. "The sooner the better, I say. This is my last job up here in the nowhere, then it's back to San Francisco for me."

A local tough glanced at Beal quizzically. "You don't like it out here?"

"Nope. It's too wide open for me. I grew up with buildings all around me. This kinda country makes me feel like I'm gonna fall right off the earth." Beal motioned to a pair of the local gang. "You two take the back. Make sure no one gets away."

Beal and the other four climbed the open, rough-hewn plank steps to the stoop. Beal took the lead, his big hand smacking the door hard enough to slam it against the inside wall. From behind the counter a man with the look of a farmer gave them a startled glance.

"Wh-what do you gentlemen need?" he asked shakily.

"You're out of business, Harper," Beal growled.

Gus Harper backed away from the counter that separated him from the hard cases. He raised both hands in protest. "Now, see here . . ."

"No, you listen and do as you are told."

"Who are you?"

Beal gave Harper a nasty smirk. "Names don't mean a lot."

"Then who sent you?"

"I think you know the answer to that. We come to give you a different outlook on what's what in this world. There ain't gonna be any competition in the freighting business."

"I have every right," Harper blustered. Then he weighed the menace in Beal's expression. His next words came in a stammered rush. "N-Now, let's not do anything hasty."

Beal pointed at the counter and rolltop desk behind. "We'll not, just so long as you put an end to this crazy notion of yours. You're a farmer, Harper. Go back to clodhoppin'." He glanced left and right to the thugs with him. "Spread out, boys. This place needs a little rearrangin'."

Harper made a fateful mistake. "Stop right there. There's law in this valley, and it's on my side."

Beal nodded to a pair of thugs. "You two take ahold of him. Now, Mr. Farmer-Turned-Freight Master, for the last time, go back to your plow. There ain't gonna be another freight company in the Central Valley."

Harper made one final, weak effort to make reason prevail. "But the railroad and Huntley's Dray Service have raised rates twice this year already and harvest is three months away."

"Don't matter how many times the prices go up, you and all the rest are going to pay and keep your mouths shut."

Beal moved in then, through the small gate at one end of the counter. He balled his big fists while the two thugs grabbed onto Harper. They spread the former farmer out so his middle was open to the vicious attack Beal leveled on him. Beal worked on Harper's belly first, pounded hard, twisting blows into the muscle of the abdomen, then worked up to the chest. A severe blow right over the heart turned Harper's face ashen. For a moment he went rigid and his eyes glazed. Slowly he came around in time for Beal to start in on his face. Knuckles protected by leather gloves, Beal put a cut on Harper's left cheekbone, and a weal on his forehead. Beal mashed his victim's lips and broke his nose. Harper went limp in the grasp of the hard cases.

Beal showed no mercy. He went back to the gut. Soft, meaty smacks sounded with each punch. Harper hung from the grip of strong hands. Beal aimed for the ribs. He felt two give on his third left hook. It gave him an idea.

"Let him go," he ordered.

Harper sank to the floor, a soft moan escaped though battered, split lips. Beal toed him onto his back and began to methodically kick Harper in the ribs. The bones broke one by one. When all on the right side had been broken, Beal went around to the other side and began to slam the toe of his boot into the vulnerable ribs. They, too, snapped with sharp pops. When the last gave, Beal went to work on Harper's stomach.

Unprotected, the internal organs suffered great damage. Sometime while Beal worked on Harper's liver, the man died. The first Beal and his henchmen knew of it was when the body, relaxed in death, voided. The outhouse stench rose around them.

"He's gone, Mr. Beal," Spencer said quietly.

"Then drag him outside. Let that be a lesson for the others. The rest of us are going to torch this place."

It did not seem like much of a plan to Smoke Jensen. Tai Chiu had described to them the dens habituated by the Tong soldiers. One was an opium parlor. There, the wretched individuals in the thrall of the evil poppy idled away their lives, many filth-encrusted and never off their rude pallets, where they smoked the black, tarlike substance that gave them their life-sapping dreams. That is how Tai Chiu described them.

At least they sounded incapable of putting up any resistance, Smoke speculated. That still left some two hundred Tong members. Tai Chiu had been quite certain of the number. The count varied from time to time, though never exceeding a hundred members for each of the three Tongs. Tai Chiu had named them the Iron Fan Tong, the Blue Lotus Tong, and the Celestial Hatchets. Smoke considered the names odd and a bit pretentious. Louis had explained the reasoning behind them.

"These Tong members choose a name based on the power a Tong has. Some of them go back centuries. Anything with 'Celestial' in it is most powerful. It is likely that Xiang Wai Lee is from this Tong."

"Quite right, Mr. Longmont," Tai Chiu confirmed. "You know much about the darker side of our ancient culture."

"There were, for a time, some Tongs in New Orleans."

Tai Chiu's eyes danced with interest. "Might I ask what happened to them?"

"Myself, and some of my friends, ah, persuaded them to depart."

"I presume you did not use gentle persuasion on them?"

"Right you are, Mr. Tai. We used six-guns and some rope."

Tai Chiu's white eyebrows rose. "I think we have the answer to why they so readily came after you. No doubt some of the survivors came here, to San Francisco. You might have been recognized the first time you were seen."

Louis considered that. "Sounds reasonable. Now, as I understand it, each of the three of us will take on one of the Tongs. When one of their meeting places has been pacified, those of us who fought there will go on to another location."

"That is correct," Tai Chiu verified. "The Celestial Hatchets are currently the strongest of the three. You do not feel uncomfortable assuming that task, Mr. Jensen?"

"Not too much. Considering I'm going to have only fifteen of your student-fighters along," Smoke answered drily.

"Be advised that it is your prowess with firearms that will tip the balance. The Tongs are not loath to use modern weapons."

Smoke looked hard at the old priest. "Thanks very much, Mr. Tai. If I thought I was goin' up against fellers armed only with hatchets, I couldn't live with myself."

Tai Chiu studied Smoke's face a moment. "Your face tells me you are serious, yet your eyes speak of a jest. You are having fun with me, yes?"

"It's that or walk away from this whole thing. Sixteen against a hundred is mighty long odds."

"Bear in mind, not all of them will be there at one time. You must deal with them as they come in answer to the rallying call. That will make your task simpler, I think."

Smoke checked the loads in his right-hand six-gun. He slid a sixth cartridge into the usually empty chamber. Then he did the same for the second revolver. "All together, I have about thirty rounds. After that, it's going to get quite interesting."

"We go now," Tai Chiu answered simply.

To their surprise, Smoke Jensen and Louis Longmont found Chinatown brightly lighted even at the midnight hour. Families streamed in and out of restaurants, many with sleepy-eyed little tykes tugged along by their small hands. Westerners as well as Chinese thronged the shops, clutching their purchases by the strings that bound the gaudy red-and-gold or green-and-silver tissue paper. Musical bursts of conversation in Cantonese and Mandarin filled the air. All of that added an unexpected complication for Smoke Jensen. Their small force had divided before entering Chinatown and Smoke felt uncomfortably exposed.

His target, the Celestial Hatchets, had a building on the far side of the market square, near the Chinese opera house. He and his volunteers would be in the open the longest. Quo Chung Wu took the lead as they rounded the corner. Two youthful Chinese lounged against the wall outside the door to the Tong headquarters. One of them roused himself when he caught sight of Quo in his saffron temple robe. He stepped out to block the walkway and raised a hand to signal that Quo should halt.

"You are in the wrong place, *shunfoo go,*" he snarled insolently.

" 'Dog of a priest,' am I?" Quo Chung Wu rasped back.

Then, in only the time it took Smoke Jensen to blink, Quo made his move. His body pivoted and bent backward. A weird birdlike sound came from his throat as he lashed out a foot in a powerful kick that knocked the Tong thug back into his companion, who had only begun to straighten up, sensing at last that trouble had come to their lair. Quo followed up the unconventional kick with a full swing that brought him back face-to-face with the Tong soldiers. Elbows akimbo, he formed his long-fingered hands into the shape of tiger claws and darted one out to rake sharp, thick nails across the face of the slow-awakening Tong man. To Smoke's surprise, the youth did not scream as long, red lines appeared on his cheek. Quo's fist closed and he smashed the injured man in the nose with a back-blow.

His left elbow struck the chest next. Then he sent a side-kick that knocked the insulting one to his knees. A pointed toe rose under the Tong hatchetman's chin and stilled his opposition. His companion had regained his feet and leaped into the air to deliver a flying kick that rocked Quo back, though it did not faze him. He pivoted to the right and drove hard fists, the middle knuckles extended, into the breastbone of his attacker. Staggering back until his shoulders collided with the wall, the thug drew a hatchet.

It gave off a musical whistle as it swung through the air. When the blade passed him, Quo stepped in and drove an open palm to the already damaged nose. Bone and cartilage cracked and popped and sliced through the thin partition into his brain. He fell twitching to the ground. Smiling sardonically, Quo stepped to one side and made a sweeping gesture of welcome to the door.

Smoke entered, his .45 Colt at the ready. Two more Tong henchmen sat on ornate plush chairs. One leaped up with a Smith American .44 in his hand. He didn't get to use it as Smoke upset him into a heap on the floor with a fat .45 slug in his chest. Beside him, his partner shrieked curses in Cantonese and loosed a round from his .38 Colt Lightning. It knocked the hat from the head of Smoke Jensen and smacked into the wall beyond.

Superior weapons skills put Smoke's round right on target. Eyes bulging, the Chinese hoodlum slammed back into his chair, which tipped over to spill him onto the hall carpet. Smoke stepped over his twitching legs and advanced along the hall. A steady drone of conversation in Chinese ended with the roar of the guns. How many would be waiting? Smoke didn't let it worry him. He stepped through the archway at the end of the hall with his Peacemaker ablaze.

A squat, rotund Chinese with a sawed-off shotgun discharged a barrel into the ceiling on his way over backward in his chair. To his left, another hurled a hatchet at the head of Smoke Jensen. Ducking below the deadly device, Smoke popped a hole in the Tong soldier's chest that broke his collarbone and severed the subclavian artery. Another Tong bully came at Smoke, his face twisted in the fury of his scream, at the same moment Quo Chung Wu stepped into the room beside Smoke.

Quo gave the thug a front kick, high in his throat, that cut off the scream like a switch. Then he pivoted and delivered a side-kick to the chest and a second to the descending head. To Smoke's surprise, he had accomplished this in less time than it took Smoke to cock his Colt. The Tong butcher dropped his hatchet and skidded on his nose to the feet of Smoke Jensen. Quo smiled and bowed slightly.

Stacks of coins and paper currency went flying as another Tong hatchetman leaped onto the table and jerked back his arm to unloose a hatchet. He pitched over on the back of his head when Smoke plunked a .45 slug into his belly, an inch above the navel. A scrabbling sound came from the corner of the room.

A youthful Tong henchman tried desperately to fling up the sash of a window. When the muzzle of Smoke Jensen's .45 Colt tracked toward him, his fear overcame him and he threw himself through the pane. Broken glass rang down musically. One of the student volunteers rushed to the gaping frame and drew a fancy carved bow. The arrow sped down the alley and took the fleeing Tong gangster between the shoulder blades. A thin, high wail ended his life. Smoke touched a finger to his bare forehead.

"Obliged," he told the archer.

Others of the young priests had fanned out through the house. The sound of breaking glass came again as a youthful Tong member made his escape. By ones and twos the volunteers began to return to this central room to report the place as empty. Smoke looked around at the havoc they had created.

"That happened too easy," Smoke told them.

Their young, happily smiling faces contradicted him. "We have no objection to that," Quo spoke for them all.

"What I'm getting at is, there are a whole lot more of them out there. They will be coming, you can be sure of that."

"Then we will not be going on to help the others?" Quo asked, uncertain.

"Not right away, Quo. We'll have our hands full any minute now," Smoke responded, as he opened the loading gate of his Peacemaker and began shucking out empty shell casings.

Louis Longmont eased his way along a dark alley in Chinatown. Close at his side came five of his fifteen volunteer priests. For all the danger they faced, these young men held uniform expressions of calm and confidence. An unusually tall, lean Chinese beside him clutched a bo stick with supple fingers. They came to a dark, recessed entrance to a cellar and the youthful martial artist tensed slightly, glided forward a step, and swung his stick.

It made a sharp *klock!* against the head of a sentry and the Tong soldier went down hard. The youth with the bo stick nodded slightly and slid on past. He raised a hand and indicated first one, then a second, ground-level doorway. The other ten young men had offered to take the place from the front. Theirs would be the risky job, Louis considered. He glanced down at the unconscious sentry as he passed the steps to the basement.

That stick, he thought. Something like a quarter-staff. Right out of the Middle Ages. Louis Longmont had been a gunfighter long enough to know that the "right" weapon did not exist. Whatever did the job when it had to be done worked. He caught up to the Chinese youth with the bo stick. Now all they had to do was wait until the rest hit the front door.

It turned out not to be a long wait. Shouts of alarm and cries of pain came from inside the Tong headquarters less than two minutes later. At first, no one showed at the rear entrance, then the door flung open and a skinny man with a waist-long pigtail rushed out. A hatchet in his left hand reflected moon-

light as he raised it defensively. One of the temple students
closed on him, a halberd with an elongated tip blade held
ready. The hatchetman changed his weapon from the defensive
to the offensive. Metal clanged as he batted the pike head with
the flat of his blade. His opponent lunged, driving the shaft of
his device forward in a lightning move.

No sound came when the slender blade drove into the gut
of the Tong soldier. His eyes went wide and his mouth formed
a pain-twisted "O." His knees went out from under him and
he dragged the halberd down as he collapsed on the steps. The
youthful volunteer wrenched his blade free. It made a soft
sucking sound as it left the dying flesh. Two more of the Iron
Fan Tong warriors burst through the open doorway. Louis took
quick aim and shot the first. He kept on running for enough
steps to pitch headlong off the stoop. Already, the high,
rounded front sight of the gun in the hand of Louis Longmont
lined up on the second target.

His revolver gave a comfortable, familiar jolt to his hand
when the hammer fell on a fresh cartridge. The Tong thug
broke stride and looked down at his chest. Surprise registered
a moment before he keeled over to one side and fell heavily
on his right shoulder. Even then, he tried to throw his hatchet
at Louis, who shot him again. The sounds of a scuffle came
from inside. Although the back hallway had been darkened,
Louis could make out the figures of two men. They flowed
rapidly through the postures of several recognizable creatures.
Now a crane, now a tiger, now a snake. With each ripple, an
arm or foot would lash out and strike at the other. Louis well
appreciated the skill they exhibited, yet he had no time to be
an interested observer.

Two Tong members came down a wooden fire escape attached to the rear wall. One paused to hurl his hand-ax at
Louis. It stuck in the siding six inches from the head of the
man from New Orleans. Louis reacted instantly. His shot
knocked the man from the ladder, and the scream he uttered
lasted until he hit the ground. The other hatchetman flung his
weapon at Louis. It struck Louis on the left shoulder with the

handle. Sharp pain, quickly stifled, radiated from the point of impact.

Louis put a bullet in the thrower's head, ending his days of ruthlessness. When the sound of the shot reverberated down the alleyway, Louis found it totally silent inside the building. He entered to find the Tong's nest in the hands of his young fighters.

"We could burn this place, but it would take the whole block," Louis informed his troops. "Five of you, stay here, in case any of the rest of the Tong comes back. The others, come with me. We'll go lend a hand to Smoke."

Tai Chiu found most of the Blue Lotus Tong at home. They boiled out of the dilapidated godown they used as a headquarters like a swarm of aroused bees. Passers-by looked away and scurried for safety as their hatchets flashed in the red-and-yellow light of lanterns strung from post to post. Without hesitation, Tai's pupils waded in.

One avoided a hatchet blow with a rising forearm block, then kicked the Tong member in the gut. Air whooshed out of a distorted mouth, only to be battered back inside by an open palm smash to the lips. Blood flew black in the colored illumination. Two of the hatchetmen came for Tai Chiu.

Their weapons did no harm as the old man melted away from in front of them. Crouched low, Tai lashed out with a side-kick that knocked the legs from under one of his attackers. Chiu's robe fluttered like wings as he spun on the ball of one foot and delivered another kick to the exposed chest of the second thug. The Tong hatched swished by just an inch short of Tai Chiu's extended leg.

Without a blink, he took a crane stance and snapped extended fingers at the face of the hatchetman. Blood sprang from four fine lines along his face. He tried another swing with the hatchet, only to have his nose smashed by a backhand blow. Before he could recover, the elderly monk kicked him three times under the chin. The hatchetman dropped to the ground to twitch out his life. Tai Chiu moved on to engage a short, stout thug with a revolver in his hand.

His first attack kicked the gun from the startled gangster's grip. The Chinese thug had not even gotten off a shot. Tai knocked him senseless with a smooth routine of fist and elbow blows and well-aimed kicks. Beyond him, two of the Blue Lotus members sprinted away from the center of the melee. There would be more coming soon, he realized regretfully.

Smoke Jensen considered it better to fight in the open, so he led his volunteers out of the Celestial Hatchets Tong headquarters to take on the reinforcements who had arrived during the past five minutes. Several of them carried swords similar to the ones with which the student priests had armed themselves. One of these darted forward and made an overhand swing at a Tong thug. The sword in the hard case's hand rose swiftly to parry the swing.

The edges met with a ring. Like lightning, the young student's left hand flashed out and slammed into his opponent's face. At once, another Tong member leaped toward the volunteer. He never made it. Breaking the engagement of their blades, the supple youth made a horizontal slash with his sword and all but decapitated the Tong thug. The last hatchetman, with an oversized cutlass, raised his weapon and set himself for a blow to the back of the exposed head of the young student.

Smoke Jensen shot the Tong member between the eyes. A shout came from down the street and Smoke looked that way to see some ten railroad detectives. In their uniforms of brown suits and derby hats, they rushed toward the scene of conflict, pick handles in their hands.

Eleven

They were in for it now, Smoke judged. A moment later, the yard bulls crashed into the line of students. The fighting spread out, two of the enemy on each one of the students. When one of Murchison's gunhawks pulled iron, Smoke Jensen stepped in. The Colt Peacemaker bucked in Smoke's hand and spat a slug that pulverized the gunman's right shoulder.

He howled and staggered off, only to be given a kick to the head by a young Chinese. Down he went, limp and unmoving. More of Heck Grange's henchmen poured into the narrow side street in Chinatown. They went after the allies of Smoke Jensen only to be knocked down and out time after time. Three closed in on Smoke. The one in the lead, a thick-chested brute with a snarling face, drew a pocket pistol and fired hastily.

His bullet cracked past Smoke's head and the last mountain man pumped a round into the man's chest. He shook himself and came on. He cocked his pistol again and took aim at Smoke. The .45 Colt in Smoke's hand bucked and a second slug ripped into his attacker's chest. Still the man remained on his feet. Smoke shot him once again.

This time, Smoke noticed that not a drop of blood flew from the wound. Smoke raised his aim and put a round in his opponent's forehead. Quickly he swung his Peacemaker to another of the armed thugs. They traded shots. The yard bull missed. Smoke Jensen didn't.

Facing only a single enemy, Smoke leveled his .45 Colt and fired the last round in the cylinder. The thug took it in his belly, an inch above his hipbone. Quickly Smoke changed re-

volvers. He made it just in time. A lance of flame spurted
from the Merwin and Hulbert the hard case carried. His bullet
punched a hole through the body of the coat worn by Smoke
Jensen and exited out the back. Too close a call.

Smoke ended the man's railroad career with a sizzling .45
slug in the heart. Smoke went forward to inspect the corpse
of the man who had absorbed so many bullets. Bending low,
he pulled open the shirt. Just as he had suspected: the dead
man wore a fitted piece of boiler plate, its backside thickly
padded with cotton quilting. Smoke's soft lead bullets had
smashed against it and spread out to the diameter of a quarter.
If he ran into too many like that one, he would really be in
trouble, Smoke reckoned. Another shout rose among the bat-
tling figures in the middle of the block. Smoke looked up in
time to see more Tong soldiers storming down the street.

Jing Gow had run all the way from the Celestial Hatchets
Tong club house to the Wu Fong theater, where most of the
members were attending a recital by a famous Chinese lute
player. They filled the balcony and two of the larger boxes to
the side of the stage. Word went around quickly and nearly
half of the audience walked out in the middle of the performance. Now, he trotted along Plum Seed Street with his Tong
brothers toward the sounds of a fight.

He did not feel the cuts made by the glass from when he had
jumped through the window. In the second floor leap he had
also sprained an ankle, and he limped painfully. All he could
think of was the huge *qua'lo* who had burst into the room during
counting time for their weekly squeeze money. That one had the
ferocity of a dragon. Jing had jumped through a curtained doorway and run upstairs. Now, blood dripped down his chest and
belly. When they rounded the corner to face the battle scene,
Jing Gow felt light-headed. How long had be been cut and not
taken care of it?

A haze seemed to settle over the street. Jing swiped at his
eyes to try to ward off the fuzzy vision. He found his hand

covered with dried blood. The fog remained. It even grew darker. Jing saw the giant foreign devil and raised his hatchet. A howl of fury ripped from his throat.

Jing Gow threw his hatchet, only the big man dodged to one side. Then a terrible force struck Jing in the chest and he saw smoke and flame gush from the *qua'lo*'s gun. Awful pain radiated from the area around his heart and the world turned dark for Jing Gow. He did not feel a thing when he fell face-first onto the cobblestones.

It appeared to Louis Longmont that every person under the age of fifty in Chinatown was a Tong member. They kept coming from buildings and down both ends of the street near the building used by the Iron Fan Tong as a headquarters. He had run dangerously low on ammunition. The thought occurred, why hadn't the police come?

It didn't matter, he decided, as he jammed a hard fist into the face of another Tong hatchetman to save on cartridges. He heard the crack of a shot from behind him and whirled to reply. In so doing, he nearly shot Brian Pullen. The young lawyer competently held a .44 Colt Lightning in his hand, a dead Tong member at his feet.

"I heard about this Tong war and thought I'd come lend a hand," Pullen explained.

Louis nodded to the corpse. "You got here just in time. I hope you brought enough ammunition."

"I have two boxes of cartridges. Will that be enough?"

"I doubt it. What we need is a shotgun. Something to clear the street with."

Brian Pullen looked blankly at Louis Longmont and snapped his fingers. "I never thought of that. Hang on, I'll be back." He ran through the back of the house before Louis could reply.

Twenty minutes went by in a frenzy of fighting the likes of which Louis had never seen. The young Chinese volunteers used a form of personal combat unlike anything he had heard of. Three of them went down, victims of hatchet blows, yet the rest continued to take a bloody, deadly toll on the Tong fighters. When Brian Pullen returned, he brought along two finely made, expensive Parker 10-gauge shotguns and a large net bag filled with brass cartridges.

Louis Longmont hid his surprise. "That should do the job."

He took one, loaded it, and blasted two Tong thugs off the stoop of the building with a single round. Pullen put the other Parker to good use, ending the career of a short, squat extortionist. Quickly the men reloaded and pushed out into the street. Four more loads of buckshot broke the fanatic assault of the Tong hatchetmen. Six of their companions had been killed in a matter of seconds. The two grim-faced *qua'lo* did not hesitate as they advanced. They reloaded on the move, paused, and then downed more Tong members. At first, a trickle of young gangsters faded away. Then the remaining street thugs abandoned the battle and fled out of sight.

"I think we should check the Blue Lotus Tong," Louis calmly suggested.

Wang Toy had successfully hidden from the enraged priests from the Golden Harmony temple. He had watched his Tong brothers being beaten and some of them killed by those led by the old priest, Tai Chiu. The aged one had never had the proper respect for those of the Triad Society. He should have been disposed of long ago. Although the killing of priests was frowned upon by Xiang Wai Lee, Wang Toy would have been pleased to carry out that assignment.

Now he skulked in the dusty attic of the Blue Lotus club house and worried about his own safety. When the last of his companions had run away, he had been left behind, unable to come out of hiding so long as the practitioners of *kung fu* remained around the building. They had left, after a short while, yet he remained in his undiscovered lair. In all his seventeen years he had never been so frightened. At last he goaded himself into opening the square hatch in the floor and lowered himself to the second-floor hallway.

Embarrassed and shamed by his cowardly behavior, Wang Toy slunk to the stairwell and started down. At the landing, he pulled his hatchet from his belt and held it at the ready. He would find his brothers and rally them. Wang reached the last step at the same time the front door flew open. The first person through it was a *qua'lo* with a double-barreled shotgun. That was the last thing Wang Toy saw because Louis Longmont blew his head off with a load of buckshot.

Smoke Jensen had barely finished counting the number of Tong gangsters when a hoard of more young Chinese men rounded the far corner. It took him a moment to realize that several of them wore the saffron robes of the student priests. They fell on the hatchetmen from behind and began to chop and kick them with terrible efficiency. Only the guns of the railroad detectives saved the Tong members from total destruction.

Two burly hard cases shot the same student at one time. One of them did not get to crow about it, for Smoke Jensen blasted the life out of him. His partner whirled and threw a shot in Smoke's direction. The bullet slammed into the doorjamb behind Smoke. His assailant tried for another round, only to be blasted to perdition by a slug from the .45 Colt in Smoke's hand. In the far distance, Smoke heard the shrill of police whistles. Recalling the incident at the bordello, he wondered whose side they would take.

He decided to leave when the first bluecoats arrived on the scene and began to club the students with their nightsticks. "Time to be moving on," he told Quo Chung Wu, who stood steadfastly at his side.

"You will run from these men?" Quo asked in disbelief.

"The last I heard, I was a wanted man. The police have gone over to the yard bulls. What do you think they will do when they reach us?"

Quo nodded and shouted to his companions in Cantonese.

"We will go to the temple. Make these men bring the fight to us.

At once the volunteers broke off their fighting and sprinted off down the street. Smoke Jensen and Quo Chung Wu formed the rear guard. It did not take much convincing to delay pursuit. Smoke shot one of the Tong henchmen in the leg and the whole crowd hung back. Smoke saw the last of them, shouting among themselves, as he rounded the corner into a wide boulevard that led to the market square.

A sharp pang of unease nearly doubled Sally Jensen over as she sat on the edge of her bed. Smoke was in dreadful danger; she had no idea from what or whom. She only knew, as clearly as the September harvest moon shone a silver pool on the braided rug which covered the smooth planks of the floor, that her man was close to losing his life. She had awakened only a few moments before, and the fragments of the dream that had disturbed her still clung to her.

She tried to make sense of the strange images which had tumbled through her dozing mind. Odd-looking lanterns bobbed in a breeze. Men in yellow robes wielded strange weapons. A heavy mist or fog hung over black water. There were screams and cries that echoed in her head. And Smoke was somehow mixed up with it all. She hadn't *seen* him in that kaleidoscope of weird impressions, only sensed his involvement. Hugging herself across her stomach, she rose and headed for the kitchen. A cup of coffee might help.

Sally scratched a lucifer to life and lighted the oil lamp on the table. Still troubled, she added wood to the stove and put water to boil in the pot. While she scooped coffee into the basket of the percolator, she tried again to piece together her premonition. To her annoyance, nothing meaningful came to the surface. She started when a soft knock came on the back door.

"Anything wrong, Miss Sally?" Cole Travis stood, hat in hand, a worried expression on his face.

"No," Sally replied promptly, then added, "yes. No, I don't know. That's what is so bothersome, Cole." She tried to force a smile and swiped at a stray lock of raven hair that hung over one cheek. "I'm not given to womanly vapors," she said lightly. "But I was awakened a while ago by the strongest impression that Smoke was in trouble."

Their winter foreman put on a sympathetic face. "Any idea what or where?"

Sally considered the shards of her dream. "In San Francisco, obviously. Only I can't make sense of what I remember of the dream." She abandoned the subject. "I was fixing coffee, Cole. Would you like a cup?"

Despite his silver hair, Cole Travis took on the expression of an impish boy. "Would you happen to have a piece of that pie left from supper to go with it?"

That brought the sunniness back to Sally's face. "Of course I do. Come on in. Maybe we can figure out what it is going on around Smoke."

People scattered before the retreating students. Their movement through the market square set off ripples like a stone dropped in water. In the forefront of those who pursued them came the railroad police. Indifferent to the Chinese citizens of San Francisco, they roughly shoved those who impeded them out of the way. Even so, they made little headway. When the men they sought veered toward the Golden Harmony Temple, they redoubled their efforts.

They looked on from halfway across the square as the last to arrive, Smoke Jensen and Quo Chung Wu, paused long enough to swing closed a spike-topped gate in the Moon arch that fronted the temple grounds. Snarling at this impediment, they pushed through the late-night shoppers. When they reached the closed partition, several of Murchison's henchmen grabbed on and began to yank it furiously.

A police sergeant and several of his subordinates shouldered their way to where the men struggled with the gateway. "Here, now," he bellowed. "We can't go in there. It's sacred ground. A sanctuary."

"Don't mean nothin' to us. Mr. Murchison wants this stopped, and we reckon to do just that," Heck Grange growled.

The sergeant scowled at him, unmoved by the declaration. "Not with our help. We got orders, all the way down from the mayor. Treat these Chinee places with respect."

"What are you going to do?"

"What we can; surround the temple and make sure no one gets out."

Granger's voice turned nasty with contempt. "While you're doing that, we'll just open up this little box and see what's inside."

Stubborn was the sergeant's middle name. "You try it and we'll arrest you. We believe there's a wanted man in there, and he belongs to the police."

For the first time, Heck Grange regretted his idea about reporting the shootings to the police. If he killed Longmont and Jensen outright, it could get sticky. No matter, his thug's brain reasoned, they wouldn't give up without a fight. And anything could happen then. He turned a disarming smile on the lawman.

"Go on, then. I'll send some of my boys along to take up the slack."

"I appreciate that," the sergeant said stiffly. "Don't worry. We'll get them if we have to wait until morning.

"What about these Chinee fellers with the hatchets?"

Looking around him, the sergeant shrugged. "If they want to go in there, there's nothing I can do about it," he dismissed.

At once, the young Tong members started for the walls.

Inside the temple, Tai Chiu urged his diminished force to take the hidden passageway so as to come out behind their enemies. Smoke Jensen considered it a moment.

"We should hold out here for as long as we can," he advised. "Everyone could use the rest. If we only had some surprises to slow down anyone coming in after us," he added wishfully.

Old Tai Chiu smiled enigmatically. "There are . . . certain defenses built into the temple. They are activated by levers. We can engage them as we leave."

Smoke began to look around. It took a while, though finally he began to recognize a number of clever obstacles, or what might be turned into such. A large log hung suspended from two ropes. It appeared to be intended for ringing a huge brass gong. The position of the line that propelled it had been placed in such a way that it could be used to draw the thick cleaned and polished tree limb upward to one side. In front of it, a too-regular line in the flooring indicated to Smoke the presence of a pressure pad. He smiled.

Other things came to his sight. A large candelabra hung suspended over the center of the worship area. Directly under it was another hidden trip device. He did not know that for centuries, this particular caste of warrior-monks had been harassed by the warlords in China. He did appreciate that they had become wise in the ways of secret defenses. Slits in the domed roof suggested that arrows could be fired through them, or objects dropped on unsuspecting heads. Well, now, that was fine and dandy with him. His thoughts took another line.

Where was Louis? Had he encountered trouble? One of the volunteers hurried up to interrupt his musings. "The Triads are scaling the walls," the young Chinese informed him.

"All we need," Smoke snapped. He quickly checked and reloaded his six-guns. His fingers told him he had only nine spare rounds. Well, let them come, he thought of the enemy outside. We'll welcome them in style.

None of the Blue Lotus Tong returned to their club house. Louis Longmont rounded up the volunteers who had come with him. "We will go to this Celestial Hatchets building. They are the largest Tong, *non?*"

He thought primarily of his friend Smoke Jensen. Smoke

had taken on the greater number because that was the way
Smoke Jensen did things. While the students had ransacked
the Tong headquarters and scrawled signs on the wall in Chinese warning the gangsters that they were no longer welcome
in Chinatown, Louis had stood guard outside. In the distance
he had heard the shrill sound of police whistles. Like Smoke,
his mind went to the visit by police to Francie's. If the law
joined in, it would hamper how they dealt with those who
opposed them. It wouldn't do to kill a legitimate policeman.

When the last of the young monks had finished smashing
furniture and breaking glass inside, Louis called them together
and made his announcement. Eagerness shined in their eyes,
though most kept their faces impassive. At once, they left in
a body.

Disappointment waited for Louis Longmont when his con-
tingent of trash collectors reached the converted warehouse
occupied by the Celestial Hatchets Tong. The place had been
demolished inside. A few bodies lay about, among them some
Occidentals Louis figured for railroad bulls. Silence filled both
floors. Not a sign of Smoke Jensen.

"If they had finished here, and heard the police come . . ."
Quo Chung Wu suggested, then added, "Yes, I heard their
whistles, too."

Louis understood at once. "The only safe place would be
back at the temple, or on the junk." He paused only a moment.
"I say the temple; it is closer."

They started that way. Along the route, Louis noted more
injured, unconscious, or dead Tong thugs and railroad detectives in their brown bowler hats. No question that the night
had taken a terrible toll on the Triad Society. It pleased him.
At the edge of the market square, Louis halted his followers
abruptly. He pointed toward the temple.

"I believe we arrived a bit too late." He noted of the swarm
of police, railroad thugs, and Tong members around the walls
of the temple courtyard.

"Not necessarily," Brian Pullen offered at the side of Louis
Longmont. "I believe that is Sergeant O'Malley over there. In

all that's happened, I forgot to tell you of one piece of good news.

"Actually, it's the reason I made such an effort to find you and Mr. Jensen. I received an injunction against the California Central Railroad, enjoining them to cease and desist in any attempt to apprehend you or Mr. Jensen." Pullen patted the breast pocket of his suit coat. "I also have a writ from the court ordering the police to disregard any complaint made against the two of you. All I have to do is serve them and the odds go down dramatically."

"What says either side will obey them?" Louis asked sensibly.

"O'Malley will. Above all other things, he is an honest cop. He'll take the writ back to the station house and give it to his lieutenant. That will effectively end the police manhunt for the both of you."

"And if Murchison's minions refuse?"

"Not a chance. They will have been served right in front of O'Malley. If they keep at it, O'Malley and the boys in blue will arrest the lot and throw them in jail."

Louis called after Pullen as the young lawyer stepped off on his errand. "I wish I shared your confidence."

"Not a problem," Pullen gave back jauntily.

Matters did not go quite so smoothly as Brian Pullen had predicted. Sgt. O'Malley spluttered and fussed awhile when handed the writ. "Ye should have delivered this to the station house."

"I tried, and was told everyone was out in the field—in Chinatown, to be exact. If your lieutenant is handy, I'll be glad to give it to him."

O'Malley looked one way and the next, then murmured, "He's at that big red an' gold gate at the front of this place, don't ye know?"

"I came in another way. What do you say, O'Malley?" He turned to Heck Grange. "I have a little something for you,

Chief." He continued after slapping the paper into Grange's hand. "It is a temporary restraining order stopping your railroad police from any punitive action against Misters Jensen and Longmont. They are to be left alone."

Grange went scarlet in the face. "I take my orders from Cyrus Murchison, not some goddamned judge."

Brian Pullen turned to Paddy O'Malley. "Sergeant, you know your duty. If these—hooligans violate this injunction, now or in the future, I'm sure you'll do it."

O'Malley's broad Irish face beamed. He had always figured this Grange feller a bit too smooth an operator. It would be his pleasure to raise a few lumps on that oversized skull. He also recalled that the big one with the six-gun had been careful not to fire on any of his policemen. Might be there was somethin' to what young Pullen said, not just some fancy lawyer tricks. He came to his decision.

"Ye'll be movin' yer men on now, Mr. Grange, won't ye, now?" His brogue thickened with the assertion of his authority.

Heck Grange found himself up against someone impossible to take odds with. He deflated and pulled a sour face. "Yes. But we'll get those two, you mark my words, O'Malley."

TWELVE

By that time, the first of the Tong members had scaled the top of the temple wall. They went over with a shout and others scrambled to follow. Heck Grange made curt gestures to two of his henchmen and sent them off to round up their number among the railroad police detachment. He'd see to an end of this, he thought furiously. Cyrus Murchison owned more than one judge. What one had done, another of them could undo.

He headed off to care for that at once, tossing behind him a curt command to Earl Rankin. "Get 'em out of here, Earl."

"Yes, sir, Chief," Rankin answered, somewhat relieved. Being around all these roused-up Chinamen with hatchets made him nervous. A chilling shout from inside the compound added speed to his feet.

Watching first the railroad police, then the city police, withdraw, Louis Longmont nodded in approval. That feisty lawyer had some sand. He spoke to Quo Chung Wu. "Now, we catch the men of the Tongs between us."

A shot came from inside the temple grounds and the volunteers in the marketplace started forward. Recognizing friends, no one made a move to get in their way. Louis Longmont had his shotgun and that of Brian Pullen. When he reached the young attorney, he handed one of the Parkers to him.

"Maybe we should have asked the police to stay to take charge of the Tong members," Brian asked.

"Sometimes, it is not wise to think like a lawyer. I don't think these students are in much of a mood to take prisoners," Louis told him grimly.

Consternation mingled with doubt on Brian's face. "But . . . these men have broken laws here for years. They deserve to be punished."

"Dead is about as punished as one can get, *mon ami,* don't you think?"

Brian paled. "I—uh—never looked at it that way before."

"Start to, or you may wind up with a hatchet between your eyes."

Unobserved, Xiang Wai Lee joined his underlings outside the cursed temple of those twice-cursed *Chau Chu* monks. His face grew thunderous as he took note of how few of the Society remained among the fighters. This could not be tolerated. His cheeks burned in sympathetic humiliation while he watched that puny lawyer take the face from both the police and their supposed allies from the railroad.

Then his expression hardened into bitter contempt. He had personally opposed the Triad Society joining forces with these foreign devils. What did they know of the honor and tradition of the Society? What, indeed, did they know of ruling by fear? A few, quick words sent new energy through his flagged-out men.

Even while the *qua'lo* argued over the meaningless bits of paper, the Tongs united and rushed the walls. A smile broke his stony expression a while as he recalled that glorious day when his Celestial Hatchets had come down through the hills and stormed that other *Chau Chu* temple. Blood had run in rivers and the riches of the frugal monks had been theirs. It had financed their journey to this strange land of foreign devils and established their power in San Francisco. Truly the Goddess of Fortune had smiled upon him that day. Just as she had done in making it his destiny to be away when these students and the two *qua'lo* had attacked.

Xiang had viewed the destruction and death only minutes before. "This must not happen," he had hissed to his second in command, Tang Hu Li. "We must find our brothers and see that they bring me the heads of these white devils."

Now, he observed that busy hands had been at work on the gate and went that way. A gunshot roared from inside and his followers ducked low. Xiang made a stately figure as he advanced without even a flinch. As he had calculated, it inspired the drove of hatchetmen. They stormed through the open gate and flowed across the lawn. Only one firearm barked in defiance.

What of the other man? Out of ammunition, or injured? Either way, it boded fortuitously for the Triad. Xiang had moved up in the Society since coming to America. Under his bloody direction, the wasteful inter-Tong warfare had been ended. Now he ruled over all three in Chinatown, and had liaison with Tongs in other cities. He had literally murdered his way to the top, with more than fifty killings to his credit. One day a network would extend from every Chinese settlement in every major city in this country. And he would rule it all. The euphoria of his recurring fantasy lifted him even now.

Then reality came crashing back as a segment of the inner face of the compound wall suddenly lost its integrity and crashed downward onto seven Tong warriors. They died, screaming horribly. Dust billowed and obscured the front of the temple. Yellow-orange flame lanced through the murk and another member shrieked and grabbed at his chest. Xiang looked anxiously around him in consternation.

A second later, two shotguns blasted from the gateway through which Xiang had walked only moments before. To his left a stout Tong hatchetman's head turned into a red pulp. Another groaned softly and sagged to the ground, his white shirt speckled with red. All Xiang could do was hurry forward into the mouth of that deadly six-gun. As he did, he broke with tradition. From his coat pocket he pulled a light-framed .38 Smith and Wesson. He had found it useful in his rise to power for the sort of killing he usually did. Right here, he had doubts of how effective it would be, though better to have it out and ready than not to have it at all.

He might have regretted that line of thought if Smoke Jensen had given him time.

Smoke saw the distinguished man with the long black queue swaying behind his head start up the steps to the temple. He also saw the small revolver in his hand and the deferential way the other Tong gangsters behaved toward him. Rage glittered in the ebony eyes, and the face held a cruel cast. This had to be the bossman of them all!

"Ho, Coolie-Boy!" Smoke taunted him. "It's me you're looking for. Face me like a man, not a dog."

Xiang Wai Lee hissed a command in Cantonese and made a harsh gesture that scattered his minions. "So, white devil, you have some courage, after all. You have a twisty mouth." His accent gave the English words an unpleasant flavor. "Are you brave enough to fight me in my own style?"

Smoke nodded at the Triad leader. "You have a gun in your hand, use it."

Insolently, Xiang thought, Smoke returned his own six-gun to its holster. It proved too much for Xiang's pride. He took another step toward Smoke Jensen and raised his gunarm. Taking careful aim, he squeezed on the trigger. Slowly the hammer started backward. Then the impossible happened.

With lightning speed, Smoke Jensen drew. Before Xiang's hammer reached its apex, the big Colt roared and blinding pain exploded in the chest of Xiang Wai Lee. He staggered and took a step back. His own weapon discharged. The slug gouged stone from a step above him. An unfamiliar numbness began to spread through him. Was this what his enemies had felt before they'd died?

He banished the thought with a Chinese curse and tried to raise his arm to fire again. A flash of excruciating pain exploded in his head and a balloon of blackness quickly filled it. Xiang Wai Lee went over backward and rolled head over heels to the bottom of the steps. His dreams of a Tong empire went with him.

* * *

With the death of Xiang Wai Lee, the fight went out of the Tong members. The three nearest to where their leader had been slain spread the word quickly. Then, shouting their defiance and rage, they spent their lives in an attempt to avenge their leader and recover his face. They made the terrible error of attacking Smoke Jensen all at once. He welcomed the first one with a bullet, his last, which split the Chinese thug's breastbone and riddled his heart with bone chips.

He went rubber-legged and sprawled halfway up on the steps. Then the hatchetmen discovered that their enemy had a hand-ax of his own. With his last round expended, Smoke re-holstered his six-gun and pulled his tomahawk free. A well-made, perfectly balanced weapon, the 'hawk had been made by a master Dakota craftsman. The head was steel and it honed down to a keen, long-lasting edge. Genuine stone beads dangled on rawhide strips from the base of the haft.

That hawk had saved the life of Smoke Jensen more times than he could recall. Old Spotted Elk Runs, who'd made it, told him; "I fashioned this in the proper time of the moon, said all the proper prayers, even gave of it a bit of my blood to drink. So long as you prove worthy to own it, this warhawk will never fail you."

Knew what he was talking about, too, Smoke reckoned. It had a fine balance and sure, deep bite. A Tong assassin named Quon Khan had learned the hard way when he'd closed in on Smoke and raised his own Tong hatchet. Quon had come up against wooden handles before, but this time his studded iron haft failed to perform its usual magic.

When he swung, Smoke Jensen parried with the Sioux warhawk. The Osage orangewood of the handle was springy and incredibly tough. It bent slightly—the best war bows were made from the same wood—and held. Smoke used the moment of stalemate to punch his enemy in the chest. Air whooshed from Quon's lungs and dark spots danced before his eyes as he tried to reply with a kick.

Then Smoke make a quick disengage by bending his knees and pivoting to his left. Every knife fighter knows that save for a period of sizing up an opponent, the actual engagement lasts only seconds. So it was for Quon Khan. As the pressure of his attack eased on Smoke's 'hawk, the mountain man struck his own blow. The keen edge of the warhawk sliced through knuckles and laid bare a long portion of forearm.

Quon screamed and dropped his weapon. Instantly, Smoke struck again. White Wolf's Fang—the Dakota craftsman had insisted that Smoke give his tomahawk a name, for strong medicine, he had maintained—struck Quon and split his skull. The blade sank to the haft. It cleaved Quon's brow and split a part of his nose. Immediately, Smoke wrenched it free, with the aid of a kick, and turned to face his third opponent, while Quon sank in a welter of gore.

Bug-eyed, the skinny teen-aged thug with a bad rash of pimples froze in astonishment. No one, especially a *qua'lo,* could move so fast and strike so hard. Only two in the Triad Society had reputations for such prowess. And this foreign devil was not one of them. He felt his knees go weak and a warm wetness spread from his crotch, down both legs, as the huge *qua'lo* turned his attentions toward him. To his consternation, the white fiend smiled, then spoke.

"Do you want to live?" Dumbly the Tong brat nodded affirmatively. "Then drop that thing and get out of here."

At first he hesitated. He raised the hatchet in a menacing manner, and the big *qua'lo* took a step forward. That decided him. His Tong hatchet clanged on the stone step and he turned tail. Black, slipperlike shoes made a soft scrabble on the walkway of crushed white rock. Quon looked neither to left nor right, and certainly not behind, as he took flight. First one, then another of his comrades saw him and joined in.

Spurred on by the steady boom of the shotguns, they cleared the temple grounds in what became the first of a concerted rush.

* * *

Apprehension began to fill Agatha Murchison when a messenger arrived from Chief Granger's railroad police. It had been at midnight, and she had awakened to the rumble of her husband's bass voice, clear down in the front hall.

"At last, by God, we've got them cornered. Get back to Grange and tell him to keep pressing. I want those two finished off tonight. Tell him I want regular reports."

Cyrus Murchison had seen the man out, then padded through the house to the two-room suite next to the kitchen that housed the cook and her husband, the butler. He roused cook and put her to preparing coffee. Agatha had managed to remain in bed for another three-quarters of an hour. A voluminous velvet robe over her nightdress, she came to where Cyrus waited further news in the breakfast room. The coffee service, her good porcelain one, sat on the table, along with three cherry tarts left over from dinner. Cyrus looked up at her entrance.

"You needn't have discomfited yourself, my dear. It is only a matter of business."

"What sort of business, Cyrus?"

"The usual," Murchison evaded, and began to demolish the tarts one after another.

"I'm worried, Cyrus," Agatha announced. "Ever since this alliance you worked up with Gaylord and Titus, you've been a changed man. It seems you never have time to rest . . . or for me."

Murchison's face crumpled and he put aside the fork, with its burden of red cherries and crust. "That's not so, my dear. I think of you always. Lord knows, there are enough reminders around my office. As you know, I have replaced that old tintype with an oil portrait of you, and there are those new-fangled glass plate photographs. And we do have many nights together." He looked miserable.

" 'Many,' " Agatha repeated. "But not like it used to be, not *most* nights. What is this about fighting in Chinatown?"

"You overheard?" Murchison asked, his face suddenly drawn and secretive.

"I could not help but hear, with all the noise you two were

making. Whatever have those heathen Chinese to do with your railroad?"

That prompted a harsh, albeit evasive, reply. "Outside of the fact that a lot of them helped build it, nothing."

"Then why are your men mixing in their affairs?"

Murchison's brow furrowed and he took a moment to contain himself. "It is not their affairs. Two very dangerous men, who mean harm to the California Central, have been seen there. Grange sent some of his men after them. Somehow it got the Chinese aroused."

"I shouldn't wonder. After all, it is the only place they may live as they are accustomed." A sudden insight came to her. "Was there any shooting?"

"*Of course* there was shooting," Murchison responded testily.

Agatha replied mildly. "Then I don't blame the Chinese for being upset." For her it was the end of the subject.

In his usual manner, Cyrus also saw it that way, this time with relief. They sat in silence a while, until the knocker resounded through the hallway loudly enough to be heard in the breakfast room. Cyrus rose to answer the summons. Agatha clutched at her lace handkerchief. Worry teased her mind. She seriously believed this alliance to be a terrible mistake. It had an aura of something illegal about it. For all his standing among the elite of San Francisco, Agatha knew that there were limits set by the power structure that could not be crossed with impunity. For a moment, a secret smile lifted the corners of her mouth.

For all the frivolous nature of the lives of society women, Agatha Marie Endicott Murchison had a fine, quick, and active mind. She had learned early to mask it under the usual vapid expressions practiced by her chums at school. Agatha Marie Endicott had been a lively, lovely young girl. She wore her long blond hair in the stylish sausage curls of her youth and had a trim figure. She had never gone through that leggy, coltish stage in her early teens. She had been lithe and graceful at her matriculation at her debutante ball at the end of May in 1860. It was there that she had met the dashing, handsome older man who would become her husband.

Cyrus Roland Murchison came from wealth. Old money had

resided in his family for three generations. His great-grandfather had made the family fortune in whaling on Nantucket Island. His grandfather had added to the vast resources by pioneering a railroad in New York State that eventually put the Erie Canal out of business. His father had answered the siren call of the California gold fields and moved his fledgling family—his wife, his eldest, Cyrus, and three siblings—to Sacramento.

Quincy Murchison soon found he had no eye or hand for prospecting. When subterranean mining began, he fell back on the family talent. He engineered and supervised the installation of tracks for ore cars. He expanded to trestle bridges and eventually worked for Leland Stanford on his Union Pacific Railroad. Cyrus Murchison had followed in his father's footsteps. He had attended Harvard and an advanced technical institute and had been working as an engineer for the UP for a year when he attended the cotillion where he met Agatha.

For her part, Agatha Endicott maintained a cool demeanor, though her heart pounded at each glance at her ardent suitor. Cyrus had fallen in love at first sight. When the ball ended, he asked permission to call on her. Coquettishly, she had stalled him, said she must consult her social calendar. Two days later, she'd sent her calling card around to the Murchison mansion, now located in San Francisco. On the back, she had penned a brief message.

"Friday? A carriage in the park? Eleven o'clock of the morning."

It had stunned her when he replied with a huge armload of long-stemmed roses and an attached note. *"My world will remain in dreariness until blessed Friday. Eleven will be delightful, my dear Miss Agatha. I shall bring a hamper."* It was signed; *"CM."*

He called for her in a spanking surrey. A dappled gray pranced in glittering harness. With consummate gallantry, Cyrus handed her into the carriage, mounted and took up the reins. They rode off with Agatha in a rosy glow of anticipation.

Now his angry voice brought Agatha out of the pink warmth of reflection.

"What the hell do you mean, they took on the Tongs?" The

answer came in a low, indistinguishable murmur. "Did the Triad Society kill Jensen and Longmont?"

This time she heard everything clearly. "No, sir. It was the other way around. By now most of them are either dead, wounded, or runned off."

"What about your men? What did Grange do?"

"We tried. We really did. Only the cops turned on us. Some mealy-mouthed lawyer feller showed up when we had 'em trapped in some Chinee church. He had papers from the court ordering us and the police to lay off this Jensen and Longmont."

Murchison exploded. "What the hell! What judge would have the grit to defy my wishes?"

"I reckon you'd have to take that up with Chief Grange, sir."

A low growl came from Cyrus. "You get back there and tell Grange I want to see him now. Not tomorrow morning, right now."

"Yes, sir. Right away, sir. An-anything else, sir?"

Agatha could hear her husband's teeth grind. "Just don't let Jensen and Longmont get away."

Cyrus Murchison returned to the breakfast room with a thunderstorm in his visage. Agatha Murchison sighed and poured more coffee.

An uneasy silence had fallen over Chinatown. Without a word, old men with wheelbarrows went about collecting the dead and wounded Tong men. The Occidentals of Murchison's railroad police waited to the last. These the elderly carted to the main entrance to Chinatown and deposited on the curb across the street. While they went about it, Smoke Jensen, Louis Longmont, and Tai Chiu discussed their situation.

"Is it to be back to the *Wang Fai?*" Louis asked.

"I'll tell you, pard, this street fighting isn't to my liking. I'm out of my element," Smoke allowed.

Tai Chiu stared at this big warrior in astonishment. Less than thirty-five Tong members, roughly divided among all three Tongs, remained in Chinatown. Yet this fighter with his gun—aha! gunfighter—said he was out of his element. What more could he do there?

Louis Longmont appeared to have read the old monk's mind. Through a low chuckle, he spoke to Smoke Jensen. "You wanted to finish them all, is that it, *mon ami?*

"At least break their backs. Have you ever seen a rattler with a broken back?"

"I do not believe I have," Tai Chiu responded hesitantly.

Louis shook his head in the negative. "There are not so many rattlesnakes in New Orleans. Now, water moccasins I know about. And other such vipers."

Smoke smiled. "Then I'm sure you know what I'm talking about. A rattler with a broken back gets so worked up about his body not doing what his brain tells it to that it begins to bite itself. Of course, rattlers are immune to their own venom."

Louis joined in with a chuckle. "It is the same with other venomous snakes, eh? What they do is use up all their poison striking at themselves. Then they can be safely picked up."

Smoke nodded. "I've been acquainted with those other deadly critters. To me, there's none of them worth picking up. Except for the rattler. His meat is mighty tasty, and a feller can always sell his skin and rattles to tenderfeet. Other than that, what use are they to anyone but themselves?"

Tai Chiu nodded enthusiastically. "Yes. Snake meat is quite a delicacy to my people. But this is not solving our immediate problem. What do you suggest we do now, Mr. Smoke Jensen?"

Smoke considered it a moment. "Going back to the ship—er—junk seems to me to be like giving up. Can your students and the other volunteers keep at it a while?" At Tai's nod in the affirmative, he went on, "Then I suggest you put them to cleaning up the last of the Tongs. It might be wise to send some of them through that tunnel of yours and hit the Tong hatchetmen by surprise. It can only serve to discompose them."

Tai Chiu smiled fleetingly. "And what will you be doing while we accomplish this?"

Smoke nodded to Louis and Brian. "The three of us have to go to the heart of this thing. We're going after Murchison and his co-conspirators."

THIRTEEN

Pearlescent light filtered through the fog of a pale dawn when Smoke Jensen, Louis Longmont, and Brian Pullen left Chinatown. Behind them, the house-to-house and shop-to-shop search for the remaining Tong members had already borne fruit. Kicking and screaming, several youths, still in the black trouser and white shirt uniforms of the Tongs, had been dragged from their homes. Frightened and helpless, parents stood uselessly to the side, looking on with shocked eyes.

Pitiful cries and pleas for mercy rose from frightened throats as these callow youths had their bottoms bared and slatted bamboo rods appeared in the hands of stern, muscular Chinese disciplinarians. Stroke after stroke fell on the exposed backsides of the former Tong terrorists. Smoke made a backward glance to take in all this. He stifled a smile and gave a satisfied nod.

Humiliation alone, from this ignominious form of punishment, would drive the Tong trash from the city, he reasoned. A loud rumble in his belly reminded the last mountain man that he had not eaten since early the previous morning. Not that he had not gone longer without food; many were the times he had been compelled to fast for three or more days. Like that time when wet powder and a horse with a broken leg had compelled him to evade a party of blood-lusting Snake warriors . . .

. . . Smoke Jensen had ridden into what had appeared to be a friendly village of the Snake tribe, along the middle fork of the Salmon River. He had been welcomed, given meat and salt, and a generous portion of roasted cammus bulbs. Years before, he had learned the traditional lore of Indian customs.

"Iffin' they feed ya'. Especially if they share their precious salt with ye," Preacher had solemnly told him. "Then ye can be certain they'll never lift yer hair while ye stay in theys camp."

"Sort of . . . safe passage?" the sixteen-year-old Kirby Jensen had offered.

"Well, naw. Once you leave their lodges an' clear the ground they count as their campsite, you jist might be fair game again."

"Ain't that sort of—ah—treacherous?"

"Nope, Kirb. It's all in how they sees things. Once you've been tooken in, they's honor bound to treat you fair and square. Once you've left the bosom of their harth, you become jist another white man an' an enemy."

And so it had proved to be for Smoke Jensen when he'd set out alone from the Snake village. Within half an hour he became aware of pursuit. He pulled off the trail, circled back, and watched. Sure enough, here came better than a dozen Snakes, war clubs, lances, and bows clutched in hands; the men's faces were painted for war.

Once they had passed him, Smoke crossed the trail, then returned to wipe out his sign. He led his stout horse, Sunfish, deep into the thick tangle of fir and bracken north of the trail he had ridden out on. He continued northward for a day.

Often he doubled back, wiped out his sign, then moved along on a parallel track. Twice he laid dead-falls. It was late in his second day when the thunderstorm formed over the mountains and sent down torrents of water. Sunfish slipped on a clay bank and went down. A squirrel gun pop sounded when the stallion's cannon bone broke. A shrill whinny told Smoke the disaster was beyond repair. Flash-flooding threatened to take the stream he traveled along out of its banks. Yet in this unending downpour, he could not cap and fire his big Hall .70 pistol.

He considered any other means of ending the suffering of Sunfish to be unacceptable cruelty to an animal that had so unstintingly served him. The suffering of the horse tore at his heart. The tempest thrashed and whipped at the man and horse for long minutes, then swept on to the east, leaving a light drizzle behind. Quickly, Smoke wiped the nipple of his pistol, capped it, and fired a .70 caliber into the brain of his faithful companion. He dared not stay here, and he could not make any time with the saddle over his back.

Regretfully, Smoke stripped the saddlebags, which contained his scant possessions, and his bedroll from the saddle and left his valiant mount behind. Even with the storm, sharp ears would have heard the report of his mercy round. It still rained too hard for Smoke to reload, so he would have to rely on his other two pistols and the Hawken rifle he had yanked from the saddle scabbard.

No matter. He had been alone, and afoot, with less. He trudged off along the edge of the roiling mountain stream, far enough into the torrent to wash out his footprints. The storm had hardly abated three hours later. That's when the Snakes caught up to him.

With triumphant whoops and yips, mud-smeared warriors materialized out of the mist of rain to one side and from behind. Their bowstrings softened to uselessness by the deluge, they relied on lances and warhawks. Smoke dropped one with a .70 Hall, then a second. The Hawken rifle at his shoulder, he aimed for the most elaborately festooned Snake, the man he remembered had been most outgoing in his welcome to the village. One who had been introduced as the greatest fighter of all the Snakes.

He needed to down this war leader to buy even a small bit of time. The Hawken fired and the ball sped toward its target. A pipebone chest plate exploded into fragments when the .54 caliber projectile slammed into it. It smashed through his chest wall and flattened somewhat before it ripped a jagged hole in his heart. He dropped like a fallen pine. Hoots of victory changed into howls of outrage and superstitious fear.

Grabbing up their dead leader, the Snake warriors flitted off through the trees. Quickly, Smoke sheltered the muzzle of the rifle and reloaded. His three pistols quickly followed. Rather than set off in a panicked run, he held his ground. Nightfall swept over the canyon and the Snakes had not returned. That didn't mean they wouldn't, Smoke reminded himself. The rain had ceased to fall an hour before, yet Smoke could not risk a small fire, even if he could find dry wood.

Back against a tree, the last mountain man settled in for a long, miserable night. From his saddlebags, he withdrew a strip of venison jerky and a ball of fry bread left from the Snake village. His munched thoughtfully while his eyes adjusted to the gathering darkness. He was not even aware of when he slipped into an uneasy slumber.

Morning brought back the Snakes. They slithered through a ground mist so thick that it obscured the cattails along the stream. Smoke saw them at the last moment and wished wistfully for at least one cup of coffee before they hit his camp. He snapped a cap on the Hawkin and downed a bold warrior who leaped at him from a huge granite boulder. Two more burst out of the brush, warhawks raised to strike. Smoke set aside his rifle and filled both hands with the butts of pistols.

First one, then the second Hall bucked and spat flame. Big, whistling .70 caliber balls cut through the air. The first cut a swath through the gut of a howling Snake. He dropped to his knees, a hand over the seeping entry wound, eyes wide. Smoke's other round found meat in the shoulder of a thick-waisted warrior of middle age. He made a grimace and gave testimony to the canine nature of Smoke's ancestry. Smoke Jensen hastily drew his remaining pistol.

He cocked the weapon and triggered it. The hammer fell on the cap, which made its characteristic flat crack. Nothing else happened, except the Snake kept coming. Quickly Smoke drew his 'hawk and hefted it. He ran his hand through the trailing thong, so it could not be wrenched from his grasp. Then he went after the wounded warrior. Four more of them, all that remained, gathered around, anticipating a quick end for this white dog . . .

. . . It had been one hell of a fight, Smoke recalled. The wet powder in his last pistol had put him in terrible danger. The wounded man had been no problem. He quickly dispatched the Snake with a feint and an overhand blow that split the warrior's skull. That still left four more. Awed by his obvious fighting ferocity, they held back. Smoke had not been granted that luxury. With a wolf-howl, he had waded in. The nearest of the four went down with a slashed belly.

His intestines spilled on the ground as Smoke whipped past him and whirled the warhawk in a circular motion that denied his enemy an opening. He spun and lashed out with a foot. His boot sole smacked solidly into the chest of a younger warrior, hardly more than a boy, who flew backward to splash noisily in the stream. He howled in frustration as the current, still high from the recent rains, rapidly whirled him out of sight. That left him with two.

Had Smoke been a seriously religious man, he might have prayed for strength, or for victory. Instead, he offered himself up to the Great Spirit. "It's a good day to die!" he had yelled into the startled face of the Snake facing him.

And, as Smoke now recalled, it had been the Snake who had done the dying. The last one had turned tail and run. That left Smoke Jensen alone to find his way on foot out of the Yellowjacket Mountains. He had made it, or he would not be in San Francisco, on the edge of Chinatown, walking down a street toward the offices of his present enemy. Another rumble of hunger reminded him again.

"What say we take on some grub before we face down Murchison?" he suggested.

"Suits," Brian Pullen readily agreed.

Louis Longmont looked around in trepidation. "Is there anyplace . . . suitable?"

Smoke made a sour face. "Louis, you disappoint me. I'm sure we can find something. Although I doubt they'll have escargots."

Smoke Jensen finished a last cup of coffee and pushed back his chair. The ham had been fresh, juicy, and thick. Three eggs and a mound of fried potatoes, liberally laced with onions, rounded out their repast. The walk to Murchison's office on Market Street took little time.

Early employees strolled toward the Murchison offices when the four grim-faced men rounded the corner and approached the building. Quo Chung Wu had caught up to the other three at the cafe. His sincerity could not be doubted, and he had been welcomed to the party determined to crush Murchison's dark scheme. Smoke Jensen signaled a halt and they stepped back against shop fronts on the opposite side of the street.

To make their presence less conspicuous, Brian Pullen purchased a copy of the morning *Chronicle* from a newsboy with a stack under one arm. He frowned at the dime Brian gave him and turned a button nose up to the well-dressed lawyer. "Don't got any change. That's the first I sold."

"Keep the change," Brian informed him.

Brightening, the kid scuffed the toe of one clodhopper over the other. "Really? Thanks, Mister." A small, newsprint-blackened hand shoved the ten-cent piece into a pocket and he set off to hawk his papers. "Read all about it! Big battle in Chinatown!"

Brian cut his eyes to Smoke Jensen. "Looks like we made the papers."

"Not by name, I hope," Smoke returned.

Quickly, Brian scanned the front page story. While he read, a fancy carriage arrived and a portly, well-dressed gentleman stepped down and entered the building. "Who is that?" Smoke asked.

Brian looked up. "Cyrus Murchison." He went back to his perusal of the article. A flicker of relieved smile lifted Brian's lips. "Not by name, anyway. It says here that it looks like a band of dockworkers invaded Chinatown for some unknown reason and laid waste to a number or residents and store owners. Promises more details to follow."

Smoke's observation came out dry and sour. "No doubt what those 'details' will be like. Unless we can make an end of this right now."

Brian grew serious "We'll have to catch them red-handed 'fore anyone will believe us."

"Murchison has that much influence?"

"Oh, hell, Smoke, they all three do," Brian advised him.

"Then we'd best be gettin' in there and find proof of what they have in mind," the last mountain man suggested.

The determined quartet crossed the street diagonally and brushed aside several California Central employees. They ignored the startled yelps of complaint, quickly silenced when the offended parties got a look at the grim faces of the four men. Smoke Jensen shoved ahead of a prissy-looking clerk type and the others followed. They entered the lobby of the California Central building and came face-to-face with a trio of burly rock-faced railroad detectives, in their brown suits and matching derbies.

Murchison's minions took in the grim, powder-grimed faces, the belligerent postures, the number of weapons, and the scarred black leather gloves on the hands of Smoke Jensen. Without any need to consult one another, they began to sidle around the edge of the room, never taking their eyes off the four intruders. Their actions did nothing to deter Smoke and his companions. They walked purposefully toward the gate behind a railing that separated the lobby from the business portion of the first floor. Behind them, the three railroad detectives bolted out the door.

A dandified secretary looked up from his desk at their approach. His eyes went wide and he knew in the depth of his heart that these men certainly had no legitimate business here. He raised a soft, well-manicured hand in a halting gesture.

"I say, there, gentlemen—you cannot go in there." He gasped in exasperation when he saw they had no intention of obeying. "Please, fellows, let's not be hasty."

Brian turned to the sissified secretary. "We're here to serve a warrant on Cyrus Murchison."

Already wide eyes rolled in pique. "I will accept service on his behalf."

"Sorry," Brian pressed. "It has to be served in person."

"Mr. Murchison is not in at the present," the defender of the gate lied smoothly.

Smoke Jensen took a menacing step forward, the fingers of his gloved right hand flexing suggestively. "Sonny, we just saw him come in. Are you going to show us the way, or do I squeeze your adam's apple until it pops outten your mouth like a skun grape?"

Defeated and demoralized, the secretary raised a feeble arm and pointed the way. "Upstairs, third floor, at the back," he bleated.

Quo Chung Wu remained behind to keep the secretary in line, while Smoke and his companions strode quickly down the hall and started up the staircase toward Murchison's office. Behind them, they heard the dulcet voice of the secretary purring.

"Ooh, a Chinese boy. How very nice. I *love* Oriental food."

Brian Pullen made gagging signs; Smoke Jensen twisted his face with a look of disgust; Louis Longmont produced a sardonic expression. Then they stood before the door. Smoke positioned Brian and Louis to either side, their shotguns at the ready. Then he raised a foot and kicked in the heavy portal. Wood shattered around the thick latch.

Moving smoothly on oiled hinges, the thick oak panel swung noiselessly until it collided with the inside wall. Beyond, Smoke saw a large expensive desk, ranks of bookshelves, an ornate sideboard with decanters of brandy and sherry, and flag poles with the United States flag and that of the California Central Railroad. He also noted heavy curtains that billowed into the room, driven by the breeze through open windows. Of Cyrus Murchison they found no sign.

"He got away," Smoke spoke plainly.

Brian gasped. "It's three stories down."

Smoke led the way to the window. Outside, an iron fire escape clung to the brick wall. Somehow, Murchison had learned of their presence and eluded them by this handy way out. From the direction of the stairwell, Smoke heard the sounds of a fight in the lobby below. He nodded that way.

"Sounds like those hard cases came back."

In the lobby, the secretary quailed under his desk while Quo Chung Wu tore into half a dozen railroad detectives. The timid

soul peeped from the legwell of the rolltop from time to time
when a strange warble or animal cry came from the lips of
the Chinese student. He could not believe his eyes.

Two men already lay on the floor, writhing in agony. The
Chinese boy moved so quickly and unpredictably that the others
were unable to get a clear shot. He whirled and pranced, then
came up on one toe and lashed out a blurred kick that rocked
back the head of one detective. Staggered, the man crashed into
the dividing rail and draped himself over it, unconscious and
bleeding from the mouth. The handsome boy, the secretary had
heard him called Quo, did not hesitate to enjoy his victory.

At once he spun and ducked and blocked a blow from an
ax handle. The owner of that deadly device stared stupidly
while Quo kicked him three times: in the chest, the gut, and
the crotch. He went to his knees with a moan. Quo moved on.
At the same time, a dozen more bully boys rushed into the
lobby. Their charge was checked by the bellow of a 12-gauge
Parker shotgun.

Brian Pullen arrived on the scene in time to drop two gunhands who had taken aim at Quo Chung Wu. The roar of the
scattergun froze everyone in the lobby for a moment. It gave
Brian time to reload. He needed it. Three hard cases turned
his way slowly, as though under water. The Parker bucked in
Brian's hands and a load of buckshot slashed into one before
he had completed his move.

He did not make a sound as he flew backward into another
railroad thug. They sprawled on the floor in a heap; the un-
wounded one squirmed and kicked to free himself. Quo had
not delayed. The moment he knew where the shotgun pointed,
he went into action.

Instead of avoiding the new threat, he waded into the middle
of it, elbow, back-fist, knee blows, and kicks rained on the
stunned henchmen of Cyrus Murchison. One of the railroad
policemen, accustomed to dealing with brawling hobos, leaped
at Quo, only to end up hurtling through the air in his original
direction bent double, his shoulder dislocated and an arm broken at the elbow. It had the affect of a bowling ball among
ninepins.

Brown suits flew in all directions. Brian butt-stroked a lantern jaw of one and stepped aside to allow the unconscious man to skid into the railing. Before the railroad detectives could organize themselves, Smoke Jensen and Louis Longmont arrived on the scene.

Smoke waded right in. He grabbed the coat of a hard case by one lapel and yanked him into a hard fist to the jaw. Saliva flew and his lips twisted into an ugly pucker. Smoke popped him again and threw him aside. A yard bull grabbed Smoke by one shoulder and heaved to spin him around.

Jensen did not even budge. Instead, he shrugged the thug off and drove an elbow into the man's gut. Air hissed out and the face of the company policeman turned scarlet. Before he could recover, Smoke gave him a right-left in the face that split one cheek and mashed his lips.

Two more turned on Smoke Jensen. One had a thick chest, with bulges of muscles for arms. He stood on tree-trunk legs, with long, wide boots to hold it all up. His partner weighed in at only a bit less menace. Growling, they went for Smoke with their bare hands. First to reach him, the smaller giant tried for a bear hug.

Smoke batted one arm away and sent a sizzling left up inside the loop it formed to crash in right under the big man's ribs. He grunted and blinked . . . and kept on coming. A quick sidestep by Smoke evaded his clutching arms. Smoke popped him on the ear with a sharp right.

Again, all he did was blink. This could get tiresome right quick, Smoke reasoned. He disliked the idea of shooting an apparently unarmed man. Yet, from the corner of his eye he saw the other brute moving to find an opening. End it now, Smoke demanded of himself.

His left hand found the haft of his tomahawk and pulled it free. He dodged back a step and swung from his toes. The flat of the blade smacked into the forehead of the colossus with a soft ringing sound. His eyes crossed and he went to his knees. Smoke reached out quickly and pushed him to one side. He fell silently. Smoke looked up in time to see a fist slam into his face.

Starbursts went off in his head and he dropped his 'hawk. Bells rang and he felt himself losing control of his legs. He gulped air, rocked back, and swung in the blind. Due to the eagerness of the huge railroad detective to follow up his advantage, Smoke landed a good one. It gave Smoke time to recover his sight.

It went quickly then. He pumped lefts and rights to the gut of the gargantuan. Liquor-tainted air boiled out over his lips. Smoke waded in. His opponent lowered his guard to protect his stomach. Smoke went for his face. The hard case recognized the need for a change of tactics and reached under his coat for a holdout gun.

Lightning fast, Smoke snatched his war hawk from the floor and swung in a circular motion. The keen edge whirred through the air and neatly severed the man's wrist. Hand and gun hit the floor. Gaping at the torrent of blood that flowed from the cut artery, the man gave a soft moan and passed out.

"Smoke, behind you," Louis Longmont warned.

Smoke whirled, his right-hand Colt appearing in his hand as he moved. A hard case with a short-barreled H&R .44 Bulldog gritted his teeth as he tightened his finger on the trigger. Fire and smoke leaped from the muzzle of Smoke's Peacemaker. His slug punched into the protruding belly behind the small revolver and its owner dropped the Bulldog to cover the hole in his gut.

"The door," Smoke yelled to his companions.

Understanding, they changed their tactics. Every move Louis, Quo, Brian and Smoke made took them closer to the tall double doors of the main entrance. By studied effort, they cut a swath through their enemy. Aching, wounded, and dead reeled in their wake. Smoke Jensen broke free first, then turned back to batter an open face and create a pathway for his friends.

He jerked two hard cases together so violently that their heads clunked together loudly and they fell as though hit with sledgehammers. It took some time for the dazed thugs to realize the purpose of their opponents. Deafened by the loud reports of shotgun and six-shooter, they reeled in confusion while the four companions fought their way clear.

Smoke and Louis barreled into the street together, followed shortly by Brian and Quo. With an angry roar, the railroad's hoodlums recognized what had happened and charged the doorway. Smoke and his Western companions laid down a blistering fire that kept the hard cases inside while the quartet backed down the street. At the corner, they rounded a building and sprinted off into the center of the city.

"Where now?" Louis asked.

"We have to find Murchison," Smoke stated the obvious. "My bet he'll be somewhere around his railroad yards. First stop is the livery to get horses. Quo, can you ride?"

A blank expression came over the young Chinese student's face. "I have never done so before. But, if I can master T'ai Chi, I can stay on top of a horse."

Smoke did not know what T'ai Chi might be, but he already had doubts about the student priest's horsemanship. Nothing for it, they had to move fast.

FOURTEEN

Not until the full extent of damage had been assessed did Cyrus Murchison realize the danger in which he found himself. With the pale pink light of dawn spreading over the hills of San Francisco, he sent urgent messages to his co-conspirators. Not a one of the judges whom he had wined and dined so lavishly, always making certain they departed with fat envelopes of large-denomination currency for their "campaign chests," would even receive Cyrus in his time of peril. Nor, he was certain, would they seriously consider overruling a decision by a colleague.

That resulted in the plain and urgent summons to Titus Hobbs and Gaylord Huntley. It urged them to gather what men they had on hand and go directly to the California Central yard office. All were to bring horses. He dispatched Heck Grange on the same errand, with additional instructions to have the yard master assemble a "special"—at least six livestock cars, four chair cars, and his private coach. It was to be stocked with food and liquor and held in readiness at the yard office.

That settled, Cyrus Murchison went about his usual morning routine. He shaved, and he brushed and patted his thick shock of white hair into place. Then removed his dressing gown. His gentlemen's gentleman assisted him in donning his usual starched white shirt, pinstriped blue-gray trousers, vest, and suit coat. He put his feet in glossy black shoes and sat patiently while his manservant adjusted pearl-gray spats. He would select a suitable hat from the rack in the front hall. On his way out the door to his bedroom, he looked back at the servant.

"Oh, Henry, will you see to packing my field clothes? That's a good man. See that they are delivered to the yard office at once."

"Yes, sir. Very good, sir."

"And while you're at it, select a rifle and brace of revolvers, with ample ammunition for a long stay, and send them along also."

Henry's eyes widened, though he reserved comment. Like all of the servants, he had become aware of the turmoil in the latter half of the night. Something boded quite wrong for the master if he made such preparations so early in the morning. Henry would bide his time and see what developed.

Downstairs, Agatha had breakfast waiting for them. A fresh pot of Arabica coffee, date muffins, a favorite of Cyrus's, eggs scrambled with sausage and topped with a lemony Hollandaise sauce, ham, fried potatoes lyonnaise, and a compote of mixed fruit. In spite of his troubled thoughts, Cyrus ate wolfishly. He and Agatha chatted of inconsequences until he had had his fill. Then, pushed back with a final cup of coffee and another muffin, Cyrus invited the remarks he felt certain would come.

"We're going to be in for some sort of change, aren't we, dear?" Agatha asked.

Cyrus considered a moment revealing the full extent of the change he anticipated. "There have been setbacks, yes," he allowed. "Nothing to concern you greatly. Although I will be required to be out of town for a while. At least until certain matters are—ah—attended to."

Agatha frowned. "You mean the killing of those two men who upset your plans," she stated flatly.

"Tut-tut, my dear, that is hardly a concern of yours."

Agatha Endicott Murchison had the proverbial bull by the horns and had no intention of letting go. "Come, Cyrus. I may choose to appear as vapid and vacant as my society sisters, but you know full well I am no fool. If you must leave town, this must be serious indeed. How badly can it affect our fortune?"

A rapid shift came to the expression of mild disdain on the face of Cyrus Murchison. A scowl replaced it. "I could be disgraced, humiliated, ruined," he listed harshly.

"Prison?" Agatha prompted.

"Possibly. It would remain to be seen how much could be traced directly to me."

"How much of what, Cyrus?"

Cyrus Murchison pressed himself up from his chair. *"That* I will not go into in detail with you, my dear. You are better off knowing nothing. I realize that women, even in your favored position, are still considered chattel. Even so, that does not exempt them from going to prison for not reporting prior knowledge of criminal events. I'm going east for a while. I'll not be home tonight, nor for some time to come, I fear. Keep your chin up, and always insist you know nothing of anything I may be accused of having done. Goodbye, my dearest."

They kissed as usual on the porch and Cyrus Murchison took his shiny carriage to the California Central Building on Market Street as he would any other day. There he found himself compelled to beat a hasty retreat far sooner than anticipated. He arrived at the railroad yard office short of breath, his usually impeccable clothes in disarray.

"Get everyone aboard at once," he demanded of the yard master.

"Horses are already loaded, Mr. Murchison," that worthy responded in his defense.

"Excellent. Did you send for my bay?"

"Chief Grange arranged for that. Oh, and Mr. Hobson and Mr. Huntley are waiting in the drawing room of your car, sir."

"Good. I'll join them. Heck," he raised his voice to summon. "Get this motley collection of ne'er-do-wells aboard. Did you arrange for food?"

"I did. And whiskey, too."

Murchison scowled. "Keep a tight lid on that. All we need is a load of drunken protectors."

Any attempt to trail Cyrus Murchison through the early morning rush of people on the way to work would be useless. Smoke Jensen announced that conclusion to the others as they stood in the alleyway behind the California Central Building. He then offered an alternate approach.

"Odds are he's headed for the trainyard. We can go directly there, or try to find if his partners in this are still around. I say we do the latter."

That received quick agreement and the four hunters set out. At the offices of Hobson's mining company, they learned that he was not in and had sent word that he would not be in that day. In the dockyard office of Huntley's maritime shipping company, one of those newfangled telephones jangled on the desk of the receptionist. He looked at it aggrievedly and assured them that Mr. Huntley had telephoned early to say he would be out of town for a few days.

"They're all at the railroad," Smoke summed up. "We'd best get over there."

They rode at what speed they could through the throng of milling pedestrians—all to no avail, they soon discovered. Reluctant to make any answer, the yard master had a change of heart when Smoke Jensen used one big hand to bunch the bib of the man's striped railroad overalls and lifted him clear of the ground.

"Y-you just missed them. Mr. Murchison and his associates had a 'special' made up. They and a whole lot of rough-looking characters rolled out of here not fifteen minutes ago."

"Headed which way?" Smoke demanded.

Newfound defiance rang in the voice of the yard master. "I don't reckon I should tell you that."

Smoke gave him a shake and got his face down close to that of the other man. "I reckon you'd better, or I'll have these fellers string you up by the ankles and I'll slit your throat and let you bleed out like a sheep."

Face suddenly gone white, the yard master bleated like one of the woolly critters. "E-E-East! Th-They went east on the Main Line. Clear to Carson City, in Nevada Territory."

"Why, thank you, Mr. Yard Master," Smoke drawled. "We're obliged. When's the next train go that way?"

"N-not until tonight. The local leaves at five o'clock, to pick up freight along the run."

"Won't do. See what you can do about rustlin' us up another train to take out right now," Smoke demanded.

"B-but that's impossible!" the yard boss stammered. "Running one train right behind the other is too dangerous."

"Suppose you let me worry about danger. Are there cars and a locomotive in the yard now?"

"Well, yes, of course. But . . ."

Smoke's gray eyes turned to black ice. "But nothing. Like I said, we'll worry about any danger. Where'd we find a likely train?"

"Out—out there," came the reply from the yard master, his eyes wide with fear.

Smoke thought on it for a minute. "Quo, you an' Louis go scout out a train that'll suit us. Let me know pronto." After they left, he turned back to the hapless captive. "I see you got one of Mr. Bell's squawk boxes." He lowered the thoroughly cowed yard boss to the floor and released him. Smoke's Green River blade appeared in his hand. "I think we'll just take that along with us. That telegraph key, too. That way, if you get the urge to send word down the line and warn Mr. Murchison about us, you'll have a hard time doing it."

"But—but that's railroad property," the man sputtered.

Smoke snorted through his aquiline nose his opinion of the severity of taking railroad property. "So's that train we're taking."

Quo Chung Wu returned, excitement lighting his face. "We found one. A locomotive, tender, baggage car, and stock car. Louis said they were just making it up."

"What's Louis doing?" Smoke asked.

Quo broke into a grin. "He's keeping the engineer and fireman peaceful. Also making them back up to a chair car."

"Now, that's nice. But we can do without the extra weight. It'll only slow us. Run tell Louis to forget it. We'll be with you shortly."

After Quo departed, Brian Pullen offered some advice. "Whatever we do, word will get out fairly soon. Even tied up, when the yard master is found, he'll spill everything."

Smoke made a tight smile. "Well, then, we take him along.

If he's not to be found, everyone will assume he's off on some business."

"I ain't goin'," the yard master blurted. Smoke glowered him into silence.

Ten minutes later, they boarded the train. The yard master cowered in one corner of the baggage car. Quo remained in the cab of the locomotive to, as he put it, "keep the engineer and fireman honest." This he did with T'ai Chi kicks and painful pressure holds. With a nervous eye on the young Chinese, the engineer opened the throttle and the train steamed out of the yard.

Five miles down the track, with San Francisco dwindling in the distance, Smoke Jensen signaled for a halt. He dismounted from the baggage car and scaled a telegraph pole. He cut the three lines and descended. He would do the same several times more.

Once under way, Smoke settled down for a strategy session with Louis and Brian. "There's not a hell of a lot we can do except chase after them. At full throttle we can close the distance, given time."

"And then?" Louis prompted.

Smoke frowned, considering it. He was not an expert on trains, even though he had worked for the Denver and Rio Grande as a right-of-way scout. He visualized the exterior of the locomotive that pulled them. "There's a walkway along both sides of the boiler on our locomotive. I reckon we can use that to board the other train. When we do that, what we have to do is take on Murchison and his partners without their hard cases mixing in."

"Easier said," Brian began, to be cut off by Louis.

"Do not despair. Once in that private car we can jam the doors at both ends so no one can enter. That will make our task much easier."

"What if there's a nest of them in there already?" Brian persisted.

Louis Longmont shrugged. "That is for Smoke and myself to deal with, *non?* For that matter, you do quite well with that shotgun. Quo Chung Wu is . . . Quo Chung Wu. He may eschew firearms, but the truth is, he is a weapon himself. We will do all right."

Brian Pullen sighed heavily, resigned. "I hope you are right."

Sally Jensen drove the dasher into her churn for the last time. She pushed back a stray lock of black hair, then removed the lid and beater. With a dainty finger, she wiped the blades clean, then reached into the conical wooden device and removed a large ball of pale white butter. She dropped it into a large crockery bowl and lifted the heavy churn, made up of wooden slats like a barrel.

From it, she poured a stream of buttermilk into a hinged-top jug. Setting it aside, she selected a large pinch of dried dandelion blossoms and powdered them between her palms. She dropped the yellow substance into the bowl with her butter, added salt, and began to knead it, to work out the last of the buttermilk. A pale, amber hue spread through the blob. Without warning, an enormous wave of relief washed through her bosom.

So intense was the dissolving of tension that her head sank to her chest and she uttered a violent sob of release. Smoke no longer faced such immense danger; she knew it. It made her heart sing. She wanted to break into a joyful ditty. In fact, she did begin to hum to herself.

"Oh, Susannah, don't you cry for me," the words rang in her head. She wanted to tell someone. Quickly she looked around. To her surprise and pleasure, she saw Monte Carson cantering up the lane from the far-off main gate to Sugarloaf.

Monte brought more substantial good news. "I've heard from Smoke. He telegraphed to say he was about to wind up his business in San Francisco. Should be home in a week."

"When did it come, Monte?" Sally asked eagerly.

"This mornin'. I come on out right away I seened it."

"Oh, thank you. I just know everything will be all right now."

Cyrus Murchison set down the brandy decanter and offered glasses to Titus Hobson and Gaylord Huntley. They had finished a sumptuous dinner at noon, in the dining room of Murchison's private car. Over coffee and rolls that morning, Murchison had explained the current situation to his partners in crime. Since then, Titus Hobson had complained about the moderate speed of the special train.

"Can't go any faster," Cyrus Murchison explained. "The *Daylight Express* is ahead of us by only half an hour. The slightest delay for them would result in a disaster when we rear-ended the other train."

Hobson frowned. "Can't word of an unexpected halt be sent to us by telegraph?"

"There's no such thing as wireless telegraphy. Won't ever be." Murchison loaded his words with scorn for the uninitiated. "One has to be attached to the wire to get a message. So we run in the blind."

"Did you send along word of our 'special'?" Gaylord Huntley asked.

"Of course I did."

"Then we could get flagged down in case of trouble, right?"

"True. But the faster we're going, the longer it takes to slow down and stop. Relax. Enjoy your brandy. There's no one chasing us. At least, none who can go as fast as we're going now."

"What do we do now?" Hobson bleated.

Murchison frowned. He had never seen this yellow streak in the mining magnate before. What caused it? He carefully chose the words he wanted. "We go as far east as we need to. Lie low, wait and see if anything is done officially. Actually, there's nothing that can be done. Only the three of us know what we have in mind. I assure you, Jensen and Longmont have no idea where we are going. *They* are our only enemy.

When we have a chance to regroup, we'll strike back at them. And believe me, the consequences for Jensen and Longmont will be dire indeed."

At the insistence of the engineer, the pirated train that bore Smoke Jensen and his allies made a water stop at a small tank-town located on the eastern downslope of the coastal range. Even though it was the gateway to the Central Valley, all the roads to be seen from the water tank were narrow and rutted. Truly, Smoke Jensen mused, the California Central could be considered the single vital artery to the area. To the south by twenty miles ran the tracks of the Union Pacific, which curved through the San Joaquin Mountains, from the first rail terminus at Sacramento to San Francisco.

No doubt the pressure of competition from the larger, more robust UP had been a factor in the decision for a power grab by Cyrus Murchison. No matter the man's reasons, he had gone far outside the law and had harmed untold innocent people in his determination to amass control over all of Central California and he had to be stopped. Smoke Jensen considered himself the right person to bring an end to Murchison's reign of bloodshed and terror.

His speculations interrupted by a hiss of steam and single hoot of the whistle, Smoke Jensen climbed back aboard the baggage car. A moment later, the train creaked and groaned and began to roll down the track. Louis had taken care of cutting the telegraph line. There would be so many breaks that it would take a week to repair them all, Smoke mused. Too bad. Catching Murchison and his partners came first. A question he had left unspoken so far came to him.

"Louis, what brought you to San Francisco in the first place?"

To Smoke's surprise, Louis flushed a deep pink. "A certain situation had become untenable for me in New Orleans. You know I had invested extensively in certain establishments in the Vieux Carré. Restaurants, a casino. Another casino on a riverboat. In fact, I had overextended. We had a run of heavy losses. Money became tight. One individual in particular, who sought to gain control of my businesses, pressed hard.

"He became obnoxious over it. Silly as it may sound, I found myself forced into an affair of honor with him. Dueling has been outlawed since the Recent Unpleasantness. One of the gifts of Reconstruction. In spite of that, we fought . . . and I killed him." Louis paused, wiped at imaginary perspiration on his forehead. "Fortunately, I was exonerated. I later found out this man worked as an agent for Cyrus Murchison of San Francisco. Digging deeper, I found out about Murchison's grand scheme. It appeared he could not be content with Central California, he wanted to expand. So I came here to find out all I could."

"Why didn't you tell me this from the git-go?" Smoke pressed.

Louis sighed. "Because I am convinced I behaved so foolishly. Like a twenty-year-old who still believes he is immortal. What could I do, alone, against such powerful men?"

"So you contacted me."

Louis eyed Smoke levelly. "Only after I learned much of the scope of their plans. Three days later, Francie was killed. I knew I had to see it out. I loved that woman, *mon ami*. She was truly *une belle femme*. We set her up in that lavish establishment, do you remember? It was after you got her out of that tight spot in Denver."

"Only so well, my friend. And I agree. Francie was indeed the lovely lady. She—deserved much better." Smoke Jensen did not waste his time on if-onlies, yet the thought flitted briefly through his mind: *If only Francie had chosen a different life.* He turned to look out the open door.

Fields ripe for the harvest flashed past as the train gained speed. A short conference with the reluctant engineer provided him the information they would reach the town of Parkerville shortly after noon. Smoke wondered what they would meet there.

* * *

When the 'special' slowed to a stop at the depot in Parkerville, Heck Grange prevailed upon Cyrus Murchison to give the men in the chair cars an opportunity to stretch their legs. With permission granted, they began to climb from the train. At once, Heck Grange spotted a familiar face.

"Ty!" he shouted above the hiss and chuff of the locomotive. "Tyrone Beal."

Beal turned, then headed his way. Before Beal could speak, Grange pushed on. "You were supposed to be back in San Fran on the *Midnight Flyer.*"

"I know. Only there was some delay. Some hick-town sheriff got on our case about the fire and the dead man at that freight company. By the time he could verify our identity as railroad detectives, I missed the train." Beal nodded to the throng of hard cases. "What's going on here?"

"We could have used you in town. One hell of a fight with Longmont and his friend Jensen. Ol' Cyrus Murchison's got some wind up his tail. Seems he thinks those two are chasin' after him and he wants to fall back and regroup. You and those others might as well throw in with us for now."

"Glad to, though except for Monk Diller, the rest ain't worth a pinch of coon crap."

"Bring who you see as best, then. And after you get them aboard, come back to Mr. Murchison's car."

In five minutes, hat in hand, Tyrone Beal stood on the observation platform of Murchison's private car. He stepped across the threshold of the rear door on invitation. Murchison sat behind a large, highly polished rosewood desk, Hobson and Huntley in wingback chairs to either side.

"Ah, Mr. Beal. I am sure Gaylord here is anxious to hear your report."

"Yes, sir. We got that farmer all right. Burned his freight office to the ground. Pounded on him hard enough to get some sense into him, too. Actually, he got a bit much of a pounding. He died."

A sardonic, cynical smile flickered on Huntley's face. "Too bad. At least that's one gnat out of our faces. You do good work, Mr. Beal."

"Thank you, sir."

"You can do some more for us. I have only this minute learned from the station master that the lines are all dead west of us. The telegrapher received only part of a message that spoke of a runaway train headed this way. It is my belief that Longmont and Jensen, and whatever ragtag band of vigilantes they could round up, are in pursuit of us. I would be obliged if you took some of Heck's men and set up a delaying action. It would mean a considerable bonus for you if you succeeded."

Ty Beal inflated his chest in sudden pride. "You can count on me, Mr. Murchison. We'll hold 'em, never you mind. Hold them long enough, anyway."

"Fine. I'm counting on you. Now I rather think we should be on our way. Pick your men, and good luck."

Forty-five minutes later, the commandeered train commanded by Smoke Jensen rolled into Parkerville. Nothing seemed untoward at first glance. Five boxcars stood coupled together on one of three sidings. On the other side, beyond the double tracks of the main line, a passenger car idled, attached to a standard caboose. Like a suckling pig, the locomotive nosed up to the water tank and took on precious liquid. The fireman hurled wood aboard the tender, aided by Quo Chung Wu and the brakeman.

Relieved to be out of their cramped quarters, if only for a little while, Smoke Jensen, Louis Longmont, and Brian Pullen walked out the kinks, stretched legs at an angle from a wooden slat bench, and breathed deeply of the country air. They had only begun to relax when a fusillade erupted from the boxcars.

FIFTEEN

Hot lead flew swift and thick. Trapped in the open, Smoke Jensen and his companions had no choice than to duck low and return fire. Smoke concentrated on the open door of a boxcar. The hardwood planking of the inner walls deflected his bullets and they ricocheted around the interior with bloody results. Yelps of pain, groans, and ouches came from the occupants.

Louis Longmont quickly duplicated Smoke Jensen's efforts. The results proved spectacular. Curses and howls came from inside the cars. Then, from the opposite sides, away from the supposedly trapped quartet of avengers, came the sound of steel wheels in roller tracks. Light shone through the opening doors. Moments later, the hard cases left by Heck Grange deserted their vantage points, which had suddenly become hot spots.

Quo Chung Wu soon became frustrated with his inability to close with the enemy enough to be effective. He turned to Brian Pullen. "How do you use one of those?" he asked, with a nod toward Brian's six-gun.

Brian gave it a moment's thought. "Best use one of these," he announced, giving a toss to his Parker and the net bag of brass cartridges. "Beginners do better with a shotgun."

Grinning, Quo hefted the weapon, shouldered it, and squeezed the trigger. Nothing happened. Brian shook his head in frustration. "You have to cock the hammer first. Then, when you've fired both barrels, open it with that lever between the barrels, take out the spent shells, and replace them with fresh."

"Oh, yes. I see. Thank you." Quo's first shot ground the shoulder of one hard case into gory hamburger. "I think I have it now," he called out cheerily.

"I suppose you do," Brian responded drily, as he watched the wounded thug stumble away.

Gunfire continued unabated from the other cars and from beyond the second siding, where the grade had been built up to keep the track level. It was from there that the charge came. Half a dozen gunmen rose up and rushed the idling train with six-guns blazing. Return fire was sporadic at best. Louis Longmont downed one hard case, then ducked low behind the steel wheels of the lead truck of one car to reload. The shotgun in the hands of Quo belched smoke and fire and another of Murchison's gang screamed his way to oblivion.

"One can apply the principles of *Chi* to shooting," Quo observed wonderingly.

That left four gunhawks. Smoke Jensen zeroed in on one and cut his legs out from under. With the enemy routed on one side, Smoke took quick stock.

"Get back on board," he commanded. He raised his voice to the engineer. "Get this thing moving!" He remained as a rear guard.

Quo seemed unhappy at having to give up on his newfound skill. He went up the ladder to the cab with agile speed, even with the shotgun in one hand.

Louis Longmont reduced the attacking force to half its original size before boarding the baggage car. The remaining trio faltered. At that moment, a burly figure stepped out of the depot, a smoking six-gun in one hand. "Which one of you is Smoke Jensen?"

Smoke answered quietly. "I am."

Eyes narrowed, Tyrone Beal took a menacing step toward the mountain man. "I want you, Jensen. I'm gonna take you down hard."

Smoke laughed. "Not likely."

"You've got a gun in your hand, Jensen. Use it."

For a moment, Smoke Jensen stared in disbelief at this cocky gunhawk. Confidence? Or was he completely loco? "If

I do, you'll die, whoever you are." Slowly and deliberately, he holstered his Colt.

"M'name's Tyrone Beal. I had a good thing goin' before you showed up. Now, I'm gonna make you pay for upsettin' my apple cart."

The more mouth a man used, the less shoot he had in him, Smoke Jensen had learned long ago from Preacher. He decided to goad this lippy one further. "Road apples, if you ask me."

Beal's face clouded. "C'mon, you loudmouthed bastid, make your play."

"You're too easy, Beal. I'd feel guilty about it. It would be like killing a kid."

Froth formed at the corners of Beal's mouth. The locomotive whistle gave a preliminary hoot and steam hissed into the driver pistons. The big drivers spun with a metallic screech. Tyrone Beal's eyes went wide and white a moment before he swung the muzzle of his six-gun up in line with the chest of Smoke Jensen. His thumb reached for the hammer.

Smoke Jensen whipped out the .45 Peacemaker and shot Tyrone Beal through the chest before the first click of Beal's sear notch sounded. Disbelief warred with agony on the face of Tyrone Beal. He made a small, tottery step toward Smoke Jensen, then abruptly sat on his rump.

"I'm kilt," he gasped. "Goddamn you . . . Smoke . . . Jensen!"

Then he died. Smoke quickly boarded the already moving train and settled down in the baggage car.

Rolling through the peaceful autumn countryside, Cyrus Murchison was almost able to forget he had been forced to flee an empire he believed to have firmly in his grasp. At least, he did until those meddling sons of mangy dogs interfered. Titus Hobson had told him that Smoke Jensen was a one-man army. Ruefully, he recalled that he had scoffed at that. He knew better now.

Louis Longmont, who was considered to be a dandy, a fop,

had proved far tougher than anticipated, also. How did a New Orleans gambler get to be so accomplished a shootist? If he moved in company like Smoke Jensen's, he must be one of the best gunmen in the country.

And that little snit Pullen. Until now, Brian Pullen had been the least-feared lawyer in San Francisco. Where did he learn to fight like that? Where did he learn to shoot?

The way the three of them had gone through the Tong gangs impressed Cyrus Murchison. For all his fine education and refined manners, he actually preferred using raw brute force to accomplish his goals. As a boy, he had dominated his friends, always been the one to decide what games they played. Later, when away from home at school, Cyrus had been fiercely competitive. He would brook not the slightest error in the work of his lab or his student engineering partners.

When at home during the summer, he worked with his father on the Union Pacific and frequently used his superior intellect, fast reactions, and utter fearlessness to knock resentful gandy dancers and other underlings into line. Yet here he sat, in his private car, running away from a fight. The mere thought of it infuriated him. A burning indignation rose within his chest and he decided to change his tactics.

At their last stop, a fragmentary message had caught up to him. It told enough. The men pursuing him had not been stopped at Parkerville. Beal had failed, and was dead in the bargain. Cyrus pounded a fist on the arm of his chair in frustration. From now on, Jensen and Longmont would have to pay for every inch of track they gained.

For the past hour, the commandeered train had been climbing a barely perceptible upgrade. The foothills of the Sierra Madre lay ahead. To keep up to the top speed safety would allow consumed far more fuel. The engineer conveyed that to Quo Chung Wu, who relayed the message via a pulley-and-rope device rigged between the baggage car and cab. Smoke

Jensen replied that the train was to stop at the next station and take on all the wood it could hold.

When the train with the four avengers aboard arrived at Grass Valley, all appeared peaceful and serene. Only the engineer recognized a familiar car on the end of a train on the main line, alongside the depot. Suddenly, a switch was thrown and their stolen train rolled onto a siding and all hell broke loose.

From the three parlor cars, a torrent of lead blasted toward the three-car train. After the first stunned moment, Smoke Jensen saw that none of the rounds seemed aimed at the stock car. Relieved for the safety of the horses, he concentrated on returning fire. At once a hard case in the window of a chair car went down behind a shower of shattered glass. Up ahead, Smoke caught a quick look at the switch. A red ball atop the upright told him the switch was set against them. Fully occupied with suppressing the volume of incoming rounds, he hadn't the time to scribble a message and send it to Quo. Fortunately, the thick, heavy desks used for sorting mail successfully absorbed the bullets flying through the doorway. It became a very dangerous waiting game.

When at last the baggage car of the slowing train rolled past the lead passenger car of the other train, Smoke seized the chance to write a brief note. *"Quo, send the switchman to throw the switch and let us through,"* it read. Smoke affixed it to the signal cord on the far side of the train and ran it forward. He did not expect a reply and did not get one. Meanwhile, the thugs in the other train were trashing the coach behind the baggage car. A shout came from two of them when they spotted the switchman headed forward to change the switch.

They fired in unison and their bullets struck the hapless man in the back. He jerked, spun, and fell in the ballast along the track. A sudden lull came in the firing and Smoke steeled himself for what he knew must come next. He alerted his companions.

* * *

Feeling quite smug, Cyrus Murchison ordered his henchmen out of the train to rush the one opposite on the siding. They ran forward eagerly, unaware of how well Smoke Jensen had instructed his three companions. With a shout, three of the hard cases rushed up to the grab-iron and ladder to the locomotive. They didn't know it at the time, but they were about to get a lesson in the etiquette of boarding a train unwelcomed.

First to reach the ladder, one thug clambered toward the cab, shouting an order for the engineer and fireman to go down the other side. For his efforts, he received a foot in the face that broke his nose and jaw. He flew off the iron rungs with a strangled cry. He hit in the gravel and cinders of the track ballast a moaning, bloodied wreck. Those with him hesitated only a second.

Six-guns crashed and bullets spanged off the metal walls and roof of the cab. Their momentary delay had given Quo time to dodge below the protecting wall of metal beside the cringing engineer. Quo looked at the terrified railroad employee with disdain. If one could not conquer fear, one could never fully know oneself. Outside, the situation quickly changed.

Covered by fire from both, one of the remaining hard cases climbed the ladder. The hand holding his six-gun came above the steel plates of the cab flooring first. Quo saw it and shifted position. When a hatless head slid up next, Quo set himself and aimed a deadly, full-thrust kick. Bushy brows followed and Quo let fly.

His training-hardened sole crashed into the exposed forehead and snapped the skull backward with such force that Quo could clearly hear the snap of vertebra. Not a sound came from the thug as he fell, twitching, to his death, his neck broken. That convinced his companion, who headed in the opposite direction. A shotgun roared from the open doorway of the

baggage car and a swath of buckshot swept the fleeing hoodlum off his feet.

A rifle and six-gun took up the defense and a withering
fire came from the riddled car that rapidly thinned the ranks.
It slowed, then halted the advance. From their exposed position, most of the hard cases saw no advantage in rushing men
barricaded behind thick counters. Several made to withdraw.
A sudden ragged volley came from both sides of the track that
slashed into the armed longshoremen and railroad police
caught between the trains.

"What the hell is this?" Cyrus Murchison bellowed at the
sight of his henchmen retreating toward the train.

Titus Hobson peered from the window, the red velvet curtain
held aside in his rough hand. "It appears to me your local
farmers and merchants have failed to be cowed by the thugs
you sent out here, Cyrus," he replied sarcastically.

A bullet hole appeared noisily in the window out of which
Gaylord Huntley gazed. He yelped and flopped on the floor.
Cyrus Murchison cast a worried glance his direction.

"Are you injured, Gaylord?"

"N-No, but it was a close call. Let's get the hell out of
here."

Cyrus Murchison cut his eyes to Heck Grange. "Get those
men back on board."

Reluctantly, then, he reached for the signal cord after
Grange left for the observation platform. Three mournful hoots
came in reply from the distant locomotive and steam hissed
from all the relief valves. Slowly the pistons began to shove
against the walking beams. The big drivers rolled forward,
spun, and regained purchase. A moment later, the creak, groan,
and jolt of the cars elongating trembled through the train. Ponderously, it began to move forward.

Only then did an expression of abject relief cross the face
of Gaylord Huntley. Some of the color returned to the features
of Titus Hobson, who reached for the brandy decanter with

trembling fingers. Cyrus Murchison covered his face with an unsteady paw and repeated the dying words of Tyrone Beal.

"Goddamn you . . . Smoke . . . Jensen!"

Agatha Murchison read with horror the bold, black headline of the afternoon *Chronicle.* Her heart fluttered in her breast.

RAILROAD POLICE AND TONGS FIGHT IT OUT!

Was this the problem that had taken Cyrus from home and office? If his police minions had clashed with those heathen Chinese, his life must be in danger. Tears stung Agatha's eyes. She did not want to read further, but she knew she must.

Late last night, elements of the California Central Railroad police clashed with members of the secret societies of Chinatown, variously called the Tongs or Triad Society. Much bloodshed resulted. More than twenty men died in the conflict, with a hundred more injured. Listed among the dead was an ominous figure known as Xiang Wai Lee, reputed Triad Society leader. When the smoke cleared, no sign could be found of the railroad police or of the sinister foreign gangsters of the Tongs.

Attempts early this morning by the *Chronicle* to contact Chief Hector Grange of the Central California Police elicited the information that the chief was not available. Likewise, attempts to reach Cyrus Murchison, President of the California Central Railroad proved fruitless. Sources in the railroad offices stated that Mr. Murchison had left the city on business and was not expected back for several days. Our Chinatown contacts responded with terse replies of "No comment." The *Chronicle*'s Chinatown reporter, Robert Gee, informed us that a sect of Buddhist priests were also attacked by the Tongs. We have often spoken out against vigilantism in our fair city, and this time is no exception. However, until we learn the motivation behind this most recent outbreak of citizen violence, we must reserve judgment.

Yet duty clearly calls for this newspaper to demand an investigation . . .

Agatha laid aside the fiery words of the editorializing journalist and swallowed to banish the tightness in her throat. Something became undeniably clear to her sharp mind: if whatever had compelled Cyrus to order his police into Chinatown had been a legitimate reason, he would have had no reason to go into hiding. Unless, of course, there had been some—some—She could not use the word "criminal." Had there been something unlawful about the association of her husband with those Chinese? Suddenly she went cold and still.

Hadn't that one in the article, that Xiang Wai Lee, been right in this very house not long ago? Slowly she lowered her head and covered her face with hands that trembled. Hadn't he?

When Murchison's train began slowly to gain momentum, Smoke Jensen climbed from the baggage car and waved his thanks to the local citizens. They cheered him and a few fired parting shots at the fleeing moguls. Smoke took his hat from his head and waved it to quiet the local vigilantes.

"If that fight didn't give you a bellyful, we could use some help. Anyone who wants to come along, put your mount on board and take a seat in that parlor car."

More cheers answered him, and men headed for their horses. Smoke went forward and swung up into the cab. His stern, powder-grimed face struck pure terror in the heart of the engineer, not a man to show yellow before anyone. But with the muzzle of Smoke Jensen's Peacemaker jammed against his head, he decided now would not be the time to show undue bravado.

"I want you to explain to my friend here how to throw that

switch when that train clears it. Don't steer him wrong, or you'll answer to me."

"I won't, Mister. I surely won't." At once he began to outline the steps to activate the switch.

Quo Chung Wu listened intently, then dismounted and ran forward. By then, Murchison's 'special' had cleared the switch. Looking down, Quo located the lever that swung the hinged tracks to give the siding access to the main line. Only minutes separated the two trains, and every second counted. Quo raised the arm into the position described and heaved on it.

Total resistance. The wrong way. Sweating, Quo reversed his stance and pushed. With a metallic creak, the steel rails swung away from the closed position and rode across the space between tracks. When the thin end of the right-hand rail mated to the inside edge of the main line track. Behind him, he heard the locomotive gather itself to rush forward.

He stood upright and gave a friendly wave. Then, fists on hips, he waited for the stolen train to come to him. More time was lost to allow horses and volunteers to board. Then Quo stepped beside to allow the locomotive to rumble past. When the grab iron came next to him, he reached out and swung aboard with all the ease of one who had had years of practice. He was surprised to see that Smoke Jensen had gone back to the bullet-riddled baggage car. Flame leaped from the open door of the firebox and Quo gave it a satisfied smile. They would catch up soon.

Speed came on the runaway as it rattled through and beyond the switch. Behind it, in the bay window section of the depot, the telegrapher frantically worked his key. The dots and dashes of Morse code sped down the line with the speed of an electric spark. Tersely, he advised stations to the east of two extras, one a stolen runaway, hurtling in their direction. Abruptly, he looked up when his sounder took on that flat buzz that came from talking to no one.

His eyes narrowed as he saw a local merchant shinny down

a telegraph pole. The line sagged to the ground in both directions from the cross arm. "Thunderation, Hiram, why in hell
did you do that?" he roared his frustration.

Hiram made an obscene gesture. "We're tired of takin' hind
tit to the likes of Cyrus Murchison. I tell you, he's up to somethin' no good, Rupe. I seed the flash of a marshal's badge on
one o' them fellers shootin' at his train. A U. S. marshal's
badge."

For the first time since he had gone to work for the railroad
at the age of twelve, Rupe gave serious thought to ending his
career.

SIXTEEN

Gaylord Huntley looked apprehensively back along the track. Greasy sweat popped out on his forehead. "By God, they're gainin' on us."

"We've still have them outgunned," Cyrus Murchison responded, with a tone of indifference he certainly did not feel.

"I don't think so anymore," Heck Grange injected. "I saw some of those local bumpkins jump on board back there."

"Well, Zach Bourchard is a trustworthy man. He'll send word along the line. Up ahead there's a siding just beyond a wide curve. When we reach it, we'll pull onto it and throw the switch against them. I don't like wrecking a locomotive, but I'll do it if it stops those damnable gunfighters."

"Sort of costly, isn't it?" Titus Hobson suggested.

Cyrus Murchison revealed his anxiety in a flash. His fist pounded the edge of his desk. "Damn the expense! These men are not dolts. That they are on the verge of ruining us right now should prove it." His eyes narrowed. "We could still lose it all, gentlemen. I have an idea. I own this fine long-range hunting rifle. It has a telescope on it. You are such an excellent shot, Gaylord, what say you stop worrying and make yourself useful? See if you can pick off the engineer of that train."

Huntley pulled a droll expression. "I thought you just finished praising his loyalty?"

Impatience at such dullness flashed on Murchison's face. "I was talking about the station master at Grass Valley. Although you have to admit, I have a point about Terry O'Brian, the engineer. Otherwise, he would not be running that locomotive, would he?"

Doubt in his face, Gaylord Huntley turned away from his vigil and reached for the rifle. He pushed in the loading gate cover and checked that a round was ready to chamber. With care he raised the muzzle to the ceiling and turned back to the platform door. His shoulders, slumped in resignation, more noticeable than his words, he opened the door and walked out on the observation deck. He knelt and brought the rifle to his shoulder.

Carefully he eased the eyepiece closer and established a field. The sway of the train made it difficult to settle the cross-hairs on the head and left shoulder of the engineer. Satisfied, Huntley worked the lever action and chambered a long, fat .45-70-500 Express round. Then he returned to his study of the target.

Steady . . . steady . . . lower now . . . easy . . . Damn it! The train lurched violently and destroyed his aim. Gaylord Huntley eased off the telescope and let the bright spot fade in his right eye. Try again. Lord, that loco must be a thousand yards off. He fined his sight picture, elevated the muzzle, and squeezed off.

The powerful Winchester Express slammed into his shoulder. A second later he saw the flash of a spark as the bullet whanged off the face plate of the cab a foot above the open window. A quick glimpse through the scope revealed that the engineer had not even flinched. Quickly he ejected the spent cartridge and chambered another.

His second shot screamed along the outside of the boiler and burst into a shower of lead fragments when it hit the thick iron plate of the cab face. Quickly he reloaded. The third round went two feet wide of the cab when the private car hurtled sharply to the left as the speeding train swung into a curve. Gaylord did some quick mental arithmetic. Four rounds left. He rose from his cramped pose and eased his numb legs.

When he returned to his position, he quickly expended two more bullets. They did no more good than the other three. Time to reload, he figured. He'd fire one more round first. A wild lurch of the car sent his bullet high; had he been on board the pursuing locomotive, he'd have heard the bell halfway down the boiler clang with a fractured tone.

Back in the plush interior of Murchison's private car, Huntley went to the gun cabinet and located and shoved fresh cartridges into the Winchester. He ran a nervous hand through his oily black hair and worked his foreshortened upper lip over his rodent-like teeth. Huntley knew what he needed and went directly to it.

Three fingers of brandy warmed the cold specter of defeat in his gut and spread calm through his limbs. Thus fortified, he returned to the observation platform and knelt to steady his aim. Huntley failed to notice that in his absence, someone else had entered the cab of the locomotive behind them. He also did not observe that the newcomer held a Winchester Express like his own.

Huntley took aim and took up the slack in the trigger. Then, through the circular rescale of the telescopic sight, he saw a lance of flame and a curl of smoke. A split second later, hot lead spanged against the brass cap of the platform rail and showered shards of metal into the face of Gaylord Huntley. Sharp pains radiated from the wounds and he screamed in horror as he felt a sliver pierce his exposed eye.

Reflexively he dropped the rifle and fell backward onto his butt. Beyond the rail, his tearing eyes took in another flash. Terrible pain erupted in his chest and he was flung backward against the doorjamb. Gaylord Huntley's mouth sagged and darkness swarmed over him. Beyond him in the parlor section, unaware of what had happened, Cyrus Murchison froze, half out of his chair, hands flat on the desk, eyes bugged, as he stared in confused astonishment at the body of his former associate.

Smoke Jensen lowered the Winchester Express from his shoulder when he saw the body of Gaylord Huntley sprawl backward in his death throes. One less, he thought grimly. The chase continued, though the gap had rapidly closed. Hauling more cars, the lead locomotive could not maintain its distance advantage for long. At the suggestion of the suddenly and surprisingly cooperative engineer, the whistle shrilled constantly, a tactic that

Smoke Jensen thought would unnerve those they pursued. Torn snatches of answering screams came from sidetracked west-bound trains as the two locomotives ran headlong through the foothills of the Sierra Nevada mountains. Train crews stared after them with eyes wide and mouths agape. Tediously, the distance shortened to half the original 1000 yards.

From there on, time was suspended as the trailing locomotive rushed toward the private car of Cyrus Murchison. Smoke judged it time to put his rough plan in motion. He left the baggage car to talk to the volunteers in the chair coach behind. The two dozen of farmers and townies who had jumped aboard Smoke's commandeered train gathered around at his summons. He eyed them with concentration.

"Now, this is going to be tricky. None of you are required to do what I'm going to ask. First off, I want to know how many among you consider yourselves surefooted."

Nearly all hands went up. Smoke suppressed a smile and nodded. "Take a look outside and forward." By turns they went to the open windows and did so. Several recoiled from the blast of wind created by their swift passage. "See that catwalk along the boiler? How many of you surefooted ones think you can walk that while the train is moving?"

Not so many hands went up this time. Smoke considered that with himself and Louis, and six of these willing volunteers, they could carry off his plan. It didn't matter to him what happened to the rest of the train. What they needed to do was isolate the rear car containing Murchison and Hobson. Now for the tricky part.

"That's good. We need six men to come with Louis and me. What we are going to try to do is close in and ram that observation car. The idea is to derail it." Startled expressions broke out among the plain country folk facing Smoke Jensen. "Failing that, those of you who come with us are to be ready to advance along the catwalks on both sides of the locomotive and board the other train while we are in motion."

"That sounds a tall order, Mister," a farmer with sun-reddened face observed.

"Yeah," a pimply store clerk picked it up. "Why should we take such a risk for you? Besides, who are you, anyway?"

"Folks call me Smoke Jensen."

Color drained from the lippy clerk's face. "Oh, Jesus. I've heard of you. Read all about you in them Ned Buntline books."

Smoke gave him a hard, straight face. "Buntline lies. I've never shot a man in the back who hadn't turned it after I squeezed the trigger."

Eyes widened, the clerk gulped, "You've read all them dime novels?"

"A fellah needs to know what others are sayin' about him," Smoke said simply. "Now, like I say, do you think you can walk that narrow track and jump, if need be?"

Seven responded in the affirmative. "Better than I expected," Louis Longmont stated drily.

Smoke let the other shoe drop. "Remember, there are still a lot of hard cases aboard that train. If we don't isolate the rear car, the fighting will be rough."

Only one of the hands went down. "All right," Smoke announced. "I'll lead you. Louis here will give you the word when the time is right."

Terence O'Brian did not mind shattering the nerves of those they pursued. Besides, he reasoned, it gave them more of a chance by warning approaching trains onto sidings. When he heard the blathering of that crazy man he knew the boy-o had slipped a cog somewhere. Jumping from one train to another? Pure madness. When the tough-faced gilly ordered the throttle opened to full again, he said, as much.

"That's a lunatic idea if I ever heard one. Why, at the speed we're goin', we could ram that train ahead of us." Smoke Jensen's reply left him thunder blasted.

"Exactly what I had in mind."

"Not with my beautiful baby, ye won't," Terry O'Brian blurted in indignation. "Ye'll derail us both!"

Smoke Jensen pulled an amused face. "The thought occurred to me. Only, I want you to just knock them off the track, not us."

Gloved hand on hip, O'Brian snapped his defiance. "Can't be done. We hit them hard enough to derail that heavy car, we go off, too."

Smoke though a moment. "You're the engineer. If you say that's the case, I'll believe you. Can you do this? Get us close enough that men can jump from the front of this locomotive to the rear car of that train?"

"Sure. Easy. If anyone is crazy enough to try makin' the leap. Thing is, I don't want to ram them."

"I understand. Only, give it a try and see what we can do."

"You're stark ravin' crazy, ye are," O'Brian offered his opinion again. Then, in exasperation, he put hand to throttle and shoved it forward.

It took a while for the big drivers to respond. With the rush of steam, they spun free of traction for a moment, then O'Brian added sand and the engine leaped forward. The gap quickly closed. At two hundred yards, four men appeared on the top of the private car. Two took up sitting positions, while one knelt and the other flattened out prone. Smoke took note of it and hefted his Express rifle.

Aiming through the forward window, opposite the engineer, Smoke squeezed off a round. One of the seated hard cases reared backward, fell to one side, and rolled off the car. The others opened fire.

"Get down!" Smoke shouted to O'Brian. "Not you," he barked at the fireman. "Keep stoking that boiler."

Bullets spanged off the metal plates of the locomotive. Smoke hunkered down and took aim again. The Winchester bucked and another thug sprang backward from his kneeling position and sprawled flat on the walkway atop Murchison's car. A slug cracked past Smoke's left ear and he reflexively jerked his head to the side. Damn, they have some good shots over there, Smoke thought. Not the time to ease up.

He fired again. As the hammer fell, the private car swayed to the left and their locomotive jinked right. Smoke's bullet sped through empty air. He cycled a fresh cartridge into the chamber. When the careening rolling stock settled down, he drew a bead on the chubby gunhand lying on his belly.

At the bullet's impact, the fat hard case jerked upward and flopped back down, shot though the top of his head. *Not bad,* Smoke judged his performance. At the last moment, before Smoke could sight in on him, the fourth of Murchison's gunmen gave it up and ran for the safety of the car ahead. Smoke held his fire as the thug's head disappeared below the lip of the roof overhang. Time to get ready, he decided, and turned away.

When he returned to the cab, the distance had narrowed to less than a hundred feet. Gingerly, O'Brian brought his behemoth up to within twenty feet, his hand playing the throttle like an organist at a mighty pipe organ console. Smoke gave him the nod. Swallowing against the lump of fear in his throat, the engineer opened the throttle again and the big Baldwin 4-6-2 sped into the rear of the Pullman-manufactured private car.

Violent impact knocked many of the volunteers off their feet. One clung desperately to the grab-rail to keep from falling down among the spinning drivers. Smoke staggered as the two vehicles slammed together. With a terrible screech, the observation platform rail sheered off and went flying to the sides of the track.

Murchison's car jolted forcefully and the rear truck raised, then slammed back. Unasked, O'Brian eased back. The blunt nose of the locomotive withdrew from its menace over the beleaguered carriage and held steady, three yards off the shattered rear platform. Terence O'Brian looked pleadingly at Smoke Jensen. Smoke nodded to him.

"Bring it in as close as possible. We'll jump."

Cyrus Murchison could not believe what he saw through the open door at the rear of his private car. Beyond the gap between it and the chase train, men stood on both sides of the locomotive boiler, slowly advancing to the nose of the steaming monster. He had been knocked out of his chair by the collision. At first he could not figure out what these lunatics had in mind. Then the reality struck him.

They intended to jump from the speeding locomotive to his car! If they made it, it would be all over, he thought in a panic. He waved to a slowly recovering Heck Grange. "Got to get some of the men in here. Those crazy bastards are coming after us."

"How?" Heck demanded.

"They are going to jump over here, you idiot. Now, do as I say. Get a dozen, no, twenty guns in here right now."

Heck started for the front door of the car. He worked the latch handle and passed through at an uneven gait. Wobbling on unsteady legs, Grange pushed into the next car. Concerned faces looked up. He stared them down, swaying with the roll of the car, one hand on the butt of his six-gun.

"We're in for it, boys. Jensen's comin' after us. Gonna jump from train to train. The boss wants twenty of you in his car right now."

"Hell, Chief, we can't get twenty men in there. Maybe eight or ten. Even then, we'd be crammed so close it would be like shootin' fish in a stock tank."

"I know that, Miller. Best thing is to be ready on the vestibule, in case those gunhawks get through. Mr. Murchison will never know if there's twenty or five in there. Now, let's get going."

Smoke Jensen looked down at the dizzying blur of ballast and cross-ties in the space between the cowcatcher of the Baldwin loco and the rocking platform ahead. He swallowed to regain his equilibrium, flexed his knees, and prepared to spring. Behind him he heard a voice raised in sincere prayer.

". . . *Holy Mary, mother of God, pray for us sinners, now and at the hour of our death . . .*"

Well, that might be right now, the last mountain man considered. What he proposed to do, what they were about to do, could easily be considered suicidal. One or all of them could be dead within the next two minutes. The rail-like bars of the cowcatcher inched closer, closer. Another foot. Two feet. Smoke Jensen reached forward with his gloved hands. Smoke took his mind off the rush of death below and sucked in a breath.

Jump! Smoke left his insecure perch and sailed over the gap between the two trains. He seemed to pause in the middle, while the gap widened. A moment later the Baldwin surged forward and Smoke hit the platform on hands and knees. He landed solidly, thankful for the gloves he wore. A burly farmer crashed to the platform beside him. Smoke looked up to see the car interior was empty.

He came to his feet as two more men landed on the observation deck. A moment later, the door at the far end flew open. Five men poured in. Smoke filled his hand with a .45 Colt and set it to barking. Crystal shattered and tinkled down on the expensive Oriental carpets that covered the floor. The hard case in the lead jerked and spilled on his face in the narrow passage that paralleled the bedrooms. The man behind him threw a wild shot and tripped over the supine corpse.

More glass shattered, this time an etched panel between the dining room and the parlor area. Smoke sidestepped and a shotgun behind him roared. Two thugs screamed and slapped at invisible wasps that stung them with buckshot fury. More gunhands pushed through the vestibule door. By now, four of the volunteers had gained the hurtling lead train.

Louis Longmont appeared at Smoke Jensen's side. "The last two are on their way."

"Good. No chance to secure that door now. No reason, really. Murchison and Hobson got away."

"They can't go far," Louis stated the obvious.

With the arrival of the last volunteers, the volume of fire became too much for the armed ruffians. Their ranks devastated, they chose to withdraw from the hail of lead that cut them down mercilessly. Smoke Jensen's last slug slammed into the thick wooden door of the private car. A muffled howl of pain came from the other side.

"Not as sturdy as I thought," Smoke said lightly to Louis. "I say we go ahead."

Louis cocked an eyebrow. "They will be waiting for us."

Smoke grinned. "Yep. I know. That's why I brought these."

From the pocket of his vest, Smoke produced half a dozen bright red packets, covered and sealed with tin foil.

"What arc thosc?" Louis askcd.

"Railroad torpedoes," Smoke explained. "I picked them up from the utility box in the cab of the other train."

Louis still did not follow. "What do you do with those?"

Smoke showed mischief in his twinkling gray eyes. "We have one of these fine gentlemen toss them through the far door, one at a time, and shoot them like clay pigeons.

"What good will that do, *mon ami?*"

"They make a hell of a bang. Enough explosive to jar the lead truck of a locomotive and be heard over the noise of the engine."

"Powerful. What gave you the idea?"

"I learned about these torpedoes when I worked for the D&RG. When a train breaks down on the main line and there is no siding, a trackwalker goes back half a mile and lays out a series of torpedoes. The number of bangs tells the engineer what is wrong and prepares him to slow and stop his train. In the construction camp we used to shoot them for sport, so I know it will work."

A sardonic smile turned down the lips of Louis Longmont. "Then, by all means, let us get to it, my friend."

Smoke turned to the volunteers. "Any of you good at Abner Doubleday's game of baseball?" Three of the Valley men nodded their heads. "One of you consider yourself a good hurler?"

"Ay bin fairly good, Mr. Yensen," a cotton-haired Swede declared with suppressed pride.

"Olie's right," one of his companions offered. "He's hell at the pitch."

Smoke smiled. "Good, then. Here, I want you to take these," he began, explaining his plan to the Swede pitcher.

Two minutes later, Smoke, Louis, and Olie crossed the gap between vestibules and got ready. Louis yanked open the door. Olie gave a slow underhand pitch that sailed one of the red torpedoes down the aisle, flat side toward the door. Smoke brought up his .45 Colt before the startled hard cases could react, and fired.

A bright flash and shattering explosion followed. Glass rang musically as windows blew out all along the car. Men screamed and clutched their ears. At Smoke's nod, Olie pitched another one. One man, blood streaming from his nose, leaped from his seat and stumbled down the passage toward the far end of the coach. A strong odor of kerosene rose from pools under the broken lamps. Smoke signaled for another.

With an expression of awe on his broad face, Olie flung another torpedo. A weakened portion of the sidewall, complete with blown-out window sash, ripped away from the side of the car. It whipped off along the rushing train. The gunhands who remained conscious could stand it no longer. Pandemonium broke out as they surged toward the next car forward.

Smoke signaled to the waiting volunteers and led the way after the fleeing enemy. He skidded to a stop and jumped to one side when a torrent of bullets ripped through the facing wall and the door. Tinted-edged glass shattered in the upper panel of the door and one clipped the shoulder of a farmer from the Central Valley.

"Ow, damn them," he complained. "Toss in some o' them bombs, Olie."

Smoke gave the nod and Olie complied. The first one went off before Smoke could fire. The startled gunhand who had shot it gaped in disbelief. Olie recovered instantly and hurled another. Smoke blasted it a third of the way down the car. Windowpanes disappeared. Men groaned and cursed. Powder smoke filled the afternoon air. Sunlight filtered through the billows of dust and burnt explosive in sickly orange shafts. Another torpedo put the defenders in panic.

They raced off to find security in the next car. Smoke watched as the last man through the entry paused to throw the lock. He cut his eyes to Louis.

"We're going to have to do this the hard way," Smoke stated flatly, as he paused to reload. The vision haunted him. Someone among his volunteers would die before this was over.

SEVENTEEN

Smoke Jensen stationed three men at the vestibule door, to keep the attention of the hard cases beyond. Then he and Louis led the others to the rear of that car and out onto the narrow platform. He pointed to a set of iron rungs which led to the roof. With difficulty they climbed the ladder, fighting against the jerk and sway of the careening train.

On top of the car, Smoke went forward with the volunteers following. Clouds had formed, Smoke noticed, as he worked his way toward the car-full of gunmen. A light misty rain fell, whipped into their faces by the rush of wind. The air smelled of woodsmoke, which gushed from the tall, grinder-fitted stack. It was filled with fine, gritty cinders and inky exhaust, which quickly blackened their faces and clothing. Footing became treacherous on the damp strips of wood that formed the walkway. When they reached the gap between cars, Smoke stopped to consider the alternatives.

Climb down, cross over and climb back up, or jump. He tested his boot soles against the wood to gauge the security of the roof walk. He took a quick, appraising glance at the strained faces behind him, then he moved back toward them, took three, quick, running steps, and jumped. At the last instant, his foot slipped.

Smoke hurtled in an awkward sprawl toward the forward chair car roof. The toe of his boot caught on the trailing lip of the walkway and sent him to his hands and knees. He hung there, painfully aware that he could have cost them the element of surprise. After two, long, worrisome minutes, he inched forward. Still challenging fire to come up through the roof, he paused again. Perhaps the idea did not occur to those below that they could penetrate the thin roof of the car. Smoke pressed himself up onto his boots and motioned for the others to follow.

To his relief, they made it without undue noise. When they had gathered as best they could, Smoke explained what he had in mind. "Spread out. We're going to fire at random through the roof. May not hit anyone, but it will stir them up some. The next coach is the smoking car. My bet is that Murchison and Hobson are in there. If we can rig the doors of the next car, jam them somehow, we can trap his gunmen there and go after the leaders with little risk."

"Sounds good," a thick-shouldered feed store owner judged.

"Then let's get to it," Smoke urged.

Smoke and Louis went forward and climbed down. Two volunteers went down the nearer ladder. Smoke used the coupler release bar to tightly jam the latch to the parlor car. To his disappointment, they could find nothing to do the same to the rear entrance to the smoking coach. Accepting the setback, they returned to the top. Seconds later, bullets punched through the roof to send showers of splinters and shards of the stamped tin ceiling down onto the unsuspecting gunhawks. Already demoralized by the exploding torpedoes, they made as one for the doors at each end. Slugs continued to snap and crack past them. More bullets smashed through the ceiling.

One man cried out in pain, shot through the top of his shoulder. His ragged breath and the pink froth on his lips told his companions the round had gone through his right lung from top to bottom. He wasn't long for this world. Another hard case uttered a groan and fell heavily to the floor. From ahead a shout of rage rang through the car when Murchison's gunsels found the latch somehow secured against them.

Shots sounded from within the car and shards of glass tinkled out onto the vestibule platform. Eager hands reached through to wrestle with the obstructing bar. After ample curses and some furious struggle, it came free. Men sprang instantly across to the smoking car. Smoke Jensen had no choice but to make the best of a failed plan. He prepared to lead the volunteers forward when a sudden jolt nearly knocked them all off their feet and over the side.

"Cut it loose! Cut it loose!" the familiar voice of Cyrus Murchison shouted from the open doorway to the smoking lounge.

Metal grated against metal, and with a lurch, the couplers opened and the front part of the train sped away from the rear portion, which began to lose forward momentum. Smoke cut his eyes behind them and saw the chase locomotive swelling rapidly in size.

"Get down and hold on!" he shouted.

Beyond Smoke, the second train plowed into the rear of the first. The force of the impact telescoped along the line of cars. The momentum drove the open couplers together, momentarily reattaching the last three cars. The men clinging to the catwalk bounced and whipped about like rag dolls in the hands of an angry child. With an explosive roar, steam exploded from the ruptured boiler of the trailing locomotive. The good and bad alike sprawled in the aisles. Men in the baggage car of the rear train slammed forward, tumbled over sorting tables and crashed into the front wall of the car. Worse was yet to come.

First, the private car of Cyrus Murchison left the rails, crumpling in on itself as it drove forward. The coach ahead teetered and began to lean to the left. It fell ponderously. Domino-like, the next chair car began to cant to one side. Only the remaining forward motion of the reconnected cars prevented total disaster. When the car under them began to waver, Smoke Jensen shouted to the men with him, "Get off of here. Jump to the right."

Unmindful of possible broken bones, the eight clinging men threw themselves away from the reeling car. The unsecured coupler twisted at the joint and separated. It let the car pitch over onto one side, to skid a distance before it came to rest at an acute angle. The eight wheels on the trucks spun as it lay in a cloud of dust. Beyond them, the train with Murchison aboard rolled serenely away. A man next to Smoke Jensen groaned.

"I think I broke my leg," he stated, his mind dulled by the sudden crisis.

"Hang on. I'll get you some help." Smoke looked beyond the billows of dirt and steam to see the occupants of the wounded locomotive leap clear to escape the explosion that would surely follow. With banshee screams, the 140 tons of iron and steel ground to a stop.

Smoke came to his boots to take stock of the disaster. He saw that the Baldwin had derailed on only one side, the lead truck of the tender dangling in empty space above the rails. Miraculously, the stock car had not jumped the track. Even more astonishing, the boiler did not explode. It hissed and belched steam, and remained intact. Gloved fists on hips, Smoke watched while Brian Pullen and the rest of the volunteers climbed shakily from the baggage car.

"What the hell happened?" Pullen asked, his tone of voice clearly conveying his disturbed condition.

Smoke's reply cut through the fog in Brian's mind. "Murchison cut the rear of the train loose. You ran into it."

Brian shook his head, as though to clear it of fog. "Well, hell's-fire, if that just don't beat all." Then he remembered the chase. "What happened to Murchison?"

"They went on. Let's get those horses out and head after them," Smoke urged. "Chances are we've lost them for now, but we can try."

Pullen took stock of the destruction all around them. "I'm not sure that's a good idea."

Cyrus Murchison, acting as conductor, signaled the engineer to slow the train when he observed the marker indicating a curve and a siding. A switchman dropped off the side and ran forward as the big 2-4-4-0 American Locomotive Works main liner slowed even more. He threw the switch and the bobtailed train rolled smoothly through the switch onto the siding.

"What are you doing?" Titus Hobson demanded.

"We do not know if the other locomotive derailed. In light of that, we cannot take the chance of remaining on this train." He turned to Heck Grange. "Off-load mounts for everyone remaining, with a spare, if possible. We'll go to Carson City by horseback."

Titus Hobson winced as he recalled how long it had been since he had sat astride a horse. The remaining—how many?— miles to Carson City would be sheer torture. His tightly squinched features reflected his thoughts. To his outrage, Cyrus Murchison read his opinion and laughed at him.

"Think of it as a pleasant outing in the bracing mountain air, Titus. Come, we'll sleep in tents, under the stars, feast on venison and bear, clear our lungs of the city's miasma, and commune with nature."

Hobson chose primness for his reply. "I hardly think this is a time for levity, Cyrus."

"Why not?" Murchison's face darkened with suspicion. "If you cannot laugh at adversity, you're doomed. Don't you know that?"

Hobson reacted from his fear-driven anger. "My God, you're priggish when you get philosophical, Cyrus."

Heck Grange's return took away a need for Cyrus Murchison to make a reply. "The horses are coming off now. We can leave in ten minutes."

"Good," Murchison snapped testily. "We may not have that much time."

"We're ten miles from where we cut loose those cars. With luck, them and their rolling stock are all busted up."

"You're right, Heck. Only we cannot rely on that."

Unaffected by the mindset of his boss, Heck came right back. "So? Even if they got out of that mess, it will take the better part of two hours to get here from there."

Murchison relented. "You're right, of course. See to everything, Heck. Be sure to off-load those chests from the baggage car."

Grange left to see to the task. Murchison set to work poking into the drawers and shelves of the smoking car. He retrieved two boxes of excellent hand-rolled cigars made in Havana, five bottles of brandy, tinned sardines, cheeses, and other delicacies. He stuffed all of it into a hinged-top box. The brandy he wrapped in bar towels. He looked up into the startled expression of Titus Hobson.

"No reason to deprive ourselves, is there, Titus? The amenities of life are what make us appreciate it."

"It will slow us down."

"No more than the tents and other supplies I had the forethought to put aboard. One more pannier on the back of a packhorse will not hinder our progress."

Titus Hobson looked at his partner with new eyes. "You anticipated this happening?"

Murchison made a deprecating gesture. "Nothing quite so drastic, old boy. But I did have grounds to suspect that all would not go smoothly. Come, we can make this small setback into a lark. How long has it been since you've been away from your wife's sharp tongue, and those cloying children?"

A wistful expression came onto Hobson's face. A man who had married late in life, he found his brood of five children, all under the age of thirteen, to be a burden he would prefer not to have to bear. And his wife had become more acid-tongued with the birth of each offspring—as though it was *his* fault she kept cropping a new brat. A tiny light began to glow in his mind. Perhaps this enforced separation would prove to be a boon.

"All right, Cyrus. I'll give you your due. This could turn out to be . . . interesting."

"Yes. But, only if we hurry. Jensen and Longmont are still back there."

Shaken, though essentially unharmed, the volunteers who had joined Smoke Jensen and Louis Longmont went quickly about saddling horses. They prowled through the kitchen of

Cyrus Murchison's ruined private car and provisioned themselves with a wide variety of expensive and exotic food. Smoke
gathered them when everything had been gotten into readiness.

"This is going to be rough. Those who have been injured
or wounded should head back. There's no telling how long we
will be on the trail."

"How far do you intend to go, Mr. Jensen?" a grizzled older
farmer asked.

"All the way to Carson City, if necessary."

The oldster shrugged. "Then I'd best go back with the rest.
My rhumatiz won't let me abide with damp ground and cold
nights for that long."

"Go ahead," Smoke prompted. "And no shame be on you.
The rest of us will start off along the tracks, see if we can
catch up to that train."

"We'll leave a few men behind, to delay them if they do
come," Murchison directed.

Heck Grange disagreed. "It will only waste lives needlessly.
Jensen's not dumb. He'll be lookin' for that. I reckon the place
to lay an ambush is up around Piney Creek, just ahead of the
upgrade into the Sierras."

Murchison considered that. He accepted that Heck Grange,
with his war experiences with the Union Army had a better
grasp of tactics than himself. Yet he was loath to appear to
not be entirely in charge. Now was not the time for vanity,
Cyrus reminded himself

"All right, let's do it that way."

They rode for two hours. Bluejays and woodpeckers flitted
from tree to tree, scolding the interlopers with shrill squawks.
Squirrels took up the protest in wild chatter. A bad moment
developed when a fat, old, near-sighted skunk waddled out
onto the trail and set the nearest horses into a panic. For men
accustomed to walking or riding everywhere in wheeled vehicles, it took some doing to bring the beasts under control. At
last, Heck Grange was compelled to shoot the skunk.

That caused more trouble as its scent glands voided. An almost visible miasma fogged over the trail, contaminating the clothing of one and sundry among the collection of thugs, riffraff, and hard cases. Curses turned the air blue and fifteen minutes were lost trying to gain the upper hand over wall-eyed horses and red-faced, tear-streaked men. A halt resulted to allow everyone to wash off the strident effluvium from Mr. Skunk.

Back in the saddle, Murchison's henchmen grumbled among themselves. The majority were city-bred and -raised. The skunk unsettled them. What more, and worse, might be out there? The grade steepened and even this complaining died out. At three o'clock the big party reached the banks of Piney Creek.

Cyrus Murchison had Heck Grange toll off nine men to set up an ambush in the rocks and cluster of willows that lined the stream bed. None of the hard cases liked being left behind, yet the possibility of ending their ongoing problem appealed to most. They dug in, arranging stones and making dirt parapets in front of scooped-out hollows in the creek bank. When all met the approval of Heck Grange, he reported to Murchison.

"We're ready. Might as well head out."

"You've done a fine job, Heck. This should rid us of Jensen and Longmont. I'll sleep better tonight knowing that."

The rumble of departing hoofbeats had barely faded out when the first uncertainties arose over the idea of the ambush. "I hear there are bears around here, Harvey," one slightly built, long-necked thug remarked to a companion who had also been left behind at the ambush site.

"Don't think so, Caleb," the other railroad cop said around a stalk of rye grass. Unlike the skinny one, who worked as a clerk in the California Central police office, he had a barrel chest, thick, corded muscles in arms and legs, and a flat belly ridged with more brawn. "They keep to the high country up in the Snowy Mountains," he added, using a rough English translation of the Spanish, "Sierra Nevada."

When the Spanish first came to California, the mountain

peaks to the east had worn a constant mantle of snow, hence the name "Sierra Nevada." In the three centuries since they had first sighted those awesome ramparts, the climate had altered enough that only the highest remained white all year. It had not done the Donner Party much good, because the snows in even the lower passes began early. The big railroad bull's assurance about bears did ease the worries of his friend. Perhaps it should not have.

Smoke Jensen kept pushing the volunteers. At his own insistence, Louis Longmont rode the drag to make certain they hadn't any stragglers. The afternoon seemed to have too few hours in it. Long red shafts of sunlight slanted through the broken overcast to warn of approaching evening. Smoke wanted to get as far along the trail as possible.

He had not had any difficulty finding signs of what direction the fleeing men had taken. Heavy-laden packhorses had left deep gouges in the soft soil of the gentle slopes, and it seemed the inexperienced riders could not keep their mounts in a single file. Within ten minutes of reaching the abandoned train, Smoke had an accurate count of the numbers they faced. It was more than he would have liked, yet far less than had started out. Now he gave consideration to the twenty-five riders and the possibility someone in charge might consider an ambush.

"We'll stop here for a while," Smoke announced, his decision made. "That map I found shows Piney Creek not far from here. The stream runs through the easiest pass leading to the high country." Smoke's eyes twinkled with suspicion. "The creek would also make a good place for an ambush."

"You are going to scout it out, I assume," Louis offered.

"That I am, my friend. You are welcome to come along."

Louis did not hesitate. "Perhaps next time."

Smoke chuckled. "I'll remember that."

"I'll see to making camp. No fires, I assume?"

"No, Louis. They are running from us. I doubt they'll turn

back and attack. A cold camp won't make our friends very happy. It'll give them a chance to cook some of those fancy victuals they took from Murchison's private larder."

Five minutes later, he rode out in a circuitous route that would take him up on the blind side of Piney Creek.

Caleb Varner cut his eyes away from the distant glow of campfires to gaze pointedly at Harvey Moran. "They ain't comin', Harvey."

Harvey let his gaze wander away from the face of his companion, to stare at where the burble of water over stones located Piney Creek. "At least, not tonight, I'd wager."

Caleb looked ghastly in the sickly light of the high-altitude twilight. "That means we have to spend the night here?"

"Sure does."

"But there's bears, Harvey."

"Dang it now, Caleb, I've done told you there are no bears anywhere around here."

Caleb considered that and found a new horror. "What about timber rattlers? I hear they like to crawl right inside a feller's bedroll with him to keep warm."

Harvey did not feel like playing this game. "String a rope around your sleepin' place. Snake won't cross a rope. Thinks it's a brother."

"Really? I don't know."

"Shut up, you two," another ambusher called harshly. "Can't a man grab a snooze in peace? What with the two of you flappin' yer jaws, ain't nobody gonna get any rest tonight."

"Don't you have first watch?" Harvey challenged. "Got no business sleepin' if you do." That should hold him, Harvey thought.

Unseen by any of the neophyte woodsmen, Smoke Jensen slipped away from the camp set up by those manning the ambush. He moved soundlessly through the underbrush with a big smirk on his face. He knew what he could do now. When he reached the ancient Sequoia where he had ground anchored his horse, he reached into one saddlebag. He rummaged around for a moment and came out with what he wanted.

Simple in construction, the first item had come from a friendly Cheyenne youngster he had often taken fishing. The boy had made it himself and proudly gave it to Smoke. It consisted of a gourd on a thin oak stick. Inside were polished pebbles. When shaken just right, it sounded like the grandfather of all rattlesnakes. The second object came from Smoke's past.

Preacher had helped him make it, on a lark, one deep, frigid winter night when they had had nothing else to do. It was a boxlike affair, with a hollowed reed for a mouthpiece. Inside Preacher had fastened an assortment of gut and sinew strings of varying length and thickness. By changes of intensity in breath and a hand waved over the open end, it could be made to produce a remarkably realistic sound. With nothing to do for several hours, Smoke waited calmly beside his 'Palouse stallion.

At near on midnight, Smoke Jensen roused himself. He dusted off his trousers and set out for the camp. When he settled on a position upstream from the enemy site, he eased back against a large granite boulder and gave his thoughts to being a giant timber rattler.

"B'zzzziiiiit! B'zzzzzzziiiiiit! B'zzzzziit!"

Smoke went still while the voices came to him from the darkness. "M'God, Harvey, you hear that?"

"Hush up, Caleb," came a muzzy reply. Then, head clearing, Harvey asked, "Hear what?"

"I heard a rattler. A *big* rattlesnake."

"Horse pucky. Ain't no snakes around here," Harvey grumbled, his patience with this tenderfoot near an end.

"B'zzzzziiiiiit!"

"Awh . . . shit," Harvey grunted out.

Blankets rustled in the darkness. "I'm gettin' outta here, Harvey. That thing sounds big enough to eat us whole."

"Where you gonna go in the dark, Caleb?"

"I dunno. Somewhere, anywhere there ain't any rattlers."

"Git in a tree. Snakes can't climb, yu'know," Harvey said calmly, trying not to let his own worry show.

A moment later, a heavy snuffling came from downwind. Even Harvey froze at that. He counted heartbeats between it and the next time. Louder now, the snuffle had a low snarl mixed in. Another pause, then the crash of brush sounded near the edge of the campsite. The full-throated roar of an enraged bear split the silence that followed.

"Oh, Jesus! *It's a bear!*" Caleb wailed. A warm wetness spread from his groin.

"Emory, Emory, do somethin' for chrissakes!" a thoroughly shaken Harvey cried.

Emory and Harvey opened fire at the same time. The grizzly roared again and charged.

EIGHTEEN

Smoke Jensen shoved on the huge boulder and sent it thundering downhill through the underbrush. Immediately he dived behind a larger slab of granite. He made it with scant seconds to spare. Six-guns roared and a Winchester cracked in the camp below. The mammoth stone careened forward on a zigzag course and splashed turbulently into Piney Creek.

A regular battlefield of gunshots boomed off the hillsides. Muzzle flashes reflected off the undersides of pine boughs. Lead cracked and whined through the air. Shouts of fright and confusion rose in a mad babble. Unable to contain his glee over the success of his toys, Smoke Jensen grinned like a kid in a vacant candy store.

Then Emory Yates spoiled it all. "Stop it! Stop it! Quit shooting at nothing, you idiots. There ain't no bear!" Slowly the discharge of weapons ceased. Emory immediately jumped on the men he led. "Don't you ever use your heads? They could hear you all the way to Parkerville. Do you think those gunfighters we're supposed to ambush can't hear? They all deef?"

He slammed his hat on the ground in disgust. "We ain't gonna surprise nobody after that dumb-ass stunt. Shootin' at shadows and funny noises."

Before he could say more, the hairs on the back of his neck rose as the awesome growl of the bear came again. "Jeeezus! First light, we're gonna pull out of here. Can't do an ambush here anymore. Four of you keep watch through the rest of the night."

"Hell, *all of us* are gonna watch. Ain't nobody gonna sleep with that bear around," Caleb stammered.

Red-faced, Emory bellowed at Caleb, up close in the man's face. "There ain't no goddamned bear."

Chuckling softly to himself, Smoke Jensen eased from behind the chunk of granite and silently stole off into the night.

In the camp established by Cyrus Murchison, the main fire had died down to a low, rose-orange glow of pulsing coals. Murchison sat with his back propped against the bole of an aged ponderosa pine. He had a half-filled bottle of brandy in one hand and an unlighted cigar in the other. He did not want to let go of the liquor in order to light his stogie, though he dearly wanted the consolation of the rich smoke. An uneasy Titus Hobson approached.

"Light me a strip of kindling and bring it, will you, Titus?" Murchison greeted his partner.

Hobson did as bidden, ignited the cigar, then settled down beside Murchison and reached for the bottle. "That thunder sound we heard a little while ago? I have a feeling it wasn't caused by the weather."

"Sorry to say, I agree. Either those people chasing us stumbled into the ambush and it's all over. Or . . ."

"Or they rode right over the men you left back there," Hobson completed the unwelcome thought.

Shortly after dark, the men left behind by Heck Grange to spy on the approaching avengers had ridden into camp to report a force of some twenty hot on the trail. That many could easily overwhelm the seven men at Piney Creek. That news had sent Cyrus Murchison to the bottle. Then, about two hours ago, the sounds of a brief, ferocious battle came to them, muffled by distance. Could it be that late?

Cyrus pulled his fat, gold-cased watch from his vest pocket. Half past two o'clock. There would be no sleep this night. A sudden crash in the brush banished his gloom. Startled from his lethargy, Murchison jerked away from the tree trunk and listened intently.

More crackling of small branches and shrubs came from above the camp. Dulled by years in large cities and aboard the locomotives of two railroads, the ears of Cyrus Murchison only dimly picked out a grunting, snuffling sound. Growls followed, growing louder. Then the full-throated bellow of an enraged grizzly split the night. Cyrus Murchison did not take time to consider that nothing larger than roly-poly brown bears still lived in the Sierra Nevada. He immediately tried to scale the trunk of the overhanging ponderosa. The slick surface of the bark gave him scant help. The smooth leather soles of his boots scrabbled for purchase, propelled by a repeat of the ferocious roar. He jammed the toes of his custom-made boots into cracks and climbed about ten feet. Sweating with effort, he clung there, paralyzed by the sting from broken fingernails. From below came the fearful bleating of Titus Hobson.

"Shoot him! Kill that bear!"

His bear act had played rather well at the ambush, Smoke allowed, so he decided to try it again. In the larger camp, it created even more pandemonium. Groggy figures jumped from blanket rolls, ghostlike in their longjohns. Blindly they fired into the darkness in all directions. Some traded shots with others equally disorganized. The cooler heads among the gang of misfits lay low in an attempt not to attract a bullet. The bear bellowed a third time.

Horses began to whinny and shy at the picket line. Several reared, their squeals of terror bright in the blackness. That brought forth another fusillade. Three horses, struck by bullets, went splay-legged and sagged down loose-limbed. From his panic-driven perch, Cyrus Murchison cried out in alarm, "Stop it! Stop! You're killing the horses."

A fourth snarling whoop from the bear removed any chance of compliance. Bullets flew in a hailstorm of deadly lead. Heck Grange, smarter than any of his men, rushed to dump wood on the firepit. He kept low to avoid the whirlwind of slugs while he added more. The blaze caught slowly, then went up with a *whoosh*.

Over its roar Heck shouted to the frenzied men. "This way. Get around the fire. Bears don't like fire. And stop that damned shooting!"

When the volume of fire reduced, Smoke Jensen crept out of his hiding place and stealthily approached the picketed horses. His Green River knife flickered in the pale starlight for a moment, then slashed upward and severed the rope to which the mounts had been tethered. He loosed half a dozen, then stepped back quickly to cup his hands around his mouth. A guttural snarl ripped up past his lips.

When the panther cough reached the ears of the horses, they lost their minds. Those who had been freed dashed off pell-mell into the night. The rest reared and stomped and jerked at the picket line until they broke it and stormed off in a loose-knit herd. Reality suddenly took root in the brain of Cyrus Murchison. Enlightenment brought with it misery. He knew . . . he *knew* the cause behind it.

"God . . . damn . . . you . . . Smoke Jensen," he groaned into the rough bark of the pine he hugged.

Morning found eyelids heavy and tempers short. Few of the hard cases had managed more than an hour's sleep. Cyrus Murchison chafed while riders went out to recover their horses. His mood did not improve when the men from the ambush straggled in reeking of defeat.

"Why aren't you lying in wait for them?" he bellowed, rising from the fire, a cup of coffee steaming in his hand.

"We got attacked," Emory Yates explained limply.

"I gathered that. We heard the shooting. Did you stop any of them?"

"It weren't men," Caleb butted in. "It was critters. A giant rattlesnake and a bear."

A cold fist closed around the heart of Cyrus Murchison. "I

think you will find that your rattler and bear are named Smoke Jensen."

"Huh?" Caleb gulped.

"You have been bamboozled, my parochial friend," Cyrus grated. "So, for that matter, have we. Smoke Jensen got around you, found your camp, and engaged in a little leg-pulling. Disastrous play, if you ask me."

"What now, Mr. Murchison?" Caleb asked.

"What? Well, once we get our horses back . . ." his face flushed crimson. "Once we get our horses back, we keep going. It is a good three days to the pass. Somewhere along the way we'll lay another ambush."

"You reckon they'll follow us?" Emory inquired, hoping to get a negative answer.

"Of course they'll follow. Louis Longmont and Smoke Jensen are determined to ruin me—ruin Titus and me," he hastily amended. "Only we'll have to outsmart them. So long as I have the support of you, my loyal employees, I am confident we will prevail."

Smoke Jensen paused long enough for the volunteers to examine the ambush site. It would help make them aware of what they faced, he reasoned. It had the desired effect. When they set out again, their usual chatter dried up by seeming mutual consent. Silence held the higher they went into the foothills. When they came to the place where Murchison had camped the previous night, the impromptu posse halted again.

Everyone listened intently while Smoke interpreted the sign left behind. Then he described what he had done to cause them to create the disorganized scuffs and gouges in the dirt. That brought full, hearty laughs. Aware now that riches and power, and a lot of hired guns, did not make anyone invincible, they resumed their good-natured ragging when the column set off again.

Three hours later, they came upon the scene of last night's disaster in the main camp. Smoke's modest recounting of what transpired delighted them and bolstered their fortitude. Smoke found the trail their enemy left to be wide and clear. He called that to the attention of Louis.

"They're not making any effort to hide their tracks. Makes a feller wonder."

Louis Longmont chuckled sardonically. "Not for long, though, eh? It seems they want us to know where they are going and follow along at all good speed."

"You've not lost your trailcraft, old friend," Smoke praised. "I think I'll take Quo Wu and scout ahead. You bring the others along, only at a nice, easy pace. Try to keep no more than a mile between us."

Louis nodded knowingly. *"Très bon, mon ami.* Very good indeed. This way, if they are brazen enough to lay another ambush, the cavalry will be close at hand to ride to the rescue."

Smoke shook his head ruefully. "I can't figure what's so funny about that, but it suits what I've got in mind. Take care, now, old friend."

"I always do," Louis replied jauntily.

To his pleased satisfaction, Smoke Jensen had already found Quo Chung Wu to be nearly as skilled at silent movement as himself. It would come in handy on this little jaunt, he felt certain. On the hunch that Murchison would want to have as much space between the main body and any ambush he might set up, Smoke called a halt a quarter short of five miles.

"We'll go on foot from here on. Circle wide of the trail they left and keep off the skyline," Smoke instructed.

Quo Wu bowed his head and spoke without the least condescension. "The art of remaining unseen is ancient in our order. It is a shame that talent does not extend to our horses," he added wryly.

Smoke was ready for that one. "Among the Spirit Walkers of the Cheyenne, it is believed that they can extend their cloak of invisibility to their ponies. It might be they have something there, after all. I've had half a dozen of them pop up on me on open prairie sort of out of nowhere."

"You are possessed of this magic?" Quo Wu asked, impressed.

A modest reply seemed called for. "Somewhat. At least, enough that if there is anyone out there waitin' for us, they won't know Thunder and me are anywhere close until it's too late."

"How does it work?"

Smoke smiled at Quo. "Accordin' to the Cheyenne, all we have to do is think of ourselves and our horses as grass. Or in our case here, as trees."

Quo seemed taken aback. "That is all? We are taught to think of ourselves as birds, flying high above the gaze of our enemies."

"Seems a mite complicated, masterin' all those motions a bird has to go through to stay in the air."

Realizing that Smoke was teasing him, Quo flushed a light pink under his pale brown cheeks. "I have . . . flown twice."

Smoke did not know what to make of that. He did have to suppress a laugh. "No foolin'?"

Quo blurted his explanation through the embarrassment of having shown such unworthy pride. "Of course, my body never left the ground. Only my spirit soared."

Considering that, Smoke clapped a big hand on one muscular thigh. "That fits with what the Cheyenne say. So, you an' your horse will be birds, an' me an' Thunder will be trees. Either way, if there's anyone out there, we'll be in among them, raisin' hell, before they have an inkling."

Orville Dooling, known as "Doolie" to his fellow railroad police, thought he caught a hint of movement from the corner of one eye. He turned his head and peered in that direction. Nothing. He switched his gaze back down the wide, well-marked trail that had been left from the camp beyond Piney Creek. Once more a flicker of motion impinged on his awareness. Orville shook his head as though to rid it of such notions.

An instant later he froze at the soft sound of a whispering voice.

"Say goodnight."

A shower of stars, quickly extinguished by a wave of darkness, filled Doolie Dooling's head. The accompanying pain lasted only a second. Smoke Jensen stepped over the supine gunman and removed his weapons. No sense in leaving them for the rest of this rabble. That accounted for the right flank guard, Smoke noted, as he moved back behind the arc of the ambush to pick another target.

Two hard cases lounged close to each other, backs supported by a thick bush. Smoke glided soundlessly up to them and reached his arms wide. With a swift, powerful sweep, he grasped them over their ears and banged their heads together. The rest of those involved in the ambush remained oblivious to his actions, particularly the one being throttled by Quo Chung Wu at that very moment. Faintly, Smoke's superb hearing picked out the drum of hooves on the spongy terrain beyond the rise where the ambush had been laid.

A second later, the lead element of the posse hove into view and a shot banged flatly from one of the hidden gunhands. Four more thugs opened up, one from so close to Smoke Jensen, he felt the heat of the muzzle blast. Smoke drew and fired.

His shot dissolved his seeming invisibility. It appeared that all five of the remaining hard cases saw him at once. Smoke flexed his legs and dived to one side, while hot lead smacked into trees and screamed off rocks where he had stood a moment before. From the opposite end of the arc of gunhawks, a shotgun boomed and two of Murchison's henchmen screamed in torment.

Immediately, the hidden shooters turned toward this new threat. That gave Smoke a chance to account for another thug. A street brawler born and bred, he reared up from his concealed position to take a shot at Quo Chung Wu. Smoke cocked his Peacemaker and called to him.

"Over here!"

The slow-witted lout began to swing his .44 Smith, eyes widening at the presence of someone right in among them.

His surprise did not get to register on his face. A bullet from Smoke Jensen's .45 Colt reached him first. The red knob of his nose turned into a black hole, its edges splashed with scarlet. He went over backward, draped across the fallen pine trunk he had used for shelter.

Disorganized by the sudden appearance of two men in their midst, the railroad police and dockwallopers completely forgot about the eighteen armed vigilantes riding down on them. That proved a fatal error. Feeding on long-accumulated anger over their mistreatment, the farmers and merchants of the Central Valley swarmed in among their would-be assassins and wrought terrible vengeance.

In less than five minutes the battle ended. Only the unconscious among the hard cases remained alive. Those were trussed up like hogs for the slaughter and left behind, to be retrieved later. "When you come back through here, don't forget these men," Smoke advised.

Nightfall found Cyrus Murchison and his henchmen in a cold, miserable camp. Considering the events of the previous night, Heck Grange had insisted on no fires. The assortment of longshoremen, railroad police, and freelance would-be gunfighters grumbled noisily while they ate cold sardines and other preserved food from tins crudely hacked open by their knives. They had not been close enough to hear the detail of the brief, furious fight at the ambush site. It had sounded like nothing more than a loosened boulder rolling downhill.

Considering the debacle of the previous night, Cyrus Murchison put another meaning on it. Now, guided only by starlight, he made his way across the encampment to find Titus Hobson and share his revelation. He found Heck Grange seated beside Titus and poured each of them a generous dollop of brandy. He opened his mouth to speak when the chilling howl of a gray wolf broke the silence of the night.

* * *

Smoke Jensen had spent four tedious hours creeping up on the area in which he had estimated Murchison would make camp. He found them within three hundred yards of his picked spot. They could have done better to have reasoned like Smoke. Yet the chosen place appeared secure enough.

On the top of a small, domed knoll, the tired, uncertain hard cases sprawled in uneasy slumber. Unlike the previous night, someone had shown sense enough not to light fires, and to put out roving sentries, with pickets posted closer in. It would make his task harder, yet Smoke Jensen flowed through them as though truly invisible. He came up behind one less-than-observant hard case with laughable ease.

Smoke's braided rawhide lariat snaked out soundlessly and settled around the rider's shoulders, pinning his arms to his sides. A swift yank whipped him out of the saddle before he could give an alarm. His butt's contact with the solid ground drove the air from his lungs and blackness swam before his eyes, while Smoke Jensen walked the rope to the captive and klonked him solidly behind one ear.

Using pigging strings from his saddlebags, he secured the unconscious man. Then he dragged the musclebound longshoreman to a shallow ravine and unceremoniously rolled him in. Soundlessly whistling a jolly tune, Smoke recoiled his lariat and strode off into the night. Near the base of the hillock, he found a lone tree, which he scaled with ease. Poised on a sturdy limb, he waited for the passage of another guard.

Within five minutes, Smoke's patience was rewarded. Dozing in the saddle, an exhausted railroad policeman approached, his unguided mount in a self-directed amble. Smoke tensed as the animal wandered by under his branch. A moment later, he launched himself. His bootheels struck solidly between the thug's shoulder blades. Smoke did an immediate backroll off the rump of the startled, shying mount and landed on his feet.

His target did not fare so well. He ended up on his head. The bones of his neck made a nasty sound when they broke. Smoke Jensen spared only a split second for regret, then moved on.

He next surprised an adenoidal youth, far too young and

green to be in the company of such reprobates as those who surrounded him. His eyes went wide and he wet his drawers when Smoke took him from behind and clamped a big, callused hand over the boy's mouth. Wisely, the youngster did not struggle. He appreciated his good sense a moment later when Smoke laid the flat of the blade of his Green River against the teenager's neck.

Smoke's urgency carried through the whisper. "If you want to live, make up your mind to take this horse I brought for you and ride clear the hell out of here. Don't stop and don't even look back. It's that, or I slit your gullet and send you off to your Maker."

If he could have, the kid would have wet himself again. He certainly wanted to. With effort, he nodded his head up and down. "Mummmf, unnnh—hunnn."

"Does that mean you agree?" Smoke whisper-probed.

"Unnnn—hunnn."

Smoke's voice hissed like Old Man Death himself in the youth's ear. "If I let you go, you won't give the alarm?"

"Nuuh-uuuh."

Smoke eased his grip and reached behind him. "All right. Here's the reins. Walk him about a mile, then hit the saddle and ride like the hounds of hell are after you." He paused for effect, then put an ominous tone in his voice, knowing what he planned next. "You never know . . . they might be."

Panting, the boy showed his gratitude. "Thank you, thankyou-thankyou-thankyou."

Smoke looked after the young man as he led the horse off from the mound. Then the last mountain man turned and started uphill. Half way to the top, he paused. He gave the kid another five minutes, then threw back his head, cupped palms around his mouth and gave the mournful howl of a timber wolf.

NINTEEN

Hairs rose at the nape of the neck of every man in the hilltop camp. This time, Heck Grange's discipline took hold and no one fired wildly into the darkness. That did not keep them from filling their hands with any close-by weapon. Eyes showing a lot of white, they peered tensely into the stygian night. Most had barely conquered their nerves when the wolf howled again.

This time it seemed to come from closer in. Another wolf answered it from the opposite side of the camp. Fear gripped all of them, especially Cyrus Murchison. His childhood had been filled with thoroughly spuriously stories about wolves carrying off children and devouring them. Now this ingrained myth came back to haunt him.

"That can't be Jensen," he stated shakily to Titus Hobson. "He couldn't move that fast. There are *real* wolves out there."

His own unease gnawing at his vitals, Titus answered in a subdued voice. "I couldn't agree more. What are we going to do?"

"Do? We'll have to build a fire. No matter those behind us will see it now. We do it or those wolves will be in among us before we know it."

"Who is going to move and draw their attention?" Hobson queried.

"Grange, of course," Murchison courageously suggested. He raised his voice. "Heck, get a fire started."

"Already under way, Mr. Murchison," the boss gunman answered blandly. "Look for the fire glow reflected in their eyes. We'll know how many there are that way."

A tiny point of light bloomed at the top of the knoll. Kindling began to blaze, and men instinctively moved that way. The two wolves howled again.

Smoke Jensen could not believe his good fortune. A live, breathing wolf had answered his call. He raised his head again and uttered another wail, answered almost at once from the other side of the mound. *Scare the be-Jazus outta them,* he thought in the manner of Paddy Flynn, an old mountain man friend of Preacher's.

Another wolf howl, answered promptly, and then he readied the three horses he had collected from the incautious sentries. He loosened their saddles and removed bits, reins, and headstalls. He got them pointed in the general direction of the hilltop camp and stepped away into the night. A fourth ululating lupine howl sent them off in a panicked canter. Smoke listened intently for the results.

Cries of alarm and consternation came from the camp moments later, when the frightened creatures blundered in among the men and raced mindlessly past the fire. Three men opened fire. Sparks rose as one of the horses blundered into the fire pit. A man's voice rose to a shriek.

"My God, they're here, they're after us."

Smoke started to make his way back to Thunder when he caught a hint of movement off to his right. A gray-white-and-black object moved stealthily through the darkness. Smoke waited patiently. Then he saw it clearly. Even the distant firelight put a yellow-green phosphorescent glow in those big, intelligent eyes.

Smoke hunkered down, extended a hand, and uttered the low whine that conveyed friendly submission among wolves. The great, shaggy beast advanced, crouched low, and came forward at a crouch. He sniffed, his educated scent telling a lot about this two-legged being. Slowly, he closed. Another inspection by nose, then the long, wet tongue shot out and licked at the hand of Smoke Jensen.

"Good boy, good boy," Smoke whispered. "You came to help. I could send you up there among them to cap this off nicely, but I'm afraid you'd get shot. Go on, now. Go run down a couple of fit raccoons for your supper." Cautiously, Smoke reached out and patted the wolf. It might be more intelligent than a domesticated dog, Smoke reminded himself but it was still wild.

A soft whine came from the long gray muzzle and the wolf rolled over on its back, exposing its vulnerable belly. Smoke petted it and then made a shooing motion. He turned and walked away, back toward Thunder. A good night's work, he reasoned. When they found the lookouts in the morning, that would spook them even more.

When the roving patrol failed to return at the end of their four-hour stint, alarm spread through the camp again. Cyrus Murchison and Heck Grange barely managed to quell the general decision to search at once. By morning's early light, the gang managed to locate the missing sentries.

Bound and gagged, all were fully conscious and furious. "It was that goddamned Jensen, I tell you," one outraged thug growled.

"There was two wolves out here last night," Monk Diller stated positively.

"They sure as hell don't carry pieces of rope an' tie up a feller," the complaining sentry countered. "It was Smoke Jensen."

"God . . . damn . . . you . . . Smoke Jensen," Cyrus Murchison thought, though he did not give voice to his impotent curse.

Those with even a scant talent toward it cooked up a breakfast of fatback, potatoes, and skillet cornbread. One man with a passing skill as a woodsman found a clump of wild onions to add to the potatoes, and another dug a huge, fat yucca root to bake in the coals. Their bellies filled, the company of hard cases rode out, headed for the distant pass and Carson City beyond. Try as they might, none of them could find evidence of the presence of Smoke Jensen beyond the bits of rope.

Winds born over the far-off Pacific Ocean pushed thick cumulus clouds toward the coast. They grew as they progressed eastward. Many with fat black bellies climbed beyond 35,000 feet, their heads flattening out into the anvil shape of cumulonimbus. Storm clouds, thunderheads. Steadily they climbed as they raced over San Francisco and beyond to the Central Valley.

Their outriders arrived over the Sierra Nevada at ten o'clock in the morning. For the past half hour, Smoke Jensen had been marking the threatening appearance of the sky to the west. When the first dirty-gray billows whisked across the sun, he nodded in understanding and acceptance. Wise in the ways of mountains, Smoke knew for certain a tremendous thunderstorm would soon sweep over them. He made his companions aware of it.

"Storm's comin'. Better get out your rain slickers."

Tyler Estes, the barber in Grass Valley, gave him a concerned look. "A lot of us don't have anything. These are borrowed horses and such."

Smoke shrugged, indifferent to physical discomfort. "You'll just get wet, then. Or you can wrap up in your ground sheets."

"Our blankets will get wet that way," Estes protested.

A quick smile flickered on Smoke's face. "One way or the other, something is going to get wet."

Half an hour later, the first fat drops of rain fell from the solid sea of gray-black clouds. The wind whipped up and whirled last winter's fallen leaves around the legs and heads of their horses. In a sudden plunge, the temperature fell twenty degrees. "Here it comes," Smoke warned.

Already in his bright yellow India rubber slicker, Smoke had only to button up and turn his collar. The brim of his sturdy 5X Stetson kept most of the water out of his face. With their backs to the storm, the posse continued on its way. A trickle of cold rain ran down the back of Smoke Jensen's collar. The wind gusted higher as he worked to snug it tighter. Then the core of the storm struck.

Thunder bellowed around then and bright streaks lanced to the ground and trees to one side. The air smelled heavily of ozone. Smoke curled from a lightning-shattered ponderosa. A big hickory smouldered on the opposite side. They had been bracketed by near simultaneous shafts of celestial electricity.

"B'God, it hit both sides of us," Estes gulped out the obvious.

With a seething rattle, like the rush of the tide on a pebbly beach, a curtain of white hurtled toward them from the rear. Visibility dropped to zero and a wall of ice pebbles swept across the huddled men.

"Owie! Ouch! Hey, this stuff is tearing me up," a young livery stable hand yelped when the line of hail rushed over the rear of the column.

"Let's get under the trees!" Tyler Estes shouted.

"No!" Smoke turned his mount to stare them down. "You saw what the lightning did to those trees back there, right? Picture bein' under one of them when it hit. You'd be right sure fried."

Estes shivered at the image created by the words of Smoke Jensen. He looked around for some escape, while the hail battered at them all. "What can we do, then?"

"Dismount and control your horses. Get on the downwind side of them and use them for what shelter it provides. It'll be over 'fore long."

It proved to be damned little protection. Quarter-sized ice balls pelted down to bruise skin protected by no more than a light coat or flannel shirt. Smoke had been right about the duration. Within ten minutes, the hailstorm crashed on to the northeast. It had been with them long enough to turn the ground a glittering white, to a thickness of some three inches.

"Give me snow any time," Brice Rucker complained. "That stuff ain't hard."

Smoke favored him with a glance. "You've never seen snow on the high plains, have you? I was there one time with Preacher. We had a heavy snow, followed by an ice storm. The wind got up so that it flung the ice-coated snow at us. It was like razors, it was so sharp. Be thankful for small favors. All we come out of this with is a few bruises."

"Few," the always complaining barber repeated. "I'll be black and blue for a month."

"Too tender a hide, Tyler," Rucker teased him.

"Go kiss yer mule, Rucker," Tyler pouted.

"One bright spot," Smoke said through the rain to defuse the testy volunteers. "Think how that storm is going to play hell with those fellers ahead of us."

Wistfulness filled the voice of Tyler Estes. "Yes. They can't fare any better than us. Worse, more likely."

Louis Longmont entered the conversation. "Murchison and Hobson are soft from years of easy living. I would imagine they are completely miserable about now."

Lacking Smoke Jensen's knowledge of the outdoors, the storm caught Cyrus Murchison and his motley crew by surprise. Instantly soaked to the skin, they had not even covered themselves with slickers before the hail had hit. Two men were driven from their saddles by now fist-sized stones of ice. Their horses ran off screaming in misery.

Turned instantly into a rabble, the men milled about in confusion. The sky turned stark white and a tremendous crash of thunder followed in the blink of an eye. The huge green top of a spectacular lone Sequoia burst into flame and the upper two thirds canted dangerously toward the trail. Then it fell with aching slowness. Fearing for their lives, the hard cases scattered.

Blazing furiously, the tree dropped across the trail to block forward progress. Its resin-rich leaves spat and hissed in the torrent of rain that fell, unable to quell the flames.

"If the wind was down, we could put up tents."

Cyrus Murchison looked blankly at Titus Hobson. Could the man have completely forgotten everything he had learned about such storms during his mining days? "What good would that do?" he demanded. "The hail would only punch holes through the canvas the minute we stretched it tight."

Titus blinked. Why had he not thought of that? He made steeples of his shoulders to hide his embarrassment. "It's a while since I've been out in anything like this."

"So I gather," his partner responded. "We might as well hold fast here until that fire goes out. No sense in taking the risk of men falling into the flames going around it." He decided to relent on his harsh outburst at Titus. "You're right, though. When the hail quits, we should set up the tents. A warm, dry camp is bound to be appreciated."

Despite the storm-induced darkness, Cyrus judged it to be no more than mid-afternoon. They would lose nearly half a day, yet it would be important to let the runoff firm up the trail. No matter how many men pursued them, they would have been caught in the open, too, he reasoned. And, it might dampen the penchant of Smoke Jensen for those childish, although dangerous, pranks. Only time would tell.

Late that night, Smoke Jensen worked quietly and alone. It had taken him a quarter of an hour to select the right tent and the most suitable sapling. He spent another fifteen minutes in attaching the end of a rope to the springy young tree. Half an hour went by while he painstakingly pulled the limber trunk downward over a pivot point made of a smooth, barkless length of ash limb. He secured it there, then took the other end of the rope and tied it off to the peak of the tent roof.

With everything in readiness, Smoke stepped back to inspect his handiwork. It pleased him. All he had to do was cut the pigging string that held the spring trap in place and nature would take care of the rest. Suddenly he stiffened at the rustle of sound from inside the tent next to the one he had rigged.

Groggy with sleep, one of the hard cases stepped through

the flap and headed for the low fire in a large stone ring. He had a coffeepot in one hand. The thug must have caught sight of Smoke from the corner of one eye. He turned that way and spoke softly.

"What's up? You drainin' yer lily?"

Smoke muffled his voice, turned three-quarters away from his challenger. "Yep."

"Too much coffee, or too small a bladder, eh?"

"Unh-huh."

"I reckon I'd best be joinin' you," his questioner suggested, as he tucked his speckled blue granite cup behind his belt and reached for his fly.

He stepped closer and Smoke tensed. The bearded thug fumbled with the buttons as he came up to Smoke. He opened his mouth to make another remark and met a fist-full of knuckles. Bright lights exploded in his head and he rocked over backward. Smoke hit him again under the hinge of his jaw and the man sighed his way into unconsciousness.

Smoke Jensen stepped quickly to where he had secured the line between the bent sapling and the tent roof. His Green River knife came out and flashed down toward the pigging string. It severed with a snap and the tree instantly swung back toward its natural position. Smoke cut loose with a panther cough and yowl while the tent tie-downs sang musically as they strained, then let go. Like the conjuring trick of a medicine show magician, the tent whisked away, skyward, exposing the sleeping men inside.

Before anyone could react, Smoke Jensen slipped away into the darkness.

Several of the volunteers gathered around Smoke Jensen the next morning at the breakfast fire. The big granite pot of coffee made its final round. They had eaten well on shaved ham and gravy over biscuits, with the ubiquitous fried potatoes and onions, and tins of peaches and cherries, courtesy of the larder in the private car of Cyrus Murchison. They laughed heartily when he recounted what he had done the night before.

"Them fellers must have filled their drawers," Brice Rucker chortled. "Those that were in them, at least. I bet more'n a few jumped right out of their longjohns."

"I didn't wait to see," Smoke answered dryly. That brought more whoops of lighter. "Saddle up, men, we've got them running scared now."

Smoke led his small force away only scant minutes after the sun broke over the distant ramparts of the Sierra Nevada. He had told them that by the next day they would be high in the mountains. Another day after that they would be able to sweep down on Murchison's gang and bring an end to it. His words received powerful support shortly before midmorning.

Four tired, harried-looking men rode toward them from up the trail. When they sighted the vigilantes, they halted and waited quietly. As Smoke Jensen and Louis Longmont came within fifty yards of them, they raised their empty hands over their heads.

"We're out of it," their self-appointed leader informed the gunfighters. "We done quit the railroad police and left Murchison to his own ends. There was sixty of us when we started. Now there's less than half." His eyes narrowed. "Which one of you is Smoke Jensen?"

"I am," Smoke told him, readying his hand to draw his .45 Colt.

A chuckle, not a challenge, came from the former railroad bull. "You sure got 'em stirred up, Mr. Jensen. Got *us* all exercised, that's for sure. Those boys up there are quaking in their boots. After what happened to that tent, we quit first thing this morning. An' there's about a dozen more ready to give it up, too."

"Good to hear, gentlemen. You're free to ride on. Only one thing," he added, a hand raised to stop them. "We'd be obliged if you left all but five rounds of ammunition with us. We're a little short as it is, and every round will be appreciated."

Their leader snickered, a gloved hand over his mustache and full lips. "And, it sort of makes certain we can't turn back and hit you in the rear, don't it?"

Smoke nodded and joined his laughter. "That possibility did occur to me. So, what do you say?" His eyes narrowed to glittering slits of gray. "Lighten your load and ride free? Or open the dance right now?"

The jovial one quickly showed both hands, open and empty. "Ain't got time to waltz, Mr. Jensen. We'll just leave some cartridges with you and be on our way."

Smoke's smile held the breezy warmth of a June day. "That's mighty thoughtful of you. I'll take you up on that and then we can ride on."

In ten minutes it was done and the volunteer posse grew richer by two hundred thirty rounds. Smoke watched the deserters from Murchison's cause from time to time until they rode out of sight. He showed a sunny mood to everyone as he picked up the pace.

Wilber Evers spoke around a hard knot of grief in his throat that night in the vigilante camp. "He was my brother. My brother, and they shot him down like a dog. One of . . . one of them took a rope to his kids and beat them. Raised welts on their backs."

Another sorrow-softened voice responded. "Yeah, I know. You hear about Ruby Benson?"

"The widow Benson?" Evers asked.

"Yep. That's the one. Only she's not so much an old widow. She's rather young. Anyway, some of these riff-raff came along from the railroad and told her to sell out the farm to Murchison. She refused. So they jumped her, had their way with her and left her a ruined woman. She—she's my sister."

"I'm sorry," Smoke Jensen added his feelings to the discussion around the supper fire. "What did you reckon to do about it?"

"She described them to me. If I find them among those with Murchison, I'm gonna hang the lot of them."

Smoke nodded. "Suits. Preacher hanged some rapists more than once. I know, because I was with him a couple of times. There's even a story going around that he one time hanged a man who messed around with children."

"Served him right, I say," the brother of Ruby Benson growled.

"What else has been done that you know of for certain?" Smoke probed.

Several voices clamored for his attention. One bull bellow overrode the others. "They burnt my barn and shot my cows. Scared my wife so much she delivered early. We lost the baby."

"Do you know them?"

"Sort of. They had flour sacks over their heads, but two of them didn't change clothes from earlier in the day. I'd know those two anywhere. They work at the depot in Parkerville. Name of Dawkins and Lusk. I meant to go shoot them when I ran into these other fellows and joined in on this little affair."

Angry mutters went around the firepit. "I had myself primed to set my sights on one of Huntley's bullies. He tormented me an' my wife until I was forced to sell two freight wagons to Huntley's outfit. I cussed myself as a yellow-belly ever since. When I heard there was trouble in Grass Valley, I hightailed it for there right away." The grayhaired man stopped there and looked around for approval from his companions.

It came quickly. "Ain't nothin' yeller about you, Paul. Why, we was right pleased to see you join us."

Paul drew himself up and came to his boots. "Well, I thank ye, Lester. Boys, I think I've got enough jawin' for one night. I'm for my bedroll. We got a bushel of work to do tomorrow."

Smoke Jensen silently agreed and pushed away from the circle of gabbers. What he had heard angered and disturbed him. All of their atrocities considered, he doubted that Murchison and his gang would be inclined to give up easily.

TWENTY

Crouched in a jumble of rocks, Smoke Jensen cracked a satisfied smile. After hearing the accounts of those victimized on Murchison's orders, he decided to try a different approach. He did not wait as long as he had for the previous night visits to the gangster camp. He wanted the men up and moving around. Smoke had selected his spot carefully and settled in to observe.

Tensions had thickened what with so many fellows forced to rub elbows for so long, he marked first. No longer did they all crowd around a large, central fire. Seven smaller blazes lighted the night, with men grouped in twos and threes, with a solitary loner at one. Smoke settled on him for his first dirty trick of the night. That determined, he slid away into the darkness around the camp.

After he had circled the campsite, he paused to relocate his target. Then, holding a deep breath, he ghosted up on the unsuspecting thug hunkered down by the fire. With panther swiftness, Smoke whipped an arm around the brute's neck and gave a sudden yank. Unseen by the comrades of the hard case, Smoke whisked him out of sight.

Using a trick of the Cheyenne Dog Soldiers, Smoke increased the pressure of his arm until he stifled the thug into unconsciousness. Then he hefted the limp form over one shoulder and carried him away. Far away. When next the man woke up, he would find himself tied to a tree in a strange place, well out of sight of the camp he had last seen. Smoke Jensen made certain it would be on the route to be taken by Murchison and the gang the next morning. Making sure that the rope that his captive could not escape on his own, Smoke returned to wipe out all trace of his presence.

"That went so smooth, there's no reason not to try for another one," Smoke muttered to himself.

He found another one easily enough. A city dude had gone out in the trees to relieve himself. And, naturally, he plain got lost. In his wandering, he blundered into Smoke Jensen. That quick he became the next to disappear without a trace.

Unaware of the doings of Smoke Jensen, and the fact that Smoke now crouched in some rocks not thirty feet away, Cyrus Murchison and his partners discussed his decision to move on to Carson City.

"We could go back to the main line," Murchison said agreeably. "Only those miserable sons of perdition are between us and it. No, Titus, Heck, it will take longer, but to continue on horseback is the wisest choice."

Titus Hobson answered testily. *"I* say the wisest thing would have been to stay in San Francisco. You own the mayor and the city fathers. And, between us, we own nearly all the judges. The chief of police plays poker with us and gets drunk in that gentlemen's club of yours. There's no way Longmont or Jensen can show any proof of our involvement in anything illegal. *They can't bring any charges."*

For the first time, Cyrus Murchison found it necessary to reveal his real fear. "You said it yourself, Titus. Smoke Jensen is a gunfighter. The best there is. And there's not a hair's breadth between him and Longmont. Listen to me, your life depends on it. Those two are not in the habit of bringing charges . . . *except the ones in their six-guns."*

Hobson paled. "You mean, they'll just . . . kill us?"

"Precisely. For men like them, justice comes out of the barrel of a gun. No, we'll keep on overland. The Central's tracks have been extended into Carson City. We can get reinforcements there. Then we'll return to California and wipe out these interfering scum." Cyrus Murchison came up on his scuffed, dusty, although once highly polished, boots. Buoyed by his self-delusion, he spoke lightly. "It is time to turn in. I'm looking forward to a sound night's sleep."

"I wish you the joy of it," Titus Hobson grumbled, uncomfortable at being reminded he was the one to identify exactly what Smoke Jensen and Louis Longmont were.

A sudden shout stopped them. "Chief! Chief, there's two of us missin'."

Heck Grange came upright. "Did you see any sign of Smoke Jensen?"

"Nope. Nothin'. Just some tracks where the boys was. They've plum disappeared."

Early the next morning, Smoke Jensen changed his tactics. In the faint gray light that preceded sunrise, he led the posse of vigilantes out at a fair pace. "We're through chasing Murchison and his mob of butchers," he informed his companions. "Today we get ahead of them and see how they enjoy an ambush." Expectant smiles answered him. "With a good early start, we can swing wide and bypass their present camp."

Everyone rode with high spirits. As the day grew brighter, Smoke increased the pace. Every hour, they dismounted and walked their horses for ten minutes. Many of those who lacked experience with saddle mounts marveled at the stamina that this provided their animals. Shortly before the noon hour, Smoke called a halt.

He gestured to where the sheer hillsides closed in on the trail. It narrowed and the grade grew much steeper. "Up there a ways is the place we'll start. Some of you see if you can locate any fallen logs. Make sure they're not bigger around than a man's body and not too dried out."

"Why don't we cut what we want?" Tyler Estes asked.

"We don't have a lot of time, Mr. Estes. The less we have to spend on this the better," Smoke informed him. "Those of you with shovels come with me. I'll show you what to do."

They worked quickly and well. Smoke supervised the building of an even dozen nasty surprises for Murchison's hirelings. Two long, narrow pits had been dug parallel to the trail, covered with leaves and brush. At a point farther along, where the mountain's breast overhung the narrow trace, Smoke saw an ideal place for a particularly nasty trap. He set men to work weaving a large net from vines and ropes.

While they did that, Smoke himself climbed to the top of the lip and sprawled out flat. Working by feel, he drove the pointed end of an arm-thick limb into the soil. He draped a double twist of lariat over the beam it formed and lowered it to the ground. Then he returned to the busy weavers.

"When you get that done, fill it with rocks and attach these ropes at the top to keep it closed. Then stick brush in the net, to make it look like a big bush."

"Then what?" Estes asked.

"We attach the trip line." Smoke turned away to check on other progress while he let them figure that one out.

Three and a half hours later, the project neared completion. Smoke Jensen made a final, careful check, then gathered the volunteers. "Everyone pick a position up above the last trap. Make sure you have a clear field of fire. And be careful going up there. You don't want to set off one of those things on yourself."

"You can say that again," Tyler Estes blurted out. When he had taken in the scope of what Smoke had in mind, his eyes bugged and the usually timid barber had thrilled in the blood lust that heated him at the thought of all these awful things going off in the midst of that gang of thugs. He remained impressed as he worked his way up above the deadly ambush site.

"Do you expect them to fall for this?" Louis Longmont asked, a critical eye roving over the concealed traps and trip lines.

Smoke gave it some thought. "For most of it. It depends on how well those boys can shoot up there whether we break them right here." Smoke cast a glance at the sun. "Either way, we'll know soon enough."

* * *

Cyrus Murchison and his army of gunslingers set out a lei-surely two hours after sunrise. Everything went well for the first three hours. Then the two men in the lead flew from the backs of their horses, driven off by a long, supple sapling that had been bent back behind a pile of rocks along the trail. They landed hard, both breaking ribs. One of them snapped a leg.

"That damn well ties it!" Heck Grange shouted. "We'll be forever getting to the top of the pass now. How many more of these things are out there waiting for us?"

Cyrus Murchison responded with an air of indifference. "Tell the men to go slow and we'll find out. But keep them going."

With the column on the move again, Murchison settled down to a gloomy contemplation of exactly *how many* such traps they would find. And worse, how much harm would be done.

Nervous, and made more cautious, the band of thugs con-tinued on toward the top of the pass. No more hidden dangers had shown up by the time Murchison's henchmen stopped for their nooning. Titus Hobson had managed to convince himself that someone other than Smoke Jensen had rigged that trap. An Indian, perhaps, to catch some form of game. He shared his thought with Cyrus Murchison. Oddly, Murchison found himself agreeing. Until now he had harbored the sneaking sus-picion that the two wily gunfighters had gotten ahead of them, yet he said nothing to Hobson. Half an hour further along the trail he quickly learned to regret that decision.

An agonized scream echoed along the high, enclosing walls of the gorge that led to the high pass of the Sierra Nevada. Its eerie wail jerked Cyrus Murchison out of his dark rumi-nations and sent a chill down his spine. Up ahead, he saw a thigh-thick log swish back and forth, after striking the lead rider. Jagged flakes of quartz protruded from the face, three of them dripped blood.

Unthinkingly, Murchison spoke his thoughts aloud. "Hideous. It's hideous. They—they're nothing but barbarians."

Heck Grange took charge. "Dismount! Walk your horses and look where you are going."

Severely shaken, his face pale, Cyrus Murchison did as the rest. He reached the spot where the man lay dead, his blood a pool around his crumpled form, when a rope twanged musically ahead and four saplings swished out to slap men and horses in the face. The hard cases shouted in alarm and jumped to the side of the trail. Fragile brush crackled and gave way under their weight. Their yells changed to screams of agony as they impaled themselves on sharpened stakes in the bottom of shallow trenches.

A voice came from one thug behind Murchison. "That does it. I'm getting out of here."

Murchison whirled. "No, wait. Stay with us. There can't be much more of this."

"Any more is too damn much for me, Mr. Murchison. You can send my pay to my house."

An idea struck Cyrus Murchison. "Anyone who deserts won't get paid!" he shouted.

"Who cares, at least we'll be alive," another truculent voice replied.

Four men took to their horses, turned tail, and fled without a backward look. Cyrus Murchison cursed and stomped his boot on the hard ground. Up ahead a trigger tripped and a loud roar filled the air. Hundreds of large rocks rained down on the men and horses below.

Whinnies of the frightened critters filled the air as the stones bruised and cut their hide. Dust rose in thick clouds. The rumble of bounding boulders drowned out the shrieks of pain from the injured hard cases. Those the farthest along the trail broke free only to be met with a wall of powder smoke. Bullets cracked through the air. Thugs died horribly.

Belatedly, those behind recovered and drew weapons. They surged forward, yelling to their fellow stupefied comrades over the tumult to keep moving forward. The thrust became a rallying point, which grew into a concerted charge. Six-guns and rifles blazing, they mounted and dashed at the ambush, indifferent to any possible traps that remained.

By sheer force of numbers, they stormed through the weak center of the hidden vigilantes. In a matter of seconds the last of Murchison's shattered column thundered over a rise and out of sight. Louis Longmont came out of the rocks where he had forted up. Smoke Jensen appeared on the slope opposite him. He quickly read the question on the face of Louis.

"We go after them, of course," Smoke said duly.

"We can't keep going on," Titus Hobson raged at Cyrus Murchison. "They've been ahead of us at every turn. Look at those poor wretches we found along the trail this morning. This is suicidal."

Murchison fought to remain calm. "No, it's not. We got through them, didn't we? The thing is, we're nearly at the summit. When we get there we'll dig in and make them come to us."

"I think it's a dangerous mistake," Titus objected.

Basically a coward at heart, Titus Hobson had been a schoolyard bully as a child. He used his strength and size to intimidate smaller children. Later, as a prospector, he had developed his brawn to an impressive degree. His bulging muscles, craggy face, and bushy brows made it easier to cow those who sought to oppose him. His confidence grew, and with it, his wealth. Not until this wild flight into the wilderness had he been effectively challenged.

Now it frightened him witless. He had been close enough to the unfortunate lout who took the log in the chest to have blood splatter on his shirt and face. He *knew* Smoke Jensen was too dangerous for them to provoke. Why had he let Cyrus drag him into this? Yet he knew that Murchison was also dangerous. A man all too quick to use the final solution of death to end any opposition. Titus knew he dare not let his true feelings be seen too clearly. He tried to placate Murchison before this discussion took a hazardous turn.

"All right, Cyrus. We have little choice anyway. I suggest we make an effort to block the trail further on. Anything to slow them. I gather that this gorge narrows, the farther up we go?" At Murchison's nod, he outlined an idea that had worked in the gold fields against a band of outlaws led by the notorious Mexican bandit Gilberto Oliveras. "When we reach the top, we should close off the entire pass. Fell trees and build firing stands of them. Move rocks, boulders, seal off the trail. Then we can hold off that scum until they run out of ammunition."

Murchison considered that a moment. "Good idea, Titus. Where did you come up with this?"

Hobson showed a hint of modesty. "I was at the Battle of Wheeler's Meadow."

"My Lord, I never knew that. Well, old fellow, I propose you take charge of our delaying actions and the fortifications. Is it true that there were only seventeen of you against nearly a hundred Mexican bandits?"

"Yes. But we had all the tools and we built well. They couldn't get to us. We held them until they ran out of powder and shot. Simple after that."

"I like that. I do like that. We'll do it your way, and watch Smoke Jensen dash his brains out against our stout walls."

Smoke Jensen stood with his right fist on his hip, his left hand on the slanted holster high on his left side. Fallen trees blocked the trail ahead. Louis Longmont joined him while the volunteers labored to clear the obstacles. With a shout from Brian Pullen, horses strained on ropes attached to the first trunk and it swung slowly, ponderously.

"What are you thinking, *mon ami?*"

"They are waiting for us up ahead. I'd bet my last cigar that we'll run into more of these roadblocks, and finally reach the place they're forted up."

Louis nodded. "I think you are right. And no doubt you are

going out there to find them tonight. This time I'm going with you."

Smoke made a fake shocked expression. "Louis, you astonish me. Whatever brought you to this? How can you think of risking that elegant neck?"

Louis produced a look of such wounded pride, only to be spoiled by the laughter that bubbled up deep inside himself. "I know you prefer to work alone, my friend. But they have grown bold after breaking out of our nice little trap, *non?* It would be well that for tonight you had someone to watch your back."

Without a show of any reluctance, Smoke agreed. His spirit lightened when the second downed pine had been dragged clear of the narrow spot in the trail. Smoke took the lead, with Louis at his side. Brian Pullen and Quo Chung Wu brought up the rear. Already Smoke's fertile imagination labored to concoct new nastiness to inflict upon Murchison and his henchmen.

Three more blockades had to be torn down by the time Smoke Jensen called a halt for the day. He had ridden ahead and scouted out the fortifications erected by Murchison's mongrels. Murchison, or someone, had chosen well. Located at the restricted point, at the crest of the high pass, it had taken little effort to build a thick, impenetrable wall. They seemed determined to stand and fight, he reasoned. It might be he could change their minds.

Smoke would have liked to use fire. If he did, he knew, he took the risk that the whole of the forest would be wiped out. Sort of like swatting a fly with a scoop shovel, he reckoned it. That left him with the three other elements as the Indians saw their universe: air, earth, and water. By the time he had returned to discuss it with Louis, he had made up his mind which they would use.

The breeze cooperated nicely, having whipped up into a stiff blow. It would mask any sounds they might make. Thankfully, it held even after the sun had set. Clouds had built up over the late afternoon, another gift of nature, and blotted out the blanket of stars and the thin crescent of moon. Smoke and Louis set out when total darkness descended.

They left their horses three hundred yards from the barrier erected by the hard cases. When they stealthily approached, they found that, rather than looming over them, the bulwark had been built only to shoulder height. All the better, Smoke saw it. He held a whispered conference with Louis and they took position near one end.

Less than five minutes went by before a roving sentry appeared on the opposite side of the barricade. Louis Longmont waited until he went past, then rose on tiptoe to stare over the wall.

"Psssst!" Louis hissed.

Galvanized by the unexpected sound, the hard case spun in Louis's direction, his rifle headed for his shoulder. Smoke Jensen came up behind him and clamped one hand over his mouth, the other on his throat, and yanked him over the wall. Louis stepped close and rapped the man on the head with the butt of his revolver. Smoke tied him tightly and they moved along the wall to wait again.

Another lookout paced his bit of the defenses, his attention wandering between the convivial firelight behind and the thick blackness beyond the bastion. Louis popped up and hissed again when the guard looked inward. He turned abruptly and Smoke hauled him off his feet. He wound up as tightly bound as the first one, unconscious on the outside of the partition.

Smoke and Louis repeated their little ruse until every watcher had been removed from the rampart. With that accomplished, they stole off into the night. When the thugs found their friends in the morning, they might not be so sure the wall would protect them.

"Here they come!" one lookout shouted from the barricade.

Cyrus Murchison and his riff-raff had only finished cussing and stomping about the waylaid sentries of the night before and gone back to breakfast. That clever bastard, Cyrus Murchison thought of Smoke Jensen. He would be smart enough to wait for the last shift to pull that. They weren't even missed until daylight. Now, before a man could even enjoy a decent breakfast, the whole lot of that rabble is attacking. With a regretful sigh, Murchison set aside his plate and reached for the rifle resting against a boulder beside him.

"Hold your fire until they get in close," Heck Grange advised. "Pick a few of them out of the saddle and the rest will turn tail. I know these bumpkins."

It turned out he didn't know them as well as he believed. Twenty-four strong, led by Smoke Jensen and Louis Longmont, the vigilante posse rode up toward the barrier. At a hundred yards, those with rifles opened fire. Anyone shooting from a moving horse had to be blessed with a lot of luck. It turned out two of the avengers were.

One hard case made a strangled cry when a bullet tore through his throat. He went down in a welter of blood. Off to the left, a second thug made a harsh grunt when a slug angled off the top of the receiver of his rifle and popped through his right eye. Already misshapen, the hunk of lead shredded a path through his brain and blew out the back of his skull.

That ended all restraint. Rifles crackled along the wall of earth and logs. One volunteer flew from his saddle, shot through the heart. He bounced twice when he reached the ground. Another took a bullet in the shoulder and slumped forward along the neck of his mount. A third, gut-shot, made a pitiful cry and turned his horse aside.

That caused several others to falter. Singly, at first, then the whole body spun their mounts and streaked off downhill to the shelter of a cluster of trees. For the time being, the fight turned into a contest of long-range sniping. Not for long, though.

After half an hour, Smoke Jensen's Winchester Express flattened a hard case who had bent over to pour a cup of coffee across the fire pit. When several of his comrades ran to his rescue, Smoke exhorted his volunteers.

"Time to hit them again. Mount up and let's ride."

TWENTY-ONE

Whooping like wild Indians, the vigilantes charged the fortifications. Caught unprepared, clearly half of the gunmen were wolfing down biscuits and gulping fresh coffee. Three of them did not make it back to the barrier.

At one hundred yards, the posse opened up again. The exposed men died in that first fusillade. At fifty yards, the toughs who manned the wall began to return fire. At first, they had little effect. Then their jangled nerves smoothed and their bullets began to find flesh.

Two of Smoke's volunteers took slugs, one in the shoulder, the other through a thigh. His horse didn't fare well, either. The hot lead punched through its hide and into a lung. Pink froth appeared on its muzzle and lips and it faltered abruptly, then its legs folded under it and the wounded rider pitched over its head.

"Get me outta here," he wailed.

A farmer, who fancied himself a good hand at horsemanship, cut to his right and bent at the waist. Arm hooked, he snagged the injured man and yanked him up behind.

"Ow, damn it!" the victim complained ungratefully. "That hurt worse than bein' shot."

"Be glad I looked out for you, you old fool," his rescuer grumped.

Tyler Estes found shooting from horseback to be rather a pain. He had just gotten the hang of it when all the targets disappeared. "Show yourselves and fight like a man," he challenged, as he jumped his horse to within thirty yards of the wall.

A head appeared, followed by shoulders and a rifle. The gunman fired and cut the hat from the head of Estes. His eyes went wide and he let out a little bleat before he clapped the cheek plate of his rifle to his face and took aim. His horse obediently halted for him and Tyler Estes released the reins for a moment to steady the barrel of his long gun. The .44 Winchester cracked sharply and the head of the thug who had shot at him snapped backward in a shower of red spray.

"That'll learn ya," Estes chortled, then wheeled away to find another target.

Another posseman cut across in front of Smoke Jensen, causing the last mountain man to rein in sharply. That saved Smoke's life, although it did not do much for the unfortunate eager one. He died in Smoke's place, drilled through the head. The suddenness of it changed Smoke Jensen's mind. They could never outlast the number of guns they faced.

"Pull back!" he shouted over the crackle of gunfire. "Pull back to the trees."

Smoke Jensen led the way to a campsite well out of sight of the forted-up gunmen. When the last of the wounded limped in, Smoke called the posse together. His face wore a serious, concerned expression. The losses they had taken preyed on his mind. These men deserved the opportunity to clean up their own yards, he reckoned. Yet they deserved to live. This fight belonged to him and Louis alone. From here on they would carry it through that way. He told that to them in a calm, quiet voice.

Brian Pullen spoke up forcefully. "Don't think you are going to get rid of me that easily. I'm in to the end."

"These . . . honored gentlemen have . . . families . . . and property . . . to care for. It is . . . reasonable that they return to them at this time. But," Quo Chung Wu went on with a fleeting smile, "it would be . . . unmanly for a priest . . . with neither wife and child . . . nor even a home . . . of my own . . . to take the path of . . . safety. I . . . too . . . will stay . . . beside you." He bowed to Smoke.

"There's no need," Smoke started his protest. Then he correctly read the expression on Quo's face. "I am honored to have your help," he amended.

Consternation ran among the men from the Central Valley. "What about us? Ain't we got a say in this?" one complained.

Smoke Jensen shook his head. "Five of you are dead and seven wounded. You've done your share. Now is the time for you to leave the rest to those who are trained for the killing game. Believe me, what we are going to have to do you don't want on your consciences."

"You mean you're goin' to lynch them all?" Tyler Estes blurted.

"No," Smoke answered levelly. "Those who give up we'll let the law handle."

"When do you want us to leave?" a disappointed posseman asked.

"You don't have to leave. Come morning, I'm sure Murchison will believe he won a big victory and pull out. We'll be going after them. You can stay here, rest up for a day or two, and give the wounded a chance to knit some before heading to your homes."

Tyler Estes scratched the balding spot on the crown of his head, and summed up for all of them. "Well, it'll be nice to get back to the shop. I reckon little Joey Pitchel will be needin' a trim, before them red locks o' his turns into long sissy curls."

That brought an understanding laugh, yet a gloomy pall settled over the volunteers, even though they faced the happy prospect of safely returning to their homes and families. Smoke Jensen sat long into the night, thinking about it.

Emboldened by their apparent easy success, particularly when nothing happened during the night, Cyrus Murchison pushed on with his surviving henchmen. He left two men behind to report of the defeated posse. They waited in the shade of a big oak a ways behind the wall, which had been left in place. The drowsy warmth of mid morning got to them and they soon dozed off.

They heard nothing when the four riders approached. Smoke Jensen saw them at once and halted. Signing the other three to remain silent, he eased over the wall and cautiously closed in on the sleeping men. A fly buzzed around a thick lock of hair that hung down on the forehead of one lout. It had made three more circles by the time Smoke reached the slumbering hard case. Then, as Smoke stepped up to him, it landed on his nose.

With a start and a sodden mutter, the thug took a blind swipe at the offending insect. His last conscious thought must have been that for a darned fly, it sure packed a wallop. Still clutching the cylinder of his .45 Colt, Smoke turned to the other snoozing lout and smacked him on the head also.

"We'll take their horses," he called back to the others. "Without mounts, they won't go forward. If they move fast, they can catch up to the posse before those fellers leave."

"That's cold, Smoke," Brian Pullen objected. "Leaving a man without a horse in this country can get him killed."

"Only if he's stupid. The old mountain men, like Preacher, walked the whole of the High Lonesome more than one time."

"Mr. Smoke . . . is right, Mr. Brian," Quo Chung Wu offered. "This is . . . the first time I know of . . . that one of our Order has . . . ever ridden anywhere. We walked . . . for centuries in China. It is . . . a requirement," he added with his cheeks flushed.

"I am sure that Tai Chiu will forgive you," Louis Longmont told Quo Chung Wu.

Quo blushed again. "He . . . already has . . . before we . . . left. I was . . . thinking . . . of the . . . Lord Buddha."

Smoke pulled a face. "Well, considerin' what we're headed

into, now's sure the time to get religion, as Preacher would say."

Louis Longmont looked from the wall to the unconscious thugs. "Too bad you knocked out those scrudy trash. Now we have to clear the trail ourselves."

"Allergic to hard, dirty work, Louis?" Smoke jibed.

Louis wrinkled his nose. "Only when I can't get a bath. We had better proceed."

It took the four companions an hour to open a pathway through the barricade. With that accomplished, they struck out on the wide trail left by Murchison and his mob. Most of the day's travel was downhill with only a single file of peaks between them and the long, deceptive grade through a lush meadow that led to Donner Pass.

Smoke estimated they would catch up to Murchison's gang at that fateful spot where less than forty years ago, men and women stranded by an early blizzard had been forced to commit the most appalling of human failings. Starving in the snow-blocked pass, they had fallen upon the corpses of their fellows to sustain their lives. How ironic it would be if Cyrus Murchison met his end there, Smoke mused.

He would find out, Smoke promised himself, two days from now.

Shouts of disgust and outrage awakened Cyrus Murchison the next morning. He pulled on trousers and boots and fumbled with sleep-numbed fingers to button his shirt. A quick splash of frigid water removed the gumminess from his eyes. He had gone to bed feeling rather better about their enforced exile.

When the two men left behind to spy out the posse had not returned by nightfall, he preferred to assume that they had nothing to report so far. Which would indicate, he convinced himself, that Jensen and Longmont and those local malcontents had turned back. Now, this, whatever it turned out to be, riling up the men. He reached for his hat as the flap opened and Heck Grange entered, his face grim, lips drawn in a hard line.

"What is it out there that has them all stirred up?"

Words clipped and sharp-edged, Heck Grange told him. "We're not shut of Smoke Jensen yet. He was here sometime last night. He left us three of my men as a warning." Finally the enormity of what he had seen overcame his forced restraint. "Goddamnit, they were strung up by the ankles, throats slit, and bled out like sheep."

For all his cruel nature, that affected Cyrus Murchison more than anything else. His face went white, his mouth sagged, and he placed the hat on his head with a shaking hand. "That's an abomination," he gasped out.

"You haven't actually seen it as yet. Which you'll have to do soon or we'll lose men like rats off a swamped barge." Grange went on to instruct his employer. "One thing you should point out is that it looks like one of the boys got a piece of Jensen. His knife is bloody."

Murchison pursed his thick lips. "More likely, Jensen used it to do for them."

Grange studied on that a moment. "I don't think so. The knife was on the ground, right below his outstretched hand, which was bloody, too."

Cyrus drew himself up. "Well, then, we'll dwell on that. Anything to keep the men together."

It proved to be too little, too late. Already, three of Huntley's remaining longshoremen had pulled stakes and left camp. By nightfall, five more would desert the cause.

Tom, Dick, and Harry Newcomb—their father obviously had a twisted sense of humor—topped the first rise outside Murchison's camp and started on the long downgrade to the valley floor. For defeated men, they showed considerable energy in the way they kept their heads up and studied their surroundings in great detail. It did them little good, though. They rode right past two men sheltered in a thicket of brush along the trail.

They swiveled their heads once more, and when they looked

forward again, two men appeared on the trace in front of them, six-guns in hand. Tom, Dick, and Harry reined their horses furiously in an attempt to turn and flee back to the camp, only to find two more people blocking their way, weapons at the ready. Desperately they spun their mounts again.

"Who are you?" Tom demanded, for want of something better to say.

The hard-faced one with cold eyes answered him. "We're your worst dream come true."

Somewhat less daunted than his brothers, Dick pushed the issue. "What's your name, Mister?"

"Smoke Jensen."

Awareness dawned. "Awh, Jesus," Tom groaned.

"We're dead men for sure," Harry concluded for his brother.

"Not necessarily," the hard-faced messenger of death told him.

"We saw what you did to those fellers last night."

Fire flashed in the ruddy eyes. "One of them came after me with a knife."

The brothers saw it then, a thickness of the left shoulder of Smoke Jensen. Tom also noted a rent in the cloth of the jacket, with red-brown stains around it. It fed him a dose of false bravado.

"What about the other two?"

"They got in the way." Then Smoke read the expression on their faces. "Don't worry, they were dead when I strung them up."

Dick, worried over the condition of his hide, asked Smoke the fateful question. "You gonna do the same to us?"

"Not unless I have to," Smoke answered calmly. "I gather you have given up on Mr. Murchison's little enterprise?"

"Yessir, yes, we sure have," Harry hastened to say. "Anyway, we worked for Mr. Huntley, an' he's long gone."

"Then you are free to go. All we ask is that you limit yourselves to a single weapon each, and leave all but five rounds with us."

Shocked by this, Tom blurted, "That ain't fair."

"I think you will find that life is not fair. Do it that way or be left for the buzzards and wolves."

"God, you're a hard man, Mr. Jensen," Tom blustered.

"Enough talk," a man with a Frenchy-sounding accent told Tom, Dick, and Harry. "Do it or die."

Quickly, Tom, Dick, and Harry divested themselves of six-guns, hideout pistols, and one spare rifle, and pockets-full of ammunition. Sweating profusely they rode off down the trail.

"That's a good start," Smoke Jensen told his companions. "Though there's a lot more where they came from."

The next dawn brought a cold, sharp wind and thick-bellied clouds Smoke Jensen knew to be laden with snow. All four ate heartily and fortified themselves with plenty of coffee. Smoke gnawed on a final biscuit while Brian Pullen covered the fire pit. The first lacy white flakes danced in the air as they took to saddle and set off.

Two miles down the trail, they encountered five disgruntled former employees of the California Central Road. The exchange went much as the one with the Newcomb brothers. None of the demoralized hard cases liked the idea of travel in this country so lightly armed, yet the alternative held not the least attraction. They did provide one gem of information. Their departure had left Murchison with only twenty-three men.

"Better odds, wouldn't you say?" Smoke Jensen quipped, as the five men rode away.

Louis Longmont answered him drily. "We have them out-numbered, *mon ami.*"

"When do you propose hitting them again?" Brian Pullen asked.

Smoke made an unusual admission. "This arm smarts like the fires of hell. I'd as soon get it over with. But I think we should let them tire themselves out a bit more. It'll be time enough at Donner Pass."

They rode on in silence for an hour, the snow falling heavier by the minute. Every tree and bush wore a mantle of white. Except for the mournful wail of the wind off the sheer rock faces, their surroundings had taken on a cotton-wool quiet. Three inches accumulated almost before they knew it. Their horses' hooves creaked eerily in that underfoot. Smoke called for a halt.

"We had better gather some wood. Otherwise it will be too wet later on."

He set the example by rounding up an armful and wrapping it in his slicker. He tied the bundle behind his saddle. When they pointed the noses of their horses east again, the snow had deepened to six inches.

"I don't like this at all," Brian Pullen lamented. "It never snows in San Francisco."

Smoke spoke through a snort of laughter. "Get used to it. I reckon we'll have a lot more before this storm moves on."

City men all, except for Titus Hobson and his mine police, the snow storm caught the column of Cyrus Murchison's men by surprise. It slowed, then halted their movement. By mid-afternoon, the horses stood knee-deep in cold discomfort. Heck Grange urged his boss to have the men keep going. He reminded Murchison of the fate of the Donner party, and again suggested that they could rig some sort of plow to clear a lane, dragging it by horseback.

"To what purpose? It will exhaust the men and animals. Have the tents set up here and we'll shelter until the storm blows over." An icy gale whipped his words away.

Folding tin stoves came from the back of one packhorse and men installed them as soon as the tents had been erected. Stove pipes poked through specially prepared openings, and before long, ribbons of blue-gray smoke rose into the air to be shattered into ragged wisps by the turning whirl of the wind. Because of their thin walls, the stoves could burn only thin twigs and small branches. Fuel went up at a rapid rate, yet the drawback held one positive side. Heat radiated quickly, warmed the men, and boiled water for coffee.

Before long, savory aromas came from each tent as pots of stew began to simmer. In his large, well-appointed shelter, Cyrus Murchison opened a bottle of sherry and poured a glass for Titus Hobson and himself. He also cracked the lid on a blue, hinge-gate Mason jar that held neat stacks of small, white spheroids.

"Pickled quail eggs," he offered them to Hobson. "Quite tasty. Only so rich, one does not want more than a few at a time." Murchison helped himself and lifted his glass. "To better times."

"Oh, quite well put," a tired, cold, and wet Titus Hobson responded. He swallowed a sip, munched an egg, and peered at the jar. "Say, what's this in the bottom?"

"What is left of the shells. After boiling the eggs, they are put in with the shells on. The vinegar dissolves the calcium and the residue falls to the bottom."

"Clever. I suppose picking the shells off of hundreds of these little things could drive someone quite dotty."

"Tedious work at best," Murchison agreed. Then he spoke the fear that still rode them both. "After the other night, there's no question Jensen and Longmont are still on our trail. I admit I am at my wits end to find a way to stop them."

"Short of losing all of our men, you mean?"

"Exactly, Titus. Has anything occurred to you?"

Hobson took his time answering. "Other than surrendering, I haven't much to say that is encouraging. You do realize we are in one damnable position, don't you? If those left with Jensen and Longmont come at us now, we are about equally matched in numbers. Our men are fighting for money. Those valley yokels are fighting for they see as a cause. They won't give up. If we have to face them we badly need reinforcements."

Cyrus Murchison scowled. "That's why we have to keep going to Carson City. It's only seventy miles, once we reach Donner Pass. There are enough track layers and more yard police there to fill our needs."

Titus canted his head to indicate the tempest outside the tent. "And if we get trapped in the pass by a storm like this? Do we feed on one another like the Donner party?"

Impatience painted lines on Murchison's face. "Spare me the grotesqueries." Then he argued from a basis of reason. "This is the first storm of the year. The snow will not last past the first few hours of sun on it. There probably won't be another until we are well down on the desert."

"You have no way of knowing that. It only seems to me that your way takes a whole lot for granted."

"Titus, Titus, you disappoint me. I always believed prospectors and mine owners were classical gamblers. Given what is at stake, don't you think that risking all is in order?"

Silently, Hobson considered this, his face a morose study. "Yes, I suppose so," he admitted reluctantly. Then he downed his sherry. "I need something stronger than this. How's the brandy supply?"

"Still holding out. Courvoisier VSOP, to be exact. I'll take one, too." With snifters poured, Murchison raised his in a toast. "Confusion to the enemy."

Smoke Jensen did not stay confused for long. Another night wasted. When the day dawned clear and cold, he rolled out of the snow-dusted blankets. The stockpile of wood soon provided a small fire to warm the stiffness from fingers and toes. He let the others sleep while he gnawed on a cold biscuit and set water to boil for coffee. Louis Longmont turned out next.

"Hell of a morning, *mon ami,*" he greeted Smoke.

"It'll pass. Sun's already got some heat in it. Way I measure, we have two feet of snow. Soon as it begins to slag down we'll head out. Coffee's ready."

Louis accepted a cup. "Is there any cornmeal?"

"Enough, I'd say," Smoke told him.

"I'll make some Southern-style mush. It will warm us and last a while."

Smoke Jensen knew all about Southern mush. It had shreds

of bacon in it, plenty of eggs, when available, and cooked to the consistency of wall plaster. Some old-timers still called it belly plaster. Smoke nodded.

"There's enough ham to fry some, if you want."

"Done. Too bad we have no eggs." Louis shrugged it off. He downed his coffee and went to work.

They left an hour later. Snow-melt trickled down summer-sun-dried water courses. Slowly the birds found new life and cause to celebrate a fresh day. Their music filled the air. As a boy, Smoke often wondered if they were telling each other about the storm that had blown away at last, sharing gossip. A foolish notion he soon abandoned in the cold light of being alone and a kid in the awesome vastness of the High Lonesome.

Now he had a scrap of that youthful fantasy return to him. Somehow it turned out to be comforting. Endless days and nights of fighting and bloodshed needed a counterpoint. For years it had been his lovely, raven-haired Sally. Out here in these strange mountains, he needed to cling to something.

"Cling to yourself, you maudlin old fool!" Preacher's voice roared at him in his head. And so he did. By one hour after noon, they came upon the site of Murchison's encampment. From the condition of the ground, he estimated the hard cases had been gone no more than three hours. There would be a little catch-up tonight.

TWENTY-TWO

Angry voices rasped around the campfires the next morning to wash away the good feelings of Cyrus Murchison on the previous evening. During the night, six more men deserted the camp. Now only seventeen gunmen remained. Cursing under his breath, Murchison stuffed himself into clothes, donned a heavy sheepskin coat, and stomped out to quell the upheaval.

"Nothing has changed, men. Nothing at all. We still outnumber them even if they all come after us."

"Yeah, and they kicked our butts right good every time before," one wag taunted.

"What's to say that the fighting and the weather haven't had a similar effect on them?" He wanted to avoid direct acknowledgment of the desertions.

No one could come up with an answer for that. Murchison seized on it to regain control. "Break camp and make ready to ride."

Muttering, some of those on the fringe of the angry assembly turned away to begin packing. Gradually, the remainder joined them, stared down by an aroused Cyrus Murchison. When the last had left, Murchison turned to his partner.

"Titus, is it going to be like this every day?"

Hobson sighed and jinked one shoulder. "Don't ask me. If they leave us alone, I don't think so. But another storm like that last one, and I won't hold out much hope."

"Bugger the weather," Murchison grumped. "If we push ourselves, we can be to the next pass before nightfall." He withheld the fateful name "Donner."

"I agree. It is critical that we make it. I'll talk to my men."

Murchison clapped him on the back. "Good. It can only help. Oh, and at noon, we won't stop to cook a meal. Have everyone bring along something they can eat in the saddle. I am going to beat Smoke Jensen at his own game."

By noon, Smoke Jensen had put his small band a good five miles beyond Murchison's overnight camp. Most of the snow had melted; only on the shady northern sides did drifts and patches still remain. In its wake it left a quagmire of slippery mud.

Smoke nodded to this. "It will slow them down more than us. Those heavy-loaded packhorses will make hard goin' of the mud."

"Shall we be visiting them tonight?" Louis asked.

"Oh, yes, I am sure we will. The ground is wet enough to use a little fire this time."

They came an hour after sundown. Smoke Jensen led the way, a flaming torch held at arm's length in his left hand. His right worked a big .45 Colt. The reins hung over the saddle horn and he steered Thunder with his knees. Louis Longmont rode to his left with another torch. Behind them came Brian Pullen and Quo Chung Wu.

Quo fired the Purdy shotgun one-handed and clung to his saddle with the other. Brian emptied one of the four revolvers he carried into one of the smaller tents as he raced past. Thugs cried in alarm and crashed through the low door flaps of other canvas lodges. Smoke reined in sharply and hurled his flambeau onto the roof of the tent that housed Cyrus Murchison. Cries of alarm came from inside as the heavy billet burned its way through. The blazing canvas illuminated the entire campsite.

Louis fired the other large tent, sheets of flame rushing up from the fringed roof overhang. This time the shouts of alarm came from outside.

"The supplies! They're burning the supplies."

"Get away. There's ammunition in there," Heck Grange shouted. "There's dynamite in there, too."

Cyrus Murchison burst clear of his doomed tent, his clothes in hasty disarray. He waved an awkward, long-barreled Smith and Wesson American in one hand and shouted for Heck Grange. Grange reached his side in a moment and the agitated railroad mogul made frantic gestures back toward the tent.

"Titus Hobson is still in there. Get some men to pull him out. A wall support hit him on the head."

"Right away, Mr. Murchison." Heck Grange sent two men into the burning tent to retrieve the unconscious form of Titus Hobson.

When they laid him on the ground, Titus Hobson swam slowly back into the real world. He coughed clear a phlegmy throat and tried to sit upright. Everything swirled around him. He caught himself with one hand before he could fall back. Fuzzily, he made out the face of Cyrus Murchison as it hovered over him.

"Are you all right, Titus?" Murchison queried.

"I think . . ." Titus Hobson began his answer, when the detonator caps in the supply tent let go.

The dynamite quickly followed from sympathetic detonation. A tremendous white flash and crushing blast followed. The ground heaved, heat waves washed over everything, and the concussion knocked Titus Hobson flat, along with nearly everyone else. A huge cloud of dust and powder smoke filled the clearing. The horrendous sound echoed off the surrounding peaks for a long time, while the stunned men tried to regain their feet.

"We should have never brought that along," Titus stated with feeling.

* * *

Quo Chung Wu found himself faced by five men made more dangerous by their desperation. He downed one with the last round in his shotgun. With no time to reload, he put the weapon aside and met their charge with fists and feet when the remaining four swarmed over him. His kicks found their targets and two men fell back. The other pair came at Quo from opposite directions.

He dodged the first lout and the other thug connected with a knife in the shoulder of the one facing him. The city trash howled and Quo jumped nimbly from between them. By then the first hard cases had recovered enough to return to the fight. They circled Quo, one with a knife, the other with his clubbed, empty revolver. Quo kept pace with them . . . at least until the knife artist who had stabbed his comrade chose to try again.

Now, Quo faced enemies on three sides. He used every bit of his martial arts skill to keep them at bay. They circled, feinted, snarled, and cursed. Quo made small whistling and warbling sounds, his hands and arms describing figures in the air, weaving his spell, lulling these dull-witted *qua'lo*. It worked rather well, until the fourth gunhand joined his companions.

Quo realized at once he had to take the offensive. He spun, lashed out a foot, and kicked one thug low in the gut. The injured dolt bent double and vomited up his supper. Quo pivoted gracefully and delivered another jolt to the side of the exposed head. The hard case went down, twitched, and lay still. The other three rushed Quo at once. The young priest's fists and feet moved in blurs. Another went down, then one with a knife got in close and drove the blade into Quo's back, over a kidney.

His mouth opened in a soundless scream and the strength left his legs. Quo stumbled forward and the knife twisted clear of his back. The grinning goon who held it thrust again, the keen edge sliding between two of Quo's ribs and into a lung. A fountain of blood gushed from his pain-twisted lips. Blackness swarmed over Quo Chung Wu as he pitched forward onto his face, never to rise again.

* * *

Smoke Jensen saw Quo Chung Wu go down and a moment of sharp regret filled him. The young Chinese priest had known the dangers involved in this battle and had come along at his own wish. Any of them, all of them, could die right here in this mountain pass, where so many had perished before. His lament for Quo ended, Smoke turned to check on Brian.

Exhibiting a skill at gunfighting unusual for a young lawyer, Brian held off three men with a coolness lacking in many a more experienced shootist. Disoriented by the wavering flames and billows of smoke, the trio of rascals threw wild shots in the general direction of Brian.

He obliged them by gunning down one of their number and smoothly replacing his spent revolver with the third of his quartet. The .45 Peacemaker in Brian's hand bucked and snorted and sent another hard case off to explain himself to his Maker. The third experienced a momentary flash of brilliance. He emptied his hands and thrust them high over his head.

Brian stepped in and smacked the man behind one ear. He dropped like a stone. Taking a deep breath, Brian turned to find another enemy. Disappointment flashed on his face as two reprobates fled from the conflict, thoroughly defeated. That left only Heck Grange, Cyrus Murchison, and Titus Hobson, who had once more regained consciousness.

Forced back on their own resources, the three candidates for hell reverted to their basic savagery. Heck Grange put a bullet through the left shoulder of Brian Pullen. A second later, he found himself facing Smoke Jensen. This would be nowhere as easy. Heck cocked his .44 Frontier Colt and the hammer dropped on a spent primer.

Frantically, he let go of the weapon and clawed for another thrust into the waistband of his trousers. Smoke Jensen waited for him. The muzzle came free and Heck Grange saw a momentary glimmer of hope. Then Smoke Jensen filled his hand with a .45 Peacemaker and triggered a round.

Smoke's bullet hit Heck in the meaty portion of his shoulder. Rocked by the slug, the chief lawman of the railroad grimly completed his intended action. Flame leapt from the muzzle of his six-gun. A solid impact rocked Smoke Jensen and he stumbled to the left, a sharp pain in his side. Gradually that numbed as he centered his Colt on the chest of Heck Grange. Smoke eared back the hammer of his Peacemaker a fraction of a second before a chunk of firewood, hurled by Titus Hobson, crashed into the side of his head.

Stars and vivid colors exploded inside the skull of Smoke Jensen. His six-gun blasted harmlessly into the ground at the feet of Heck Grange. That gave Grange a chance to fire again. The hot slug broke skin on the side of Smoke Jensen's neck. A sheet of blood washed warmly downward. Through the throbbing in his head, Smoke tried to steady himself.

Concentrating desperately, he willed his vision to return. Heck Grange swam erratically in the involuntary tears that filled Smoke's eyes when he could at last see. He steadied his hand and eared back the hammer. The Peacemaker roared once more. Heck Grange's knees buckled and he went down hard.

He caught himself with his free hand and cried out at the pain that lanced through his body from his wounded shoulder. Once again he tried to finish off Smoke Jensen. The six-gun in Smoke's hand spoke first.

Hot lead spat from the muzzle and caught Heck Grange in his left nostril. Grange reared backward and kept on going to land on the back of his head, which had been blown off along with his hat.

Smoke spared the hard case no more time. He felt dizzy and light-headed. Dimly he saw Louis Longmont turn toward Titus Hobson as though wading under the ocean. Hobson also moved in slow motion. He pulled a .44 Colt Lightning from his Coggshell Saddlery shoulder holster and fired almost immediately.

His bullet struck Louis Longmont in the upper right thigh. Louis went to one knee, although he continued his swing. His own six-gun bucked in his hand and the slug sped true. The eyes of Titus Hobson went wide and white when pain exploded in his chest. He tried to cycle the double-action revolver again. This time the projectile missed Longmont entirely.

Weakened by rapid blood loss, Louis Longmont fired his last bullet and missed. He sank to his side on the ground. Head still whirling, Smoke Jensen went to the side of his friend. Hobson, light-headed from his wound, came at the two of them, firing recklessly. Smoke returned the favor and his bullet tore a chunk from the heaving side of Hobson. The Colt Lightning struck an expended cartridge and a expression of shock washed Hobson's face white.

Smoke Jensen knew that he had fired his last round. When the wounded Hobson recovered himself, he snatched up another stick of firewood and advanced on Smoke. Determined to save the life of his friend, Smoke Jensen drew his war-hawk and readied himself. Hobson, though unsteady on his feet, gave him little time for that.

Titus Hobson swung the billet like an ax handle. It swished past over the head of Smoke Jensen, who had ducked. Smoke feinted with the tomahawk and the fighters separated. They appeared to be nothing more than two vicious predators quarreling over a choice bit of carrion. Smoke carefully kept himself between Hobson and Louis. Titus Hobson tried a fake on Smoke Jensen.

It failed and the war-hawk sailed by dangerously close to the face of Hobson. They backed off. Smoke risked a glance at Louis and saw the light in those gray eyes begin to dim.

"Louis, if you can hear me, cover that wound and use your belt for a tourniquet. Do it now!"

His concern for Longmont almost cost Smoke that fight that moment. Titus Hobson lunged and swung the wrist-thick stick at the side of Smoke's head. Smoke spun and parried the blow, did a quick reverse, and cleaved the length of wood in half. Hobson let out a startled yelp and jumped back.

"Damn you, Smoke Jensen. Damn you straight to hell."

Smoke laughed at Hobson. His side had become a continuous lightning strike. Quickly he changed hands with his war-hawk. The movement confused Titus Hobson and he stood blinking. That hesitation proved enough for Smoke Jensen.

Swiftly he swung the deadly 'hawk and felt the solid impact as the keen edge sank into flesh and bone near the base of the neck of Titus Hobson. Muscles and tendon severed, Hobson's head drooped to the opposite side at an odd angle.

A gurgle came from deep in his throat and his eyes rolled up. The foreshortened piece of wood fell from numb fingers and Titus Hobson spilled onto the ground, taking Smoke Jensen's tomahawk with him. Smoke took time only for two quick, deep gulps of air, then turned to Louis.

Louis Longmont sat upright now, shoulders drooped, chest heaving with the effort to breathe. His leg wore a tightly drawn belt above the wound and a square of impeccably white linen kerchief covered the bullet hole. He raised his head and cut his eyes to Smoke Jensen.

"You know, we're getting too old for this sort of thing, *mon ami.*"

"Speak for yourself, Louis," Smoke panted. Then he remembered Cyrus Murchison.

Quickly as his injured body would obey, Smoke Jensen turned to his left to find Cyrus Murchison on his knees, trembling hands raised in abject surrender. His lips quivered as he spoke.

"I—I've never seen anyone fight so ferociously. D-Don't hurt me. I'm giving myself up. I'll fight the charges in court." A sardonic smile replaced the fear in the man. "And I'll win, too."

Smoke Jensen looked from him to Louis Longmont, then cut his eyes to Brian Pullen. Pullen's expression told Smoke volumes. Smoke sighed. "With his money, he likely will win." Then he returned to the matter at hand. "Let's patch one another up and take in our prisoner. There's been enough blood shed in the Donner Pass."

A day's journey to the east and those who had come out of the Donner Pass alive turned south. At the insistence of Smoke Jensen, they had brought along the bodies of Quo Chung Wu,

Titus Hobson, and Heck Grange. The rest they buried as well as they could. Two more long, hard days to the south put them alongside the tracks of the California Central Railroad.

Cyrus Murchison proved entirely cooperative. He instructed Smoke Jensen in how to rig a signal that would stop the first westbound train. Half a day went by before the distant wail of a steam whistle announced the approach of the daily express run. To the relief of them all, the signal worked.

"We could be in a tight spot rather fast," a weakened Louis Longmont advised from the travois on which he rode as he and the others studied the hard faces of the crew.

"We still have a few things going for us, old friend," Smoke Jensen advised him lightly.

"Such as what?"

"We do have their boss as a prisoner," Smoke suggested.

"That is precisely what I see as the source of our problems," Louis stated drily.

Smoke showed no reaction. "Let's see what they say . . . or do first."

The engineer braced them first. "Isn't that Mr. Murchison you have trussed up like a Christmas goose?" Smoke Jensen allowed as how it was indeed. "What the hell is that all about?" the locomotive driver demanded.

This time, Louis Longmont replied. "He is under arrest."

"By whose authority?" the truculent engineer snapped.

Smoke took a step forward. "By mine. We are going to board your train and ride to San Francisco and turn him over to the police."

A defiant curl came to the thick lips of the trainman. "You will, like hell."

Smoke flashed his badge. "I think we will. I'm a deputy U. S. marshal. If I'm forced to, I'll simply commandeer the train, throw your ass in irons and run it myself."

Two burly switchmen grumbled at this, yet they made no move to interfere. That quickly decided the engineer. "All right, all right. You can board. But you'll have to ride in a chair car. Ain't got no fancy coach hooked up."

"I'm sure Mr. Murchison won't mind," Smoke quipped.

* * *

They arrived in San Francisco an hour before sundown. The huge red-orange globe rested a finger's width above the flat, glassy sea and sent long shafts of magenta over the rippling water of the bay. The first order of business was to take Cyrus Murchison to the police station. Smoke surrendered him directly to the chief of police and listed the charges.

After a sad journey to the Golden Harmony temple in Chinatown with the body of Quo Chung Wu, Smoke, Louis, and Brian headed for the bordello. Two of their hired protectors met them on the porch. A minute later, Lucy Glover dashed out to join them.

"I was afraid something had happened to you," she blurted, staring directly into the face of Brian Pullen.

It instantly became obvious to Smoke and Louis that the pair shared mutual stars in their eyes. Smoke cleared his throat. That broke the thick web of enthrallment. Reluctantly, Lucy and Brian turned their attention to the big man with a white bandage on his neck.

"Brian and I have been talking about the future of this—er—establishment. I have decided to ask you to continue in charge of the—ah—operation. Louis is going to stay in San Francisco and make arrangements to sell my latest acquisition."

Shock and worry clouded Lucy's face. "You're going to *sell?*"

Smoke chuckled softly. "Yes, and as quickly and quietly as possible."

"Don't you realize that this place can make a fortune for you?"

"Granted," Smoke declared. "And if my dear Sally ever found out about it, she would have a fit."

"But—but, what will I—I and the girls—*do* after it's sold?"

"The girls can pool their resources and make a bid. Anything reasonable will be considered. For your own part, if I'm not mistaken, young woman, you have a career change ahead in the near future."

Lucy Clover cut her eyes from Smoke Jensen to Brian Pullen, who blushed furiously. "You're right, Smoke, if I have anything to say about it," the young lawyer said softly.

The two gunfighters chuckled indulgently. Then Smoke Jensen ended their embarrassment. "I'll just gather my things and be on my way."

Lucy was shaken. "You're leaving so soon?"

"I have to. I've been away from the Sugarloaf too long."

"But your wounds," Lucy and Brian protested together.

Smoke gave Lucy a sunny smile. "They'll heal better in the High Lonesome. Especially with Sally there to pamper me." He turned to Louis Longmont. "Louis, it's been good working with you again. After you have this out of the way, come up to the Sugarloaf for a while. The latch-string is always out."

"I appreciate, that, *mon ami,* and I will give the invitation serious consideration. For now, then, I will only say *adieu.*"

"Farewell, old friend, and ride an easy saddle."

With that, Smoke Jensen was gone.

THE MOUNTAIN MAN SERIES BY
WILLIAM W. JOHNSTONE

__The Last Mountain Man	0-8217-6856-5	**$5.99**US/**$7.99**CAN
__Return of the Mountain Man	0-7860-1296-X	**$5.99**US/**$7.99**CAN
__Trail of the Mountain Man	0-7860-1297-8	**$5.99**US/**$7.99**CAN
__Revenge of the Mountain Man	0-7860-1133-1	**$5.99**US/**$7.99**CAN
__Law of the Mountain Man	0-7860-1301-X	**$5.99**US/**$7.99**CAN
__Journey of the Mountain Man	0-7860-1302-8	**$5.99**US/**$7.99**CAN
__War of the Mountain Man	0-7860-1303-6	**$5.99**US/**$7.99**CAN
Code of the Mountain Man	0-7860-1304-4	**$5.99**US/**$7.99**CAN
__Pursuit of the Mountain Man	0-7860-1305-2	**$5.99**US/**$7.99**CAN
__Courage of the Mountain Man	0-7860-1306-0	**$5.99**US/**$7.99**CAN
__Blood of the Mountain Man	0-7860-1307-9	**$5.99**US/**$7.99**CAN
__Fury of the Mountain Man	0-7860-1308-7	**$5.99**US/**$7.99**CAN
__Rage of the Mountain Man	0-7860-1555-1	**$5.99**US/**$7.99**CAN
__Cunning of the Mountain Man	0-7860-1512-8	**$5.99**US/**$7.99**CAN
__Power of the Mountain Man	0-7860-1530-6	**$5.99**US/**$7.99**CAN
__Spirit of the Mountain Man	0-7860-1450-4	**$5.99**US/**$7.99**CAN
__Ordeal of the Mountain Man	0-7860-1533-0	**$5.99**US/**$7.99**CAN
__Triumph of the Mountain Man	0-7860-1532-2	**$5.99**US/**$7.99**CAN
__Vengeance of the Mountain Man	0-7860-1529-2	**$5.99**US/**$7.99**CAN
__Honor of the Mountain Man	0-8217-5820-9	**$5.99**US/**$7.99**CAN
__Battle of the Mountain Man	0-8217-5925-6	**$5.99**US/**$7.99**CAN
__Pride of the Mountain Man	0-8217-6057-2	**$4.99**US/**$6.50**CAN
__Creed of the Mountain Man	0-7860-1531-4	**$5.99**US/**$7.99**CAN
__Guns of the Mountain Man	0-8217-6407-1	**$5.99**US/**$7.99**CAN
__Heart of the Mountain Man	0-8217-6618-X	**$5.99**US/**$7.99**CAN
__Justice of the Mountain Man	0-7860-1298-6	**$5.99**US/**$7.99**CAN
__Valor of the Mountain Man	0-7860-1299-4	**$5.99**US/**$7.99**CAN
__Warpath of the Mountain Man	0-7860-1330-3	**$5.99**US/**$7.99**CAN
__Trek of the Mountain Man	0-7860-1331-1	**$5.99**US/**$7.99**CAN

Available Wherever Books Are Sold!

Visit our website at **www.kensingtonbooks.com**

THE LAST GUNFIGHTER SERIES BY
WILLIAM W. JOHNSTONE